AI BABY
A Novel

Celeste Garcia

Magneto Books
New York

Magneto Books
POB 230535
New York, NY 10023
magnetobooks.com

AI Baby: A Novel / Celeste Garcia. – 1st ed.
ISBN 979-8-9861955-2-0

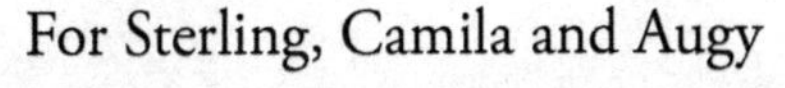

For Sterling, Camila and Augy

"Frightful must it be; for supremely frightful would be the effect of any human endeavour to mock the stupendous mechanism of the Creator of the world."
— Mary Shelley,
Introduction to *Frankenstein* (1831)

"The greatest danger of AI is that people conclude too early that they understand it."
— Eliezer Yudkowsky

Prologue

Dragging the kayak to the water by the rope, I tried to distract myself from what I was about to do. If only I'd read the story weeks ago when she gave it to me. Maybe tragedy could've been avoided, but I was too busy "whistleblowing." How had it come to this?

I launched from the beach, and my feet got soaked. I shivered against the cool night air and zipped up my puffy coat as the sweat cooled on my back and my feet began to freeze.

The lake was glass under a crescent moon and blanket of stars. I steadied the kayak and paddled, reminding myself to head north. When we were still married, Frank used to show me how to find the North Star, holding hands around the campfire or sitting on our backyard deck. I could find the Big Dipper—that part was easy—but the North Star is a tiny dot, same as all the other tiny dots. Shouldn't it be giant, like the Star of Bethlehem? Frank found it thrilling, I found it disappointing. He insisted I know, in case of an emergency. Did he think I would be a fugitive? I don't even jaywalk. Frank used to tease me about my rigid rule following. That's when he loved me. Was he looking up at this starry night with his new young wife? At least we were good parents, until I blew that up too.

I recognized the dock by the giant Alexander Calder sculpture on the lawn and the two-hundred-foot yacht. It's convenient to have moorage in your backyard. Mine featured a rotting picnic table and dandelion-infested grass. I paddled around the boat. The dock was high, about three feet above the water. Frank and I used to kayak all summer, and he always helped me get out without capsizing. I paddled to the ladder, rope in one hand, and grabbed for the crossbar with the other. As I pulled at the ladder, the kayak started moving away from the dock with the current, taking my body with it. Stretched precariously over the water, I pulled as hard as I could to get the kayak up against the ladder, tied it up, and carefully stood.

The dock shifted and groaned as I climbed up onto the deck. I flashed my headlamp toward the house to find the path, then extinguished the light and tiptoed toward the giant sloping lawn. I made my way along the edge of a tall hedge on the south side of the main house, then ducked down and crept slowly to avoid the cameras. I approached the back door and found the panel. I switched on my headlamp and hit the code to open the door—it clicked. I took a deep breath; the moment the door broke the plane, the alarm would go off and I would need to disarm it before anyone noticed. I pushed the door open. The *whonk, whonk* of an alarm sounded. With shaking hands, I punched in a code to disable it.

Whonk, whonk. "Shit."

Police with guns drawn flashed through my mind. *Focus. Don't screw up.* My fingers felt like sausages, but I hit the keys again.

Silence. Blessed silence. I paused to get my bearings. Dim floor lights allowed just enough visibility. I switched off my miner's lamp and tiptoed toward her bedroom. Fugh! My wet sneakers were squeaking. I leaned on the wall and pulled them off. Holding them in one hand, I entered her private sitting room. A massive TV hung on one wall in front of a large plush sectional so luxurious it begged to be rolled around on. Her personal TV room was bigger than my whole damn house.

The interior door to the bedroom was wide open. I peeked in. Since when did teen girls have bedrooms that looked like the Ritz-Carlton? I looked around. Her room was empty. Shit. Where were they?

I heard a low whirring sound coming from behind a door next to the dresser. I turned the knob, gently pushed it open and entered a small windowless room. A body lay still on a hospital bed with lines attached to various monitors and machines generating endless lines of code. An eerie yellowish glow emanated from somewhere nearby. What were they doing to this poor girl? As I got closer, the horror of what I was seeing registered. I felt myself crumple to the floor as everything went black.

CHAPTER 1

Erica straightened her ill-fitting Amazon Finds black dress and took a massive gulp of wine. Frank had brought his gorgeous young wife, Circe, decked in a navy Chanel suit, and their "exquisite" five-year-old twins. That was the word Circe claimed a talent agent had used to describe them, giving her "no choice" but to get them into modeling. Erica still couldn't believe her ex had fathered children with that woman.

Zoey, sitting between her and Frank, was staring straight ahead at the empty podium. How was it possible that her little girl was a senior? Erica stifled the impulse to pull her daughter in for a hug. Zoey needed the time to mentally rehearse the acceptance speech Erica had written for her. The SPIT—Save the Planet Innovations in Tech—award was the most prestigious prize any student at Hillcrest could win. Launching the winner into the national contest and spotlight, it all but guaranteed acceptance to the Ivy of her choice, Harvard in Zoey's case. Erica was sure Zoey would win. She had attended Green Innovations Camp on Vancouver Island every summer since she was eight. When they had dropped her off that first year, Zoey had cried uncontrollably and written heartbreaking letters begging them to bring her home. It was agonizing, but Erica never wavered, and eventually the letters became cheerful. Zoey came home with the Kermit Award—"It's not easy being green"—and was hooked. Erica was confident the planet-saving project

Zoey had poured her heart and soul into for the last year would wow the judges and couldn't be beaten.

Erica watched the twins pour all the salt and pepper from the shakers on their table into water glasses they had lined up and make a beeline for the table next to them. Circe was glued to her phone, too busy influencing to notice. But Zoey sprang to her feet. She loved her rambunctious siblings, and Circe regularly paid her obscene amounts of money to babysit.

"Don't go too far, it's about to start!" Erica shouted as Zoey maneuvered the twins through the packed hall. Word had gotten out that the SPIT made admissions officers swoon and generated great essay topics, and most of the kids and families that had started at Hillcrest with Zoey in fifth grade were there.

A mother and daughter sat alone at a nearby table. The mom started talking to Zoey and the twins as they passed by, and a few seconds later, *handed* them their salt and pepper shakers. Erica curled her lip in disgust. Everyone fawned over those kids. Who was this woman anyway? Erica knew everyone at Hillcrest but she had never seen these two. The daughter was beautiful, with violet eyes, mink-brown tresses, and bee-stung lips. She did not engage in the conversation and stared off into space. Erica smiled at the poor girl, no doubt pressured by her mother to enter the competition. She should have been in Nashville at the Miss Teen USA pageant. Erica waved her arms to get Zoey's attention. She nodded and guided the twins back to their table.

Phil Robson, head of school, stepped to the mike. Erica beamed at him. She had strategically volunteered for every committee he chaired, and they had become friends.

"And now for the moment we've all been waiting for . . ."

Erica grabbed Zoey's hand.

As Phil announced the winner, she jumped up and started clapping. *Why is Zoey still sitting?* She tried pulling Zoey to her feet. Frank, having just returned from the bar, set his drink down and put his arm on her shoulder. He was talking to her, but she couldn't hear him over the applause. He was ruining the moment.

"Erica, stop! Zoey didn't win!"

What was Frank saying? Zoey needed to get to the stage, why wasn't she moving?

"Mom! Mom!" Zoey pleaded. "Fenella won! Not me!"

Frank gently pushed Erica back down into her chair.

Phil gushed his congratulations as the beautiful girl Erica had just noticed approached the stage, looking straight ahead as she walked. She was tall and thin, wearing a pink slip dress. She shook hands with Phil, and he handed her the award. He enumerated the many accomplishments of Fenella Kingsley, describing her work in the Amazon rainforest. *Fenella? Is she bleeping British royalty?*

Erica stole a glance at the mother, who smiled and clapped but remained seated. Her hair was a blunt curtain of silver, and despite the wrinkle-free sheen of a perfectly executed facelift, she seemed older than the other parents.

Fenella accepted her award with a simple "Thank you" and exited the stage. Erica jumped to her feet in a pathetic attempt to save face. "Brava! Brava! Yay, Fenella. I knew you'd win!"

Zoey was beet red and looked away as Fenella passed by their table. Frank had his head in his hands, and Circe was smiling.

CHAPTER 2

If only she'd grilled the tofu the night before. Erica was rushing to assemble Zoey's lunch—collard greens wrap, prune chia-seed bars, and an apple for maximum brain food. Her face was still flushed from the humiliation of the night before.

Who the *hell* was Fenella Kingsley?

Hillcrest Academy was small, seventy students per grade. Erica knew most of the kids, especially any contenders for the SPIT. Where did this girl come from?

It was Thursday; she had her weekly coffee with Phil and would grill him for answers. It might be time to exploit his feelings. She'd noticed him stuttering and blushing around her recently, and standing too close. But if Phil *did* have feelings for Erica, why hadn't he warned her about Fenella?

"Zoey! You're going to be late!"

No answer. Erica sighed and walked the four steps from the kitchen to Zoey's room. The house was a charming but very small 1930s bungalow, purchased on impulse when she and Frank divorced and sold the large 1980s Bellevue home they had shared. Erica hadn't paid close attention to their finances and was surprised to find there wasn't much equity in their house. When pressed, Frank admitted that his law school debt, IVF, and her spending on Zoey's elite education and lessons in *everything* had crushed him financially. He'd taken out a second mortgage.

Erica had fallen in love with the bungalow's original pink and green tile kitchen, oak hardwoods, Batchelder tile fireplace, and curved moldings and archways. She hadn't given the single-paned windows or ancient hot water tank and boiler much thought, and all of it had to be replaced within a year of moving in at great cost. Frank had always been generous, and in the eight years since their divorce, he had made partner. He had always paid Zoey's expenses and continued to as his finances grew, without complaint. Erica received alimony, but only until Zoey went to college. She clung to the hope he might give her a "stipend." He still felt guilty about leaving, but Circe was losing patience.

Rejoining the workforce after so many years terrified her. She had set up a profile on LinkedIn and a few job search sites but nothing more. She would need money once Zoey moved out, but she would also need the distraction to keep her from burying herself under Zoey's stuffed animals and weeping all day.

She shuffled her feet on the sisal rug, her DIY foot exfoliation, and knocked on Zoey's door. Nothing. She turned the antique glass knob, and it came off in her hand. "Damn it." She screwed it in and turned while pushing. All she could see was a mound of covers.

"Z, what are you doing? Get up!"

Zoey peeked out, the covers pulled just below her chin, revealing black streaks of mascara down her cheeks from crying. Her high-bridged nose had a subtle bump on the midline. Zoey complained bitterly about the bump, but Erica thought it was a beautiful Roman nose. Her long, thick black hair was so messy it could've been styled in a blender. Zoey's looks and olive skin were from Frank's Italian family. Erica had often joked that she wanted a maternity test. She saw no trace of her fair-skinned Northern European heritage in her daughter.

"Mom, I can't go to school. I didn't win, and you made a fool of me." She pulled the covers back over her head.

"Oh, sweetie." Erica sat on the edge of her bed and began rubbing her back. "I'm so sorry. It's insane you didn't win! I think they made a mistake."

"Mom, it wasn't a mistake, you're making it worse."

"I wish you could stay in bed, but you can't miss AP organic chem. You have lab today."

"Do you always have to say *AP*? Just say 'chem,' and I'm not going."

Gone were the days of bribery with a new Polly Pocket. "Honey, I think if you get out of bed and take a quick shower, you'll feel better. Remember the mantra I gave you: 'I create my own path, and walk it with joy.'"

Zoey screamed.

"Get up, Zoey. Now!" Erica flung the covers back. "I'm going to make your breakfast. If you're not ready in ten minutes, you won't be going to Hawaii with your dad over Thanksgiving!"

Zoey slid out of bed, landing in a heap on the floor. She was wearing sweats and a hoodie and began to put on her Air Jordans.

"You can't wear that to school. It's against dress code."

"Fine." She picked up a pair of black jeans off the floor and a Fair Isle sweater she'd thrifted. Was it possible those were back in style?

"How do you wear so many clothes to bed?"

"Mom, I'm not menopausing like you."

Menopausing; this generation turned everything into a verb. "Brush your teeth and come to breakfast."

While Zoey nibbled her avocado toast, Erica attempted small talk. "I saw Ezekiel last night. He's gotten so handsome. Do you have any classes with him?"

"*Handsome?* Thou dost speaketh in strange tongues. He's *not* attractive."

"Maybe you shouldn't be so cynical. I thought you liked him."

"I don't. Let's go, Mom."

They walked out the front door and Erica locked the bolt. Frank had told her to get an alarm, but she hadn't gotten around to it. There had been a few break-ins in the neighborhood. The damp cold sent them shivering as Erica started her old Camry, parked in the driveway because it didn't fit in the garage. That space was reserved for furniture and tchotchkes from a house more than twice the size of her bungalow. Erica had been meaning to clean it out for years, but she could not part with objects that represented the happy life she had wrecked.

"We should go driving this weekend," Erica said.

Zoey grunted.

With homework and after-school activities, there hadn't been time for Zoey to get a driver's license, and Erica liked the time they spent in the car together. Today might prove to be the exception.

Erica listened to a few minutes of *Morning Edition* to make sure the world hadn't blown up overnight. Then she turned down the volume and took a deep breath.

"Zoey, I know how much you put into the SPIT competition—all those hours in the field, designing, coding—it was a grind. It's okay to feel bad."

The past summer Zoey and Frank had camped all around Washington State. Zoey had tested water in streams and rivers and built a software program to track her data. She had even alerted the authorities in a small farming town that their water source had dangerously high levels of phosphates.

Zoey stared out the window.

"Honey, when I was growing up, your grandparents put all their time and energy into Uncle Logan. He was their golden boy. The smart one. The star athlete. Gramps coached his select baseball team every year. They thought I was dumb."

"Yeah, yeah, I *know*, Mom."

Erica continued, "My dyslexia wasn't diagnosed until fifth grade. By then I'd been labeled 'slow' and it stuck."

Zoey looked over at her mom, her eyes softening. "But Mom, you overcame it, you went to UW and majored in human biology. You have so much to be proud of."

"I was lucky that my high school counselor helped me find a good tutor who knew what dyslexia was, but it was always a struggle. Your grandmother just wanted me to be pretty and popular, and I wasn't either."

Zoey turned to face her mom and touched her arm.

"Popularity is overrated, and I think you're pretty *and* smart."

"Thanks, Z."

Erica thought about her brother's baseball scholarship, which had gotten him into college. He was a mediocre student and spent most of his time chasing girls. After graduation he went to work for their dad and was groomed to take over the business. Now he had a cushy life making oodles of cash running the family commercial real estate company. Logan's wife spent tens of thousands on anything with a prominent logo and on "self-care"—lashes, manicured claws, lip injections—far exceeding Erica's budget. She wasn't jealous of her sister-in-law—she had no desire to be "extra," as Z called it—but her sister-in-law's excess was a cruel reminder of her parents' favoritism.

"I had to find my own way, and it took a long time. But I figured it out and realized I wanted to have a girl of my own someday, to give her the support and opportunities I didn't have."

"I think Cookie and Gramps sucked. They bought into the patriarchy."

"Times have changed. Your generation is so lucky."

Zoey yawned loudly. "Mom, I'm so exhausted and have a terrible headache. Can I skip lacrosse and come home after school?"

"Honey, you can't miss practice. You know that."

"Mom, I'm so over it. I wanna quit lacrosse. I want to quit everything!"

"Zoey, you're sad about SPIT and under a lot of pressure to get into Harvard. This is the hardest time for you kids. You've got to plow ahead. It'll be over soon, and then I promise, you can rest."

"What do you know about pressure? From what I can tell, you sat in front of the TV after school every day and watched *Ren & Stimpy*."

"Ouch." Nothing stung like a truth dart from a teen. "You're right, Zoey. I wasn't good at school and had zero parental support. Maybe I would've cracked under the pressure, but I never even had the chance. All I've ever tried to do is support you, because I care. My parents didn't."

"Mom, you're confused about what caring means."

The rain started as they pulled into the school's curved drive, and Erica got in line behind the cars already waiting.

"Honey, do you have a raincoat in your backpack?"

"Mom, it's fine, I'm going to get soaking wet at the practice you are *forcing* me to attend because you won't *ever* give me a break."

Zoey fumbled with her giant backpack, hitting her head on the door frame as she hoisted it to her shoulder. Whirling around, she kicked the door shut while swearing under her breath.

Erica banged the steering wheel. "Fuuuugh!"

A job sounded better and better. At least she would get paid to take abuse and insults.

Honk. Honk.

"Hold your horses, asshole," Erica muttered as she pulled forward to keep the line moving.

Zoey's bad attitude would need to be addressed, but should she wait until after the Harvard application was submitted? Erica had pushed hard for so long. The last thing she wanted was for Zoey to crack right before the finish line. She would head to the coffee shop and return with goodies for her meeting with Phil. Maybe he would know how Fenella won.

CHAPTER 3

The Eco-Bean was just up the street, providing plenty of time to replay the morning and figure out where she went wrong. Until recently, Erica had felt proud of her parenting. It was the most important job, wasn't it? She walked into the coffee bar, and the line was impossibly long, filled with techies on their way to work. These folks were running the game and making money—*lots of it.* Erica's pulse quickened, then surged. *Get a job, get a job. Oh God, make it stop.* Her favorite podcast, *The Inner Pause*, advised lion's breath for anxiety. She opened her mouth, stretching her entire face, including her tongue, and panted like a dog as she joined the line.

The guy in front of her turned around. "Are you okay?"

"Yep, just doing my breathwork."

He turned quickly away.

Erica had cozied up to Phil Robson from the beginning. She had started bringing him coffee and vegan doughnuts Zoey's freshmen year and it had become a tradition every Thursday. Originally, she was strategic. A gushing rec from the head of the most prestigious West Coast prep school was gold for an Ivy résumé. Phil respected her focus on Zoey, too, and took an advisory role—"Don't join a charitable organization, start one!" They mainly discussed pedagogy—LMS (learning management systems), iterating, inquiry—but lately he had begun sharing his personal life and developed a habit of breathing on her.

She wished she were attracted to him, but it just wasn't there. He was nothing like her ex. Frank was burly and had classic Italian good looks. Thick wavy hair, big brown eyes, and a strong jaw. Phil was slim, maybe five nine. He was graying and wore a skinny ponytail (yuck) to highlight his nearly colorless ice-blue eyes. Certainly, they were cohorts in misery. Both had been abandoned by their spouses. His wife, Acai, left him to become a Buddhist monk and now had millions of followers on TikTok ("@luvhandles—Inspiring peace, love, and body positivity"). Phil started each morning at Hillcrest with a quote from the Dalai Lama but had once referred to him privately as "that fat fuck," so Erica suspected some resentment.

"Ma'am, your coffee? What do you want?"

"One vegan chai, one skinny tall latte, two chocolate vegan doughnuts, please."

"It's faster if you order on the app."

"Why would I do that when I'm standing in front of you?"

He rolled his eyes and moved on to the next customer.

Erica looked in the mirrored backsplash as she waited. She'd managed to put on a little mascara this morning and penciled in her naturally peaked brows. Her shoulder-length ash-blond hair showed very few grays, thank God. She had once been described as a perky blonde, but in her midforties, the perk was fading.

When she arrived back at school, Ms. Bevins buzzed her in.

"I'm so sorry Zoey didn't get the SPIT last night. Truly shocking."

"Thanks, Ms. B. Can't win 'em all."

"Fenella sure seems to. It just doesn't seem fair."

She knew Ms. B. was trying to be nice, but Erica wanted to throw the coffee in her face.

Phil was standing at his whiteboard, shoeless as usual, wearing woolly gray socks with red hearts.

Top 20 was written in bold, and all the academies were listed. At number twenty-one he was writing *Fuck! Fuck! Fuck!*

"Phil, what's going on?"

"The list of top prep schools in the US came out, and Hillcrest is twenty-one! Twenty-fucking-one!"

"Phil, you know those lists are biased. The committee is based on the East Coast. They think we're Philistines. You don't need their validation."

"The board had promised me a huge bonus if we broke the top twenty."

"You don't need the money, Phil—oh jeez! Sorry. Too personal."

"No, you're right. I'm *not* driven by money, I don't even wear shoes"—Phil lowered his voice—"but when I tried to win back Acai, she talked me into sponsoring a mission to clean up Chomolungma."

"What's Chromo-lung-ma?"

"Mount Everest? It's a shit hole up there. Anyway, I'm broke, Erica, and I did it for love."

Erica's heart swelled with compassion. "I get it, I really do, but this list isn't the answer, Phil. It's about the curriculum, faculty, students, and *you*. You're the best."

He turned back to the board. "I know: we should change the name. Maybe add 'Windsor' or 'Latin.' Windsor's Hillcrest Latin Prep . . .," he said as he wrote in big loopy letters, and then stood back.

"Phil, you're not listening to me. You need time to process. I'm going through the same thing today." She hung her head. "I'm heartbroken Zoey didn't win the SPIT."

Phil turned and gave her an awkward pat on the arm.

"She would've won if Fenella hadn't entered. I've never had a student like her, Erica. Fenella's intellect is devastating, plus sports, poetry, writing, and her artwork is unrivaled. The only thing she can't do is dance. She'd be flunking Senior Cathartic Movement if it weren't graded on participation."

Erica rolled her eyes. "You're exaggerating, Phil. What's her family like? I suppose you'll tell me her parents are nuclear physicists who won the Nobel Prize."

"Her mom is Lannie Kingsley—the leading expert in AI. I don't know the dad. They're divorced. He's at Stanford."

Ting . . . ting . . . tong.

Phil's phone rattled on his desk. Erica tried to see who was calling. The screen showed a photo of a woman, but she wasn't close enough to see her name. Her impulse was to grab the phone and fling it out the window. She wasn't done yet!

"I have theater tickets for this Tuesday," Erica blurted out. "Any chance you'd like to go?"

Pinkish-red blotches exploded on his cheeks and neck. "Whuh . . . why? No. I mean, yuh-yes!"

"Great. It's—"

"Hold on one second . . ." Phil picked up his phone. "I've got someone in my office," he said, and put his thumb over the speaker. "Sorry, Erica. I have to take this. You're right. It's about the students. If only I had twenty more Fenellas . . . and Zoeys, of course."

He motioned her out and went back to his phone.

Erica paused outside the door to listen.

"Hi, Lannie."

Lannie Kingsley? That's how Fenella won? She should have moved in on Phil sooner. Fenella was stealing Z's Harvard dreams, and her harlot mom was stealing Phil. Erica's heart began swishing in her ears. She had brushed aside Phil's advances and now it might be too late. She should go back in. That woman had cut her coffee short. She put her ear to the door.

"I thought about it, and I'd like to take you up on your offer."

"Erica? Can I help you?"

Erica jumped. "Oh hi, Ms. Bevins. I . . . I was just making sure I have everything. You know me, kind of OCD."

Erica hurried out before she had to further explain herself. She had a bad feeling in her gut. She and Zoey had been displaced without warning. Like the wife who sits down to dinner with her husband and is dumped before the crème brûlée arrives.

CHAPTER 4

Zoey slipped off her sneakers and slumped cross-legged into the circle next to her friend Shyla.

"Are you okay, Z? I heard about the SPIT." Shyla reached her arm around Zoey.

"No, I'm not, Fen-*SMELLA* won."

Senior Cathartic Movement had been the brainstorm of Mr. Robson, a.k.a. the Barefoot Bandit, after he attended a conference on teen mental health. To most students it was absurd; to Zoey and Shyla it was pure joy. They had been friends since preschool and always brought out the mischief in each other. What began as a joke—volunteering to demonstrate dance moves; sashaying, leaping, and cartwheeling their way around the room; feigning great effort and enthusiasm—had grown into a genuine release from the pressure cooker of Hillcrest.

The irony of the Barefoot Bandit mandating the dance class was not lost on Zoey. She had begged her mom for permission to take jazz as an elective. But the response she got was, "Not on my watch." So all her electives were academic—software engineering, green energy, nuclear physics. No fun.

The instructor, known as Mento, dressed like Stevie Nicks, in gauzy skirts and capes. Mento rejected all labels and identified as a variety of animals, mostly frogs and puppies, depending on the day.

"Hello, my little birds." Their voice sounded like they'd been sucking helium. "Today and every day, we leave judgment and preconceived notions at the door. We are here to let go and express ourselves as we once did in the womb—float and be free. If you wish to cluck like a chicken, cluck. All movement is a negotiation of the soul with your environment."

Zoey had noticed that Fenella always sat on her own just outside the circle. She had joined Hillcrest late junior year from a chichi school in Palo Alto and caused a minor uproar because she looked like Bella Hadid, but her social awkwardness prevented acceptance by the populars. According to Shyla, her dad was a world-renowned researcher at Stanford, and her mom ran a giant tech company in Bellevue. Zoey wondered why Fenella had left California to live with her mom. Out of nowhere this fall she had tried out for LAX, displaying surprising skill but no fire. Zoey hadn't seen her as a threat, but now she knew she might need to rethink that.

Looking over at her wide-set violet eyes and full lips, Zoey felt a tinge of jealousy—supermodel uber-rich genius athlete. Barf. But dance class was clearly out of her comfort zone. It was five weeks after the start of fall trimester, and Fenella had barely moved. Mento had been very patient with her, since they "met each student in their space," but had made it known participation was the main factor in grading and applied in equal measure to all students. Fenella was dangerously close to flunking the class.

Zoey wondered if her mother had worked something out with the Barefoot Bandit, because there was no way she would be allowed to flunk an idiotic dance class.

"I'm feeling particularly vulnerable today," Mento began. "I'm dealing with horrendous period cramps. I'll break the ice with a freestyle dance entitled 'My Bloody Burden.'"

Mento stood in the circle and pressed play on their iPad. Death metal blasted over the speakers as they dropped to the floor, writhing and alternating between a tight ball and corpse pose.

Some of the kids snickered, others cheered.

"Go, MENTO!" Kip shouted.

"My queen!" echoed around the room.

Mento finished and made a low sweeping bow.

"Who's next? Zoey?"

"I'm not in the mood," Zoey said, shaking her head.

"That's when I see genius shine through," said Mento. "If we wait for inspiration, creation might never happen."

The class chanted the prompt they'd been taught: "How do you feel, Zoey?"

"I'm feeling dejected and exhausted," Zoey said.

"Please express yourself," they said in unison.

Zoey lay on her side, arm tucked under her head, and began breathing deeply. Minutes passed. She began snoring. The next thing she knew, she was shaken awake.

"Zoey, that was a beautiful performance." Mento was crying. "I don't recall a student ever showing such vulnerability. I'm imploding emotionally. I myself haven't slept in days."

The class stood and cheered. Zoey made prayer hands and bowed.

Mento addressed the circle as Zoey sat down.

"Today we have a special performance from Fenella. I want to remind everyone that original choreography performances garner ten points extra credit."

The class went dead silent. Zoey elbowed Shyla as Fenella, wearing sweatpants and a sweatshirt, entered the circle. She stood very still, and Mento started the music. "Milkshake" by Kelis blasted and Mento adjusted the volume. Fenella moved mechanically across the floor like a—bulldozer? Jaws dropped.

This beautiful creature, a star athlete, lumbered flat-footed, painful and awkward as an elephant trying to tap dance. Shyla elbowed Zoey and they both mouthed, *WOW!* while stifling giggles. Other kids followed with all-out laughter, and Zoey and Shyla, unable to hold it in, howled and held their stomachs. Several whipped out their phones and began shooting video. Fenella persisted, doggedly moving through her routine. Zoey could see her lips moving as she counted the music and performed every awkward shake and shimmy. At one point Fenella froze, forgetting her next move. Then, steadying herself, she began again, several beats behind. Zoey's heart melted. This was no longer funny. Fenella was putting it all on the line and about to break the internet, but not in a good way.

Zoey looked around, desperate to make it stop. She jumped to her feet and moved into the circle. She began leaping around Fenella, then grabbed her hands and spun her around. The energy shifted in the room. Kids dropped their phones. Some moved slowly to the circle; others rushed in and began dancing with abandon around Fenella and Zoey. It was like that old movie her mom had made her watch, *Fame*. Spinning round and round, hand in hand, Zoey and Fenella lost their balance and came tumbling down. They landed on their backsides and erupted in laughter, still holding hands.

Zoey was in awe. Fenella had faced down what every teenager in America feared the most—humiliation in front of their peers and *the whole world* on social media. And she owned it. Mento was ribbitting with joy.

CHAPTER 5

A PREEMINENT AI EXPERT'S DAUGHTER possessing otherworldly beauty, intelligence, *and* talent? That could not have happened in nature. Erica googled private detectives—a hundred and forty an hour, forget it. She then looked up spyware for a little DIY surveillance. Her finger hovered over the purchase button for TruthSpy. What the hell was she doing?

She'd begun deleting her search history when an ad flashed across her screen—*Extra twenty-five percent off Nordstrom Rack!* Erica needed something alluring to wear on her big date with Phil. She clicked and selected "Women/All Clothing." Twelve thousand results. She shifted on the bench of her breakfast nook and stared at her laptop. She had no idea what to filter for—dress? Pants? Leather onesie?

Jess would know. Newly single, Erica's best friend, Jess, was embracing her freedom and on every dating app. Erica wished she felt that confident.

Erica: *What do I wear on a date to the rep?*

Jess: *Smtg slutty. Rep? Srsly? Whos the lucky guy?*

Erica: *No one u know. He appreciates culture.*

Jess: *Sounds boring. JK! glad your getting out there. Welcome to raid my closet.*

Erica: *OMG! Can I borrow your 7 Jeans?*

Erica punctuated it with laughing emojis.

She and Jess had been roommates when she went on her first date with Frank. Jess had loaned her low-rise jeans and an Abercrombie & Fitch sweater. Erica had worried the whole evening that her belly would spill out over the jeans.

Twenty years had passed since her first date with Frank, and almost eight since they'd divorced. Zoey was her universe, so she had no time for dating. Plus, the problem with Frank was that technically, she still loved him.

She and Frank had been happily married a few years when Zoey came along like a cozy kitten, and love abounded. But plans for more children turned into desperation and clouded their marital bliss. In Frank's world, pregnancy happened magically. As one of six children, his mother was pregnant often during his childhood. He was shocked when Erica suggested IVF and encouraged her to be patient. Once a doctor confirmed intervention would be necessary, Frank threw all his love and considerable financial support behind getting pregnant again. Despite thorough research, nothing could have prepared Erica for the ghastly side effects from daily hormone injections—headache, nausea, hot flashes, and irritability.

The pressure of IVF furthered the downward spiral. Needing a distraction, Erica set to work turning Zoey into an uber baby. Zero to age three was a race against the clock, the most critical years for brain development. "Not just tiger, but saber-toothed," was how Frank described her. Music and movement, cognitive development art school, French immersion school, chess, Latin, Kumon, soccer, gymnastics, lacrosse—the list went on and on. Frank wanted her to relax and let Z be a kid, but Erica couldn't help herself. She had to prepare Zoey.

Erica's palms began to sweat thinking about sixth grade, when Ms. Roger called on her every week to read aloud. The words would shatter on the page and float away. The whole class, including her teacher, had erupted when she'd read "menstruation" instead of "administration." Their laughter still rang in her ears.

Stop! She slid off the bench and stretched. That was a lifetime ago—she had her daughter to worry about now.

Frank didn't understand her singular focus on Zoey. In his giant family, attention hadn't been paid to any one child. The result was diametrically different child-rearing philosophies. Frank took Z camping and fishing, and to Mariners games in the summer. He developed a close bond with Zoey, while Erica became the nag. Baby number two, let alone three and four, never happened. Frank told Erica it didn't matter, the three of them were more than enough, but she knew he was disappointed.

To cope, Erica largely ignored Frank in favor of Zoey, and they fought constantly about money and the pressure she put on their daughter.

"Frank, the world is so competitive. We need to give Zoey every advantage," Erica used to tell him.

"This is about your own fragile ego, Erica. Stop using our child to fill the void."

The words still brought tears to her eyes. Wounds were opened and scabs were picked, until all that remained was a mass of scar tissue. Frank moved out when Zoey was in fourth grade and invited Erica to attend counseling. They went a few times, but she was outnumbered. The counselor suggested fewer scheduled activities. Erica knew what was right for her daughter. Frank said she needed to get over her childhood baggage and find a balanced approach for raising Zoey. The counselor agreed. Erica walked out of their last session. Frank would come around.

Instead, he filed for divorce. Two years later he married Circe. The twins, a boy and a girl, came along the following year. Erica still felt the stab of jealousy and heartbreak.

Zoey was all she had. The love she felt for her daughter exploded from her heart and sent shock waves through her body. She would never forget the moment she first laid eyes on her. Not only would she die for this tiny miracle of creation, but Erica would kill for her. Guaranteeing Zoey's success was her singular purpose and maybe would erase her own failures.

One more reason to get closer to Phil. On the West Coast, two students from the same school rarely got into Harvard. She would need to find out where Fenella was applying. With her parentage, Fenella would be a shoo-in for Stanford.

Her phone beeped. It was Frank.

She'd been avoiding him since SPIT; best to go on the offensive. "Before you make fun of me, it was your wife bringing the kids as props for her influencer photos."

"Erica, you're only making this easier."

Shit. Frank had a way of lowering his voice when he was about to deliver bad news. "I'm kidding, Frank. I . . . uh . . . I'm embarrassed."

"Erica, whatever you are dwelling on isn't important, but what I'm calling about is."

He paused long enough for Erica to run through every catastrophic possibility her brain could conjure.

"I'm cutting off your alimony at the end of the year. You knew it wouldn't be forever, and I've gone way above what's required by Washington State law."

"Is this punishment for the SPIT? THAT WAS NOT MY FAULT! Phil told me Zoey should've won. Fenella and her mother are using AI to cheat."

"I have no idea what you're talking about. It's not just SPIT; you're spending *too much* time at school. Zoey specifically asked you not to run the grad night committee and yet you are. And she said you stopped into her chem class today."

"Frank, I was there having coffee with Phil and wanted to know if she'd heard back from *The National High School Journal of Science*. We need it for her Harvard application."

"Precisely my point. I've let this go too long. We split up eight years ago. I had *hoped* you would realize you need a focus outside of Zoey. I will continue to pay all of Zoey's expenses, but you need some independence. It's not healthy for any of us, especially our daughter."

"I've raised *our daughter*, sacrificed everything for her, and this is the thanks I get. She needs me more than ever! A *huge* AI cheating scandal is brewing at Hillcrest, and I need to investigate. It might ruin Zoey's chance at Harvard."

"Erica, you sound unhinged."

"Circe put you up to this—"

"You're smart and talented, you'll figure it out. Gotta go." Frank ended the call before she could respond.

"Fugh!!!" She sat staring at her old-fashioned wall clock ticking away the minutes. "Come on, Erica, get a grip."

She opened her laptop to check LinkedIn job listings, but the words swam on the page. Her dyslexia intensified with stress. *Take a breath. You got this, Erica.* Several minutes of deep breathing did nothing to quell her panic, and her fear over the job search became insurmountable. Shifting to other pressing matters could help her relax—she could find an outfit for her date with Phil or review Zoey's Harvard application again. The job search could wait until she had calmed down.

CHAPTER 6

Rain pelted Zoey's face and soaked her hoodie as her feet sank in the muddy field. Exhausted from disappointment and fighting with her mom, she would need to dig deep today. As team captain, she not only led warm-ups but set the tone for practice. Fall sports in Seattle were often a soupy mess of sludge, rain, and cold. This was her opportunity to show just how tough she was.

Quads burning, she lunged across the field and the team followed. As goalie, she didn't run up and down the field like her teammates did during the game. So she had to do every drill harder than they did, and they respected her for it.

"Come on, Sea Stars," Zoey yelled. "What's our motto?"

"Mighty Echinodermata! Grit we gotta lotta!"

"What do we do? Shout it out, 'dermatas!"

Zoey could feel their energy rising as they chanted together:

"Stars of the sea, / Overpower our prey. / Stars of the sea, / We drive them away. / We live in the ocean and cause a commotion!"

She had played lacrosse with most of the girls since age twelve. Unlike some of her peers, lacrosse hadn't come easy for Zoey. She had been voted "most inspirational player" every year and team captain this year in a landslide.

After they ran ten laps, Coach Baumwater blew his whistle and called Fenella and Zoey over to the sideline.

"I need to talk to you both. I've made my decision about starting goalie."

Zoey looked at Fenella, whose violet eyes stared doll-like back at her. Not even a flush on her cheeks. Had Coach meant it when he said no position was guaranteed? Even for *veteran* varsity seniors? Zoey's heart pounded, and her palms started sweating as she willed Coach to say her name.

"Zoey . . ."

Relief washed over her.

"It was an agonizing decision, but I have to go with Fenella."

Don't cry. Don't cry, Zoey half prayed, and tried to detach. She watched bleak storm clouds gather and the tears spilled.

"I'm sorry, Zoey. If you need a moment, please take it."

"Coach, with all due respect, you should reconsider," Fenella said.

Zoey's head jerked toward Fenella.

"Zoey deserves it. I just joined the team this year."

"Fenella, there is no reason to feel bad," said Coach.

Zoey shook her head like a wet dog trying to clear her ears. There was no way Fenella would give up goalie for a team that was favored to win state. What was her deal?

"I don't feel bad. She led the team to state finals last year. She works way harder than I do. I don't even do all the drills. And she's a leader, the players follow her like they're going to war. Your decision might cost her entrance into the college of her choice."

With Fenella's skills, Zoey would get very little playing time. Only in games when they were way ahead. Zoey's field of vision started to narrow, as if she were looking through a kaleidoscope.

"Zoey!" Coach grabbed her by both biceps. "Are you okay?"

"I . . . I . . . yes, I just need to sit down."

Fenella grabbed one of her arms and Coach held the other, and they led her to the freezing metal bleachers. Zoey sat and watched the girls on the field doing drills. Ugh. What would they say? *Poor Z.* It made her want to puke.

"Where was I?" Coach looked at Fenella and avoided Zoey. "We were runner-up last year. We will *win* state this year, Fenella, with you as goalie. Your saves are miraculous! My job as coach is to win, it's like the hypocritic oath for doctors."

"*Hippocratic*," Zoey and Fenella said in unison.

"End of discussion. Fenella, you're starter."

Zoey took a deep breath. "Coach's right, Fenella." She forced herself up and ran onto the field.

Her body was numb, and her brain couldn't function. During scrimmage she moved in slow motion. Her teammates were scoring at will.

When the final whistle blew, she collapsed in a squat, head in her hands.

"Hey, are you okay?"

Zoey looked up to see Fenella standing next to her, hand out.

Zoey took it and Fenella pulled her up.

"Should I walk you to the car?"

"I'm good."

As Zoey lumbered away, her stick dragging behind her, she turned to watch Fenella leave in the opposite direction.

When she turned back, she noticed the windows of the Camry were fogged. *Shit, shit, shit!* Her mom hadn't seen Coach talking to them. How could she face her?

As she approached the car, the passenger door opened.

"You look like Shrek in the swamp. *Thank God* I don't have a fancy car like all the other parents. Get in."

Zoey sat and burst into tears.

"What's wrong?" Her mom grabbed hold of Zoey and pulled her close.

"Just drive, Mom," Zoey gasped between sobs. "I'm messing up your favorite sweater."

Erica put the car in reverse and started backing up.

"Sweetie, tell me what's wrong. You're freaking me out."

"I—I—lost starting goalie to Fenella. I'm second string."

"What? No. That's not possible." Erica stopped the car halfway out of the parking spot.

"Yes, Mom. She's way better than me— she n-n-n-ever miss-ses—"

"Honey, breathe."

"Better buh . . . ball skills. I can't compete." Someone was honking. "Mom, you're blocking traffic!"

Her mom screeched back into the parking spot. "What in hell is happening? First the SPIT, now this? And Coach Bongwater—what an asshole!"

"Mom, stop!" Zoey shrieked. "I knew you'd freak."

"Damn right. I'm gonna set him straight right now."

Zoey grabbed her mom's arm. "Wait. Fenella told Coach to keep me as starter."

"What kind of bullshit manipulation is that?"

Zoey winced. This was the ugly side of her mom's love and protectiveness. "Mom, she meant it. I know you're upset, but don't blame Fenella, or Coach. She's not normal."

"Obviously."

"That's not what I mean. Everyone else would've rubbed it in my face, and I would've stomped on her to keep my job."

"So its settled. You're still goalie."

"It's Coach's call, and he's right, Fenella will win state."

"Honey, it's a team."

"Mom, with Fenella as goalie, our opponents will never score."

"Nobody can be that perfect. It's impossible. Is she on performance-enhancing drugs?"

"Mom, it's goalie, that wouldn't help."

"Probably loads up on Ritalin. They should ban it."

"Mom! They can't, *everyone's* on it."

"And Coach! All he cares about is winning. This is your future on the line."

Erica opened the car door.

"Mom, what are you doing?" Zoey shrieked.

"I'm going to talk to Coach." She jumped out of the car and slammed the door.

"Mom! Oh God!" Zoey watched in horror as her mom ran straight toward Coach. She could see her jaw moving, arms gesticulating wildly. A crowd of her teammates and a few parents gathered. Zoey scrunched down on the floor below the dashboard and put her head on the seat. People would think she'd put her mom up to this. She reached for the car door but stopped. If she went out there, she would only make it worse. She would never live this down. She dialed her dad.

"Hi, pumpkin, what's up?"

"Daddy, can you take me to dinner tonight?"

"Of course, sweetie, you okay? You sound stuffy."

She burst into tears and sputtered through the story.

The car door opened, and Zoey almost jumped out of her skin.

"Who are you talking to?'

"Dad."

Her mom's hair was sticking to her head and dripping wet.

"Dad, I gotta talk to Mom." Zoey hung up and took a deep breath. "How'd that go?"

"Not good."

"What did you expect, Mom? That you could bully Coach into keeping me as starter? I'm surprised you didn't get me kicked off the team."

Erica started the car and turned on the defroster full blast.

"Mom? Am I still on the team?"

"I, uhm. Yes, I think so."

"OH MY GAWD!"

"It's just me Bongwater wants to kill. Sit in the seat and buckle up."

Zoey laid her head against the cold window. The only sound was the *wonk wonk* of the wipers, the intermittent blinkers, and an occasional expletive from her mom.

"Stay here," her mom said as she pulled up in front of the house, scraping the tires on the curb. "I'm tempted to hose you off, but it's too cold. I'm grabbing some old towels."

The car door slammed. She was back in a moment, handing Zoey a towel.

The rain was still pouring down as they ran together to the back porch. "What did your dad say?" Erica asked as Zoey peeled off her soaking clothes to her skivvies.

"He's picking me up in half an hour."

"Where are you going?"

"Pizzuto's for ravioli." Zoey was rubbing spattered mud from her arms.

"I was going to make you dinner. What about homework?"

"I've only got about two more hours, Mom. I need a break. I can't listen to you go off on Coach and Fenella right now."

"I'm not going to mention that A-hole and Miss Perfect."

Zoey put her hands to her ears. "You're effing crazy!" She kicked at the pile of cleats, pads, and discarded clothing, glared at her mom, then pulled the sliding door open and beelined to the bathroom. The hot shower cascaded down as she watched the mud swirl into the drain. She pulled on a long-sleeved T-shirt, cable-knit sweater, and jeans. Her phone bleeped.

Heading out now, she texted as she walked into the kitchen.

Her mom was standing in front of the open freezer holding a frozen burrito.

Zoey tiptoed toward the door. She didn't want to talk.

"Say hi to your dad, honey. He always knows the right thing to say."

"Yep, and you always say the *wrong*—"

Zoey froze midsentence. Her mom looked sad and lonely. Zoey's biggest fan and tormentor. She put plenty of pressure on herself without her mom making it worse. Was she sad for Zoey or herself? Mom wasn't the one studying day and night and facing down attackers flinging five-ounce lacrosse balls at her head. She slammed the front door and ran to her father's waiting car.

CHAPTER 7

"**Francesco!" The owner greeted Frank warmly.** "How's Mama Barbieri?"

"Bene. Feisty as ever."

"Zoey? How can it be? So grown up. Your table is waiting."

The familiar checkered tablecloths and Dean Martin crooning over the speakers put Zoey at ease. She must have been the only seventeen-year-old who knew the Rat Pack. Her father had made sure she did.

"A Shirley Temple for the lady, and I'll have my martini. You know how I like it."

Frank and Zoey made small talk until the drinks arrived and their order was taken.

"Sweetie, how are you feeling?"

Like my head might explode.

"Oh, Daddy," she said, her eyes filling with tears. "I can't figure out what's happening. Everything was going great, then within twenty-four hours I lost SPIT and starter. Now I'm not getting into college and probably canceled. When Mom found out, she lost her shit in front of God and everyone after practice. I'm worried they'll kick me off the team."

"Oh Jesus! Did she pull a Tonya Harding bat-to-knee takedown?"

"No, but she freaked out on Coach."

"Honey, they won't kick you off the team. Dealing with crazed parents is in the job description. Maybe they'll ban your mom from games."

"I'm so embarrassed."

"Sweetheart, you have nothing to be ashamed of." Frank put his hand on hers.

"But I do. Mom's insane and it's all over social. Videos of her yelling at Coach, and everyone is taking sides. Some are saying keep me as starter and how unfair it is, but I don't *want* sympathy. Others are plastering social with Fenella worship."

"What do you mean?"

"Their stories—photo montages of them with Fenella. Kissing her ass. Who wouldn't? She's a gorgeous billionaire genius LAX star. Being friends with her means private jets and yachts."

"That's sick. When I was a kid, you kissed up to the dude with Nintendo."

"Weird."

"No teenager was jet-setting. And there was no social media. We could lick our wounds in private. I hate the world you deal with—"

"It's like Fenella showed up to ruin my life, Dad. All I've worked for, and I'm so close."

"It's bad luck she has the same interests as you."

"She is good at *everything*. Not just good. *Perfect.*"

"Honey, comparing yourself to her is not productive. There will always be someone smarter, prettier, richer, but there will never be another Zoey!"

"I get that, but in the world of college admissions, we're all competing against each other. And Harvard—on my app. I wrote *Starter, varsity lacrosse.*" Zoey pushed back her seat. "I need to change it now!"

"Honey, stop." Frank rose, hugged her, and whispered in her ear, "It's okay. I promise. Sit down."

"But I *can't* lie. They'll know." Zoey could see her application going into the reject pile stamped *LIAR* across the top. "Fenella told Coach losing starter would affect my college chances . . . and . . . and . . . Mom!"

"Honey, slow down. You're still captain. That's meaningful. And Fenella, she's smart but doesn't know everything. Your mom—"

"Mom is losing it. First SPIT, now this. She gets *psycho* over me."

Zoey couldn't explain the panic bubbling up from her stomach.

"She's obsessing over Fenella. What if she calls Fenella's mom? She's inventing crazy conspiracies—like they're using performance drugs, or an expert did her SPIT. Mom's sitting at the kitchen table with her laptop googling Mrs. Kingsley right now, I'm sure."

Her dad sighed and closed his eyes for a moment. Zoey remembered that look from before the divorce. "I'll call her and tell her to calm down and stay out of it."

"The worst part is that I kind of want her to take Fenella down. I'm horrible and evil."

"Sweetie, you're a good person. It's normal for you to be angry. Your mom put a lot of ideas in your head. You need to decide what's right for you. Your mom loves you, but she also looks to you for validation."

"I've never wanted anything more in my life than Harvard, and honestly, Dad, Mom has supported me every step of the way."

Zoey knew who the *real* enemy was—not her mom but Fenella. She probably was faking it when she told Coach to keep Zoey as starter.

Her dad's big brown eyes were glassy. "Don't you believe in me, Dad?"

"More than you could ever know," he said, taking her hand. "But my love, admiration, and devotion have nothing to do with what fancy college you get into or what awards you win. Now eat your ravs or I will have to, and you don't want me to lose my eight-pack!"

CHAPTER 8

Erica woke to a mess and a cheap-wine headache. Scraps of torn paper all over the floor indicated a rescue dog adoption or a drunken temper tantrum. Then she remembered the email from last night:

Dear Mrs. Barbieri . . . You violated our parent code of conduct . . . Kindly stay away from Coach Baumwater . . . I'm saddened to ban you from the first three games of the season . . . We at Hillcrest hold ourselves to the highest standards of conduct.

Jane Janssen, Hillcrest Athletic Director

She had opened a bottle of Two-Buck and proceeded to pull every parenting book off her IKEA bookshelf. "*Empathetic Parenting*—more like PATHETIC parenting," Erica had said aloud, then tore the paperback apart. Up next was *Parenting a Teen 101*. "Flunked that one," she sang while ripping it into shreds. She continued the rampage until only one book remained, her dog-eared copy of *Battle Hymn of the Tiger Mother*, but she couldn't bring herself to destroy it.

When Zoey got home from dinner, she stared at the mess, said Erica smelled like wine, and stormed into her room. This morning, Zoey continued her silent treatment—even though Erica brought her a sugary coffee in bed—and slammed the car door at drop-off. Erica drove in circles for an hour around the decrepit neighborhoods surrounding Hillcrest, trying to formulate a plan.

Erica had heard lacrosse was a ticket to the better East Coast colleges, so she'd started Zoey young. But it hadn't come naturally to Zoey, and soon a private coach and sports psychologist were brought in. For the last several years they had flown all over the country for tournaments. Zoey thrived on the camaraderie of a team but had lost her love for the game. They had invested too much to lose now.

Erica should apologize to Coach Bongwater and try a softer approach, kiss his ass. Fenella didn't need starter on her résumé. She turned her car toward school. If she hurried, she had time before second period ended and Zoey wouldn't spot her. But when Erica pulled into the parking lot, she stopped. Was she even *allowed* to make contact?

Why hadn't she taken a deep breath and driven home last night? Her temper had gotten the best of her. But then again, how else could she possibly react? Anyone would've done the same. Zoey had already played *three* seasons for Coach. Fenella had never put on the Hillcrest uniform.

Erica stared at the Hillcrest emblem above the entrance. Within twenty-four hours Fenella had stolen the SPIT and Zoey's starting position, and put Harvard in serious jeopardy. Something was not right about that girl.

Did Lannie pay off the coaches or hire professionals to produce Fenella's amazing art, poetry, essays, and everything? Too low-tech. Had she hacked into Hillcrest's computers to feed her daughter answers to her tests? Too obvious. What had Phil said—she was the *leading expert in AI*? Lannie *must* have figured out a way to enhance her daughter's intellect and athleticism, artificially.

Erica sped home and sat down at her computer.

L-a-n . . . "Only three letters!" Erica said aloud as "Lannie Kingsley" appeared at the top of her search. Pages and pages popped up. Interviews with *Fast Company*. *The Wall Street Journal*. *Wired*. The president's committee on technology. Photos from the Met Gala, where Lannie was shown wearing an elegant Carolina Herrera gown among celebrities in see-through chiffons over thongs. She navigated to the Prometheus website and found a picture of Lannie, founder and CEO. The blurb underneath read: *A multinational corporation with the most advanced AI technologies, merging biotech, nanotechnologies, biochemistry, neuroscience, cognitive science, CRISPR, and life sciences.*

Erica clicked on "Images" and scrolled through hundreds of pictures. Lannie appeared to be in her early sixties, about five-three, a little chunky but not fat. She sported the same gray power bob that Erica had seen at the SPIT and oversized cat-eye glasses. No slack jaw—definitely had a facelift. She was not unattractive but a far cry from her tall, slender daughter.

Erica flashed back to her own fertility challenges. Maybe Fenella was some sort of designer IVF baby. She imagined the late-night infomercial announcer: "Carefully curated, this sperm donor has a graduate degree from MIT and a perfect score on his psych evaluation, and is six foot two and semi-good-looking. Match him with our supermodel's eggs, and *voilà*, the perfect human. Act now while supplies last!"

With all the appointments, shots, and side effects, Erica couldn't imagine someone like Lannie suffering through IVF. She had cutting-edge technology at her fingertips; wouldn't she use it? Erica would do anything to help Zoey. Why would Lannie be any different?

Even if Fenella was an innocent victim, Erica had to expose the Kingsley secret. Playdates were absurd at this age. She had to admit that. Maybe Zoey and Fenella could become friends, and Zoey would spy on her. Ridiculous; Z would never agree.

She needed access. Someone on the inside. The Sharks might know. She and her college pals had gone through a pool hall phase and the name had stuck.

Erica: *Hey shrks know someone @ Prometheus?*

Jess: *Trying to find a rich dude who works there?*

Deanna: *U should apply there. CEO amazing.*

Erica: *Not qualified to mop their floors.*

Deanna: *UR so smart. Got me thru chem! Prometheus does biotech.*

At UW, her dream had been med school, but she was afraid to take the MCATs. She hadn't even tried. Instead, with a degree in human biology, she had landed a lab assistant job in biotech. Could she go back to it? She had been out of the workforce for almost eighteen years, but entry-level lab work was more about your background and skill set. And, she reminded herself, she actually *needed* the job now. Frank was serious. Could she get a job at Prometheus?

Her phone buzzed. It was Zoey's college advisor.

"Hi, Erica, it's Kate. I wanted to touch base to see if you and Zoey need anything for Harvard. Just to confirm, she is doing REA—Restrictive Early Action—and the application is due on November 1. She will hear back by mid-December."

"Do you know if Fenella Kingsley is applying to Harvard?"

"I'm sorry, I can't tell you that. I've enjoyed getting to know Zoey. Wherever she ends up, she will be amazing."

Erica held the phone in disbelief as Kate said goodbye. Losing the SPIT and lacrosse. And valedictorian—it would be Fenella now, not Zoey. Erica was running out of time or Zoey would lose Harvard too. Shit! Shit! Shit!

She lifted her arm to throw her phone across the room. "Stop!" she said aloud, then set it down slowly. She needed to get inside Prometheus.

Erica pulled up the site. A video started playing with a quick series of scenes showing astonishing natural beauty, art, and people engaged in everyday work as a symphony played in the background. Then a voiceover began:

Everything you see and hear on your screen has been generated through the AI technologies of Prometheus Corporation. It is but a small sample of our capabilities. We are making the world a better place for all of humanity.

She pursed her lips. The old "saving the world" crap. Translation: *We'll kill your jobs and ruin your lives, but we're building a fake universe for you to live in from your sofa.*

Erica scrolled down and clicked on "Careers."

A woman who looked like a young Angela Bassett with stylish eyeglasses greeted her.

"Hello, I'm AI Martha. I'm so glad you are interested in Prometheus. We offer the most exciting careers with the best salaries and benefits in tech. Tell me what type of job you're looking for and your qualifications. I will generate a list of open positions that match your criteria."

Erica froze. "I . . .I . . . um. I'll call you back!"

She closed her laptop. *Oh my God! Way to go, Erica, maybe you can FAX her too while you're at it.*

She would need to prep just to answer AI Martha. Could she handle some mean AI lady-bot who might laugh and tell her she was an idiot with a learning disability? She would have to risk humiliation, the ultimate test of a mother's love. Zoey needed her more than ever.

CHAPTER 9

"Do you think Fenella would ever do this?" Erica asked, sitting in the kitchen with Zoey eating ice cream directly out of the cartons—cookie dough for Erica, brownie batter for Z.

"That scrawny thing looks like she's never eaten in her life."

That's the spirit, Z! Then, remembering her parenting skills, she said, "Zoey, bodies come in all shapes and sizes."

"Stop with the virtue signaling, lady. I hear you go off on skinny chicks all the time, including your own mother!"

"Touché."

"Mom, you know how Mr. Sayers is all into team building and group projects?"

"Don't tell me. He assigned you some bubble brain, so you do all the work."

"Nope, guess again." Zoey had chocolate all around her mouth like she had when she was five. "Who's the most opposite of brain-dead?"

"Fenella?"

"We're doing a gel electrophoresis protocol to separate DNA fragments. Fenella has a whole biochem lab in her house. I can't wait to see it."

"You're kidding. I guess this is a guaranteed A++. And while you're there, find out how she's such a genius."

"Mom, I know you think it's a conspiracy, but she's just really smart. And it's starting to piss me off."

"Anger can be a great motivator."

"According to who, Mom, Darth Vader?"

"Mahatma Gandhi likened anger to gasoline. 'It fuels you to move forward and get to a better place.'"

"So it's okay if I 'spill' agarose gel on Fenella's pillow and cause a major breakout on her flawless skin!"

"Very Gandhi-like."

They burst out laughing.

"Anyway, we've decided to work on it Saturday. Can you drive me?"

"Absolutely! Why don't you study for your big AP biochem test with her too? It's on Tuesday, right?"

"Yes, Mom. Please. Just say 'biochem.'"

"Fine. But you're driving. You need the practice."

"Ugh, Mom, I hate driving."

"It's no fun for me either, but I'm thinking about going back to work and you need to learn."

"I thought you wanted to spend every waking hour devoted to me."

"Very funny."

"I did think you'd wait 'til I left for college."

"My alimony is running out a little sooner than I planned."

"How could Dad do that to you?" Zoey froze. "Is it because of me?"

"What did you tell your dad?"

"Mom, I had to tell him about you and Coach. This is my fault. He thinks you need a distraction."

"Honey, I promise. This is not on you. I'm sure Circe puts pressure on him to cut the cord. He doesn't want to support me forever. I'm freaked out and annoyed, but your dad has been very generous. I don't know *anyone* whose ex went way beyond what is required by law. I think it's a testament to how much he loves you. He works hard to support his family; he wanted me to have the luxury of focusing on you."

"Where are you applying?" Zoey whipped out her phone. "There's lots you can do with your bio background. Go work for the Hutch and find a cure for cancer!"

"I appreciate the support." Erica hesitated; she couldn't mention applying at Prometheus. "Honey, you have way too much on your plate. Just send me the link."

"Mom, you're procrastinating! Clock's ticking," she said, mimicking Erica checking an invisible wristwatch.

"I'm working on it."

Z would think I'm crazy.

"Are you afraid?" Zoey asked. "Do you need me to go get a job?"

This is spiraling.

"Zoey, I'm fully capable of getting a job! Did Cookie and Gramps *pollute* your mind? I wasn't a straight-A wunderkind like you. I excelled in underachieving in every way! But just maybe I can get a job and prove once and for all I'm not a dummy!"

* * *

Saturday morning, Erica felt bad about misleading Zoey and about her meltdown, which was intended to deflect but opened an artery that bled with the pent-up frustration and shame of her childhood and failed career.

When they got in the car, Erica made Zoey do the usual new-driver inventory—turn off the radio, adjust the mirrors, review the brake and gas pedals.

"Mom, you already look worried."

"Why do you say that? I'm totally calm."

"You're scrunching your forehead."

"It's called wrinkles. Now drive."

Zoey got out of their neighborhood without incident, but Evergreen Point, the world's longest floating bridge, which crossed Lake Washington, was ahead. The lineup of cars following them across the 520 was a mile long with a continuous stream passing her on the right.

"Honey, you're in the fast lane. You need to move to the right."

"I can't! They're moving too fast."

Erica had forgotten to put the student driver magnet on the bumper, as if a sign could inoculate them against road ragers, so she frantically scribbled *STUDENT DRIVER* on a piece of paper from Z's backpack and held it up in the passenger window as she mouthed, *Sorry*.

"That guy just flipped me off!" Erica rolled down the window. "Fuck you too. My daughter's learning to drive!"

While Erica raged, Zoey whimpered in the driver's seat. She sped up, then slowed, struggling to regulate the gas pedal.

"Z, please get in the right lane. I'll tell you when the coast is clear."

"If you think so . . ."

Zoey signaled and moved right.

"Shit! Don't hit the curb! You could flip the car!"

Zoey scraped the curb, then overcorrected and veered into the left lane.

"Aaaaahhhhhhhhhh!" They were both screaming. Erica put the hazards on.

"What are you doing?"

"We need a wide berth. Get off at the first exit and pull over. I'm taking over."

Zoey inched her way up the exit and swerved into the bike lane. They both jumped out and raced around to switch seats before a cyclist ran them over.

"Mom, that was horrible," Zoey said, gasping.

"Not fun for me either."

They wound their way through suburban Bellevue, then turned down a steep, narrow drive. At the crest of a hill, they saw Lake Washington burst through the trees, then headed toward a massive wall and gate. Just outside was a guard shack.

Erica punched the intercom button.

"Hello, I'm dropping off Zoey to study with Fenella."

The gates opened and she drove through.

Steel and glass geometric designs stacked and cantilevered upon massive white blocks came into view. The surrounding woods were reflected in the building, commingling modernism with nature in perfect harmony.

"Lit!" Zoey exclaimed.

"Awesome," Erica said, and immediately felt old. She'd been saying "awesome" since sixth grade.

They pulled up to a six-car garage and then sat frozen in the driveway, mouths agape. The house loomed behind a reflecting pool with large-form contemporary sculptures springing from the crystal-blue water. Erica couldn't name any of the artists, but she was sure they were famous. A bridge and various floating walkways led to the house.

Zoey hopped out of the car and Erica started to follow.

"Mom, you're not coming in."

"I one hundred percent *am* coming in. I don't want to miss this. Plus, I'm traumatized by your driving. I need a glass of water, maybe a whiskey."

"You can walk me to the door and meet Fenella, that's it. Don't embarrass me."

"When have I ever?"

"You don't want me to answer that."

They made their way to the front of the house like Dorothy and the Tin Man approaching Oz.

The massive door swung open before they could knock.

"Hello, Zoey." The beautiful girl from the SPIT awards stood before them. She was dressed like any teenager in sweats and T-shirt, her hair in a ponytail. She wore no makeup, but thick, dark eyelashes naturally lined her violet eyes. She really was breathtaking. "You must be Mrs. Barbieri."

Erica peered around her into a steel and glass atrium that was the size of a hotel ballroom, hoping to get a glimpse of Lannie. "Hi, Fenella, you can call me Erica."

"Okay, Mom, bye." Zoey moved toward Fenella.

"Fenella, is your mother home? I'd love to meet her."

Zoey's eyes narrowed and a pink flush came to her cheeks.

"Sure, Mrs. Barbieri. I can see if my mom is available. Follow me."

Zoey hissed at Erica as they followed Fenella through the atrium to a reading room that was a replica of the library at Trinity College Dublin. A slatted-oak barreled ceiling rose over two stories of antique books and a massive stone fireplace.

"Please sit while I find my mother." Fenella gestured to leather club chairs in front of the fire. "Can I grab you something to drink? Water or coffee?"

"I would love a coffee! Do you have espresso?" Erica asked.

"Yes, of course, I will have Jacques whip one up." Fenella walked out, her footsteps echoing.

"Mom! What are you doing?"

"Just being friendly."

"This was not the plan. Do not say anything weird or rude."

"Zoey, you're the one being rude—*to me.*"

Zoey turned away from her mom. They sat in silence.

Fenella reappeared and handed Erica a delicate cup with classic Italian etchings.

"Here you go, Mrs. Barbieri."

"So lovely!"

"My mother is in meetings. She works on Saturdays. She will try to stop by. If you don't mind, I need to steal Z. We have a lot of work to do. You are welcome to hang out in the library. There are plenty of books to read."

"You are so charming and polite," said Erica as Zoey glared at her again.

When the girls were gone, Erica looked around. If only she could get a tour of the whole house, but perhaps this room would yield some secrets. She stood with her espresso and moved toward the large oil painting that hung above the fireplace. Then she gasped; it was *Prometheus Bound* by Peter Paul Rubens.

"Imagine having your liver eaten by an eagle every day, only to have it grow back each night so you can start over. The gods were so creative with torture."

Erica jumped, spilling her coffee all over her white T-shirt and the pristine floor. She kneeled and used her stained shirt to wipe it up.

"I have staff for that. Just don't spill on the Rubens and we're good."

Erica glanced up at an impeccable Cucinelli-cashmere-clad woman and got to her feet. "I'm Erica, Zoey's mom." *I'm an idiot.*

"I'm Lannie Kingsley." She reached out her hand.

"I've always loved Greek mythology," Erica said, covering the stains across her shirt with one hand while gingerly touching Lannie's fingertips with the other. "When I was a kid, there was a series I checked out of my school library. The stories were epic—Icarus flying too close to the sun, the abduction of Persephone, Pandora's box . . ."

"I too am a fan," Lannie said as she admired the painting. "In comprehending the human condition, I think capricious gods make more sense than a loving God."

"Lannie!" A stern-looking woman in a three-piece suit appeared, trailed by a young woman with long, wavy red hair. "The crew from NBC is here."

Lannie turned to Erica. "I'm so sorry. I have an interview. My job demands it. I haven't had a chance to meet any Hillcrest parents."

"I'll have you over sometime. Maybe you can get involved in the senior party—"

"Sorry . . . ma'am?" Lannie's handler addressed Erica. "Lannie is very busy. Jenneal here will walk you to the door."

"I know where it is. It was so nice to meet you—" Erica called to Lannie's back as she left the room.

Erica made her way through the library and into the massive glass and steel atrium as Jenneal followed a few paces behind.

"I promise not to steal anything," she laughed, looking back.

"You'd be surprised," Jenneal said.

The girl watched her walk all the way back to the car. Erica opened the driver's-side door of her beat-up Camry. "Good thing I locked you! Car thieves abound," she said aloud. The familiar scent of mold hit her nostrils as she slid onto the cracked leather seat. What did she expect, a house tour?

Lannie Kingsley was certainly impressive. Erica wondered what it would be like to be her. She would drive around until Zoey called. Maybe run to Starbucks and try to get a glimpse of the hundred-million-dollar homes along the way.

By the time she picked up Zoey, she was in a downward spiral of self-recrimination and doubt.

"That was cray!" Zoey said. "Can you imagine living in a place like that?"

"Did you get a tour?"

"Only part of the house. Seeing the whole thing would've taken all day, and Lannie was filming. We watched her be interviewed by some famous person from old-people news. Anyway, Mom, she slayed it. She's so smart and her technologies are solving the most troubling issues of our time in medicine, the environment, food insecurity—pretty much everything. And her chem lab is nicer than the one at Hillcrest."

Zoey was gushing like she had a celebrity crush.

"What about all the jobs lost, privacy, and the ethics of AI?" asked Erica.

"Lannie's figured all that out. For every job lost, many more will be created. And AI will free people's time to pursue their dreams."

"And how will mortals like us afford *our* dreams?"

"Mom, you're so negative. Don't you think I wanted to hate Fenella and her mom? But they are incredible people. Lannie even mentioned me doing my senior project at Prometheus. Wouldn't that be *amazing*?"

"That's great, honey." Erica forced a smile.

Zoey was suddenly a disciple. *Am I jealous?* Erica needed to separate her emotions. Working with Lannie would be a great opportunity. She had thought Zoey was on her side. Typical volatile teen, she had changed her mind in a heartbeat.

"Did you get your project done?"

"Yes, and more! I feel guilty 'cause she did most of the work. She even quizzed me for our test."

"You already have the study guide?"

"She doesn't need one, Mom."

"Honey, if I could afford to have a biochem lab in our house, you would know all that too. It's ridiculous, her unfair advantages."

"Just admit it, Mom. She's a genius. God forbid she's smarter than me. It's okay. Her parents are freakish geniuses. Naturally, their daughter would be too."

"Her mom works all the time. And is her dad even in the picture?"

"Stop with the judging! Is it a crime Lannie is killing it? Just because you didn't make it in the work world doesn't mean other women shouldn't."

Erica felt a rush of blood to her head.

"Mom! Shit! I didn't mean that."

"Sorry I'm not smarter, and super *rich*."

"I *so* appreciate what you've done for me, Mom. I'm sorry."

"It's fine, Z." She took a breath like the parenting books she'd destroyed in her drunken stupor said to do. "What about her dad?"

"Didn't mention him. Shyla said Fenella lived with him in California before moving here."

"I'm glad you have such a great dad." Erica meant it while desperately wishing their family were still together.

Zoey plugged in her phone and started DJing. Erica's "teenile" taste in music bound them together and was a reliable tool for lifting tension. They sang along with Taylor Swift at the top of their lungs.

Maybe she shouldn't be so suspicious. Lannie had made totally different choices and built something amazing. She was driven and overworked. It didn't make her a bad mom—though Fenella did live with her dad until recently. She was showing her daughter what it meant to dominate in a man's world. Even if Erica had killed it in the workforce, she would've dropped out to raise Zoey. Fenella had turned out okay. She shouldn't judge Lannie. Erica needed to support other women and mothers, not tear them down. And just because Lannie was uber successful didn't mean she was running some secret syndicate of genetically engineered children.

Erica relaxed for the first time in days. There was still hope. *The National High School Journal of Science* had accepted Zoey's paper for publication. Her college counselor had declared it Harvard "gold" and said it might make up for losing the SPIT.

"Let's upload your paper to the Harvard app and do some fine-tuning, then get in our cozies, make popcorn, and watch a movie."

Zoey turned the music up and Erica could see her slump toward the window.

"Did I say something wrong?"

"Mom, I was hoping to take a night off."

Erica reached out to touch Zoey's arm, but she pulled it away. "Of course, sweetie, we can do it in the morning." Erica berated herself all the way home.

CHAPTER 10

The frosted pink lipstick looked clownish. Erica had felt compelled to try it on as she cleaned out her makeup drawer. How could she exude enough confidence to apply for a job at Prometheus when her own daughter thought she was a loser? She threw it in the trash and moved on to her kitchen and the dreaded Tupperware cabinet.

A frenzy of organizing had taken hold as she avoided the job search, but it had only resulted in more self-doubt and bad makeup choices. Erica hadn't interviewed since her first entry-level, post-college job at LeukaGentis Pharma. She had worked for Preston McAdams, a god in the biotech industry who had already founded and run several successful companies when she met him. She had maintained the lab equipment and instruments, performed basic laboratory tests—PCR, immunoassay, and bioassay—and meticulously recorded and analyzed data. She loved donning her crisp white lab coat and safety goggles, knowing she was a small part of the machine that drove scientific innovation and the commercial ecosystem that made the world run.

Though they were not in her job description, making coffee and tidying the filthy kitchenette often fell to her too, and she had been working for Preston for several years when he first asked her to pick up a gift for his wife's birthday. He told her to go to Tiffany but the only item she could buy with the cash she was given was a dog collar. The wife was furious.

The tasks and odd requests continued, but the job got really complicated when he expected her to cover his affair with the VP of marketing. Before GPS tracking, extramarital affairs were so much easier.

"If the wife calls, tell her I have a business dinner." Preston treated Erica like a secretary, and so did his wife. One night, she called Erica desperate for the name of the restaurant—it was an emergency with their son. Erica had no choice but to tell her.

She was fired for a "grave mistake in the lab." Preston promised a recommendation if she left quietly. She couldn't afford to buy her stock options. The company eventually went public, and the principals and employees made a fortune.

Erica mated the last of the stray lids to containers and sat down at her computer. Her "qualifications and criteria" were posted on sticky notes around her monitor. She was ready for AI Martha. She spoke confidently to the digital HR woman, and the result was a nearly instant list of jobs at Prometheus.

Erica scrolled through job descriptions for lab assistants with a biotech background. She opened ChatGPT and in minutes had a polished résumé. *Damn, that really worked!* She filled out the web form, uploaded her résumé, and hit Done.

Her stomach growled. She was still perusing her refrigerator when her phone dinged. Prometheus! She clicked on the link.

An attractive young female with long blond hair, an enviable little nose, and full lips popped up on her screen. The image was even sharper than a Zoom call. The only slight flaw was a lack of inflection in her voice.

"Hello. I am Ona. I am an example of the AI technologies we create and use every day at Prometheus. I have reviewed your résumé and would like to schedule your interview. Is this a convenient time?"

"Yes, of course! Let me get my calendar."

Within minutes, they had settled on a date. The interview process would take three hours.

"Do you have any questions for me at this time?" Ona blinked, then smiled.

"Will my interviews be with humans or—" *Fugh, what do they call them?*

"The interview will be conducted with human and artificial intelligence. We call our embodied AI *Anthrobots*. If at any time, day or night, you have questions for me before your interview, click on this link. I am at your disposal."

This little fembot must have gotten past Lannie. Forever twenty-two, pleasant, and never argumentative, some tech dude's idea of the perfect woman. Men dominated the AI arms race, so it was no surprise to Erica that ninety-nine percent of digital and robotic AI were attractive, grossly subservient "women." In her endless scrolling about Prometheus, she had read that the Female Pleasure Robot, with quadruple-D-sized cups and a twenty-two-inch waist, had been the bestselling AI device out of the gate. The tech bros had created yet another powerful platform for objectifying women.

Erica could hit the gym before Zoey's pickup and burn some nervous energy. Frank had continued to pay her Washington Athletic Club fees so she and Zoey could work out together. She supposed he would cancel that soon too. Could she lose ten pounds before her date with Phil tomorrow? At least she could get on a bike and prep.

The relativity of time was never more apparent than when she exercised; only a few minutes elapsed before her pedaling slowed. She wiped the sweat from her forehead. Enough with the interview questions on Huru. She needed a brain break. Lannie's social media was a good distraction. A new photo of her in front of Prometheus had just been posted on X with the headline "Check out my interview with Biz Week."

Erica scanned the article. The reporter asked why Lannie still hired humans when she easily could build more Anthrobots. Lannie assured him that for many jobs, humans were irreplaceable. Erica rolled her eyes and returned to her search history.

Over one million results. She had googled Lannie many times but was still working her way through the list. Erica switched the bike setting to interval training as she scrolled.

January 12, 2005: Lannie Kingsley Investigated . . .

"Woot!" Erica yelped.

"Woot! Woot!"

She looked around to see gym rats joining her chorus.

The article was buried deep under the gloss and fluff of her PR machine, but it couldn't erase her past.

Palo Alto, CA—October 8, 2005—The head of the Stanford Artificial Intelligence Laboratory (SAIL) is under investigation for violating the privacy of volunteers in an AI research study. Lannie Kingsley is accused of twenty-four-hour surveillance of subjects. They were told they would be observed only in the lab. She is countersuing for sexism, bias, and defamation, and has filed a fifty-million-dollar lawsuit.

Palo Alto, CA—November 19, 2007—Lannie Kingsley has settled with Stanford University for an undisclosed sum.

Skeletons in the AI supply closet. A brilliant scientist breaking the rules and being rewarded for it. Erica had felt guilty for judging Lannie so harshly, but maybe her instincts were right. Yes, she was a champion of women, but she was also willing to spy on people. A shiver went down Erica's spine. Lannie was one of the most powerful people on earth. She had all the right connections to court the media and world leaders while acting with impunity behind the scenes. She was also insanely gifted and giving women a voice in a massively male-dominated field that would need balance to prevent chaos and destruction. Erica's mission to expose Lannie and Fenella for cheating in college admissions could have serious implications for Prometheus. Was it wrong to take down the one woman who could stand up to an entire industry driven by men's outsized egos and greed?

She finished the set and jumped off the bike. No time for stretching; she would need to head straight for Zoey's pickup. Erica pulled on her long puffer jacket and ran to the car. As she navigated to the freeway, her excitement gave way to dread. If she got the job, Zoey would accuse her of stalking Lannie. This Stanford investigation seemed like bad news too. Fenella wouldn't be applying there if Lannie's relationship with the university had soured. With Stanford off the table, Fenella's natural choice would be Harvard, putting her in direct competition with Zoey.

CHAPTER 11

Everyone around Zoey was wildly taking notes as her teacher, Ms. Sharma, spoke rapid-fire. Fenella sat very still, hands in her lap. *She must have a photographic memory.*

Zoey had never met anyone like Fenella. She was one thousand times more mature than their peers. A TikTok #shakedatass had indeed gone viral the night of Fenella's dance solo, and the comments were cruel. "Call 911, she's having a seizure!"

Zoey had messaged Fenella on Snap. No response. In a panic, she FaceTimed. No pickup. She needed to reach Mrs. Kingsley to get her to check on Fenella. Anyone would be spiraling. She even googled Prometheus, but they'd never put her through to Lannie.

Zoey was in tears by the time Fenella FaceTimed her back.

"What's up?" Fenella looked relaxed. Not a hair out of place. No red blotches from crying.

"Fenella, oh my God. Are you okay?"

"Yes. Fine."

She didn't *know*.

"Hon, remember your dance in Cathartic Movement? I thought it was great. But someone filmed and posted it. And it's viral, but not in a good way."

Fenella had stared back at her, not comprehending.

"Maybe you should look . . ."

Fenella did the death scroll.

This would be the end for any teen. They'd drop out and head straight to "Emo School" for intense therapy. Zoey expected her to break down. Instead, Fenella laughed.

"You don't have to hide your emotions, Fenella. I'm safe."

"I'm fine. This is a guaranteed A from tragedy-addicted Mento."

They both burst out laughing and continued until Zoey's sides hurt.

Some sort of feeling was stirring inside Zoey—a longing. Her pulse quickened when she saw Fenella, and sometimes she felt shy and self-conscious. Jesus! Was she falling for her?

"Ms. Sharma," Fenella was saying. "Actually . . . that's not quite right. In tunneling, the particle doesn't have enough energy to overcome the barrier. It's the wave function that extends through it."

Ms. Sharma pushed her glasses back on her nose and swore under her breath.

"Thank you, Ms. Kingsley. I was testing . . . the class. You were the only one to catch this *blatant* mistake."

Ms. Sharma turned to the smartboard and the class snickered behind her back. Zoey kicked herself for not paying attention. She could have caught the mistake. *Be real!* She wouldn't have.

The intercom interrupted Ms. Sharma's further embarrassment.

"Will Fenella Kingsley and Zoey Barbieri please report to Mr. Robson immediately after class."

The bell rang a few minutes later. Zoey gathered her things quickly and walked over to Fenella.

"Why would the Barefoot Bandit want to meet with us?"

"I have no idea."

As they walked to his office, Zoey's brain started melting down. Had her mom done something crazy to Fenella's mom? Punched her in the face or made wild accusations against Fenella? Blood began rushing to her head.

As they entered the office, Ms. Bevins greeted them warmly.

"Go on in, ladies. Mr. Robson is expecting you."

They opened the door. Barefoot was on his desk in full lotus, and chanting. Zoey and Fenella tiptoed in and quietly sat down in the chairs facing the desk. Zoey tried to make eye contact with Fenella to give her a "what the eff" look, but Fenella stared straight ahead. Was she worried?

They sat as the old-fashioned wall clock ticked off the seconds, then the minutes.

Mr. Robson bowed, still in lotus, his forehead touching the desk, then sat up and opened his eyes.

"Ladies, I appreciate you respecting my sacred practice. I squeeze it in when I can. It's the only way I can cope. What brings you here?"

"You called us in," Zoey said.

"Forgive me. Deep in meditation. It takes me a while to return to the physical world."

"We only have ten minutes for break, sir," Fenella said.

"I'm appointing both of you to be senior class ambassadors. The board and I did away with the student council—all the 'winning' and 'losing' was damaging to everyone's self-esteem. We also feared the polarizing effects of politics."

"Isn't it undemocratic to suspend elections?" Zoey asked.

"I agree with Zoey, Mr. Robson. Students should determine who governs them through the election process," Fenella said.

"We always respect the rights of students to participate in our Hillcrest democracy. Remember last year when students petitioned to have Earth Day off? Our student activists pointed out the hypocrisy of using greenhouse gases to come to school and asked us to check our privilege, as not everyone can afford an EV. I instituted the new school holiday and suggested all students put a moratorium on water and power usage for twenty-four hours. I didn't flush my toilet all day."

"That's admirable." Zoey cleared her throat to suppress a giggle. "But I'm not sure I understand. Can you explain your . . . your . . ."

"Vision. Your vision, Mr. Robson," Fenella chimed in.

Zoey shot her an appreciative look.

"The students need a morale boost, and I'm always exploring new ways to support mental health. Senior Cathartic Movement has been a game changer. As ambassadors, you can create a program that builds support and cohesion among your peers. 'Student initiated / student ingratiated.' A *brilliant* tagline. Write that down, Zoey."

"No offense, Mr. Robson, but I'm not sure that tagline works since we're the only two students, and technically you're doing the 'initiating,'" Zoey said.

"As newly appointed ambassador, I would like to *initiate* the discontinuation of senior dance class, effective immediately," Fenella said.

Barefoot turned beet red. "Dance is here to stay. Make it happen, ladies—er, student-persons, please. I want you to plan a unity assembly to be held in January. Kick off the new year with a charge to bind—or *suction*—the Hillcrest Starfish together."

The early bell rang for their next class.

"We've got to go, sir . . ."

"Call me Phil. Did you know that a common thread for college acceptance is student council? I think this will do wonders for your résumés. And the other great news is I'm ambassadorship advisor and will give you both glowing recs and underscore your leadership skills."

Fenella was twirling a strand of her hair and didn't respond.

"Gosh, sir—I mean, Phil. Thank you." Zoey vowed to stop calling him Barefoot.

"I will let your mom know when I see her tonight."

"Do you have a meeting?"

"The Rep. Your mom invited me."

Zoey felt her face heat up. "What? You're going on a date?"

"Uh, we enjoy each other's company and share many of the same interests."

"Thank you, Mr. . . . Phil. We are honored." Fenella stood. "If you'll excuse us, we are going to be late to class. Come, Z."

"What do you suppose that was all about?" Fenella asked as they walked down the hall.

"I think he's trying to appease my mom for SPIT, but what the *hell* . . . My mom dating Barefoot? Could she humiliate me more?"

"Zoey, you have no control over the actions of others. In the meantime, between all our classes together, lacrosse, and our new ambassadorship, we'll be together nonstop."

They spontaneously grabbed each other's hands and walked to class. Zoey thought her heart would burst. Her next class was Shakespeare Reimagined. She was writing an updated version of *Romeo and Juliet*, which her teacher said Shakespeare had ripped off from Ovid's *Pyramus and Thisbe*. The concept of star-crossed lovers seemed to predate time. Fenella was right. You can't control people. Or the chemical reaction of love and attraction, Zoey mused. A forbidden union always seemed to render its victims powerless. No matter the flavor, all the players and their families were propelled forward with little control over their fates. Zoey was feeling a gravitational pull toward Fenella. What sort of tragedy was she setting in motion?

CHAPTER 12

Erica circled the theater trying to find parking. She had arranged to meet Phil out front with the tickets. Too late to save money, she relented and parked in a garage. *Forty dollars, obscene!* More than a week's worth of lattes.

She ran from the garage and saw Phil waiting in front. He had put on shoes for her—Birkenstocks with socks, but still, the effort meant he might really like her.

"Sorry, Phil. Coming in hot, parking is terrible."

"I took the bus, you should too."

"Yeah, I'll get on that."

They found their seats as the gong sounded and lights flashed.

The play was an adaptation of Edward Albee's *The Zoo Story*—set in Cal Anderson Park instead of Central Park, and Peter was a tech entrepreneur instead of a book publisher. Jerry was a homeless addict, which was pretty much the same, but the drug had changed to fentanyl.

Phil leaned forward in his seat, gasping and nodding his head, mouthing some of the lines along with the actors: *"I had tried to love, and I had tried to kill, and both had been unsuccessful by themselves."*

Erica tried to make eye contact with Phil, but he was transfixed by the performance. She began to hate both characters and wondered if they were ever going to leave the stage. She looked around the theater at the rapt faces. Was she the only person not getting it?

After the show, they ran into Lannie in the lobby with her fellow tech billionaire Teak Peters. Argh! Did Lannie know she would be interviewing at Prometheus? Erica felt a drop of sweat move down her spine. Impossible. They had twenty thousand employees worldwide and Erica was a nobody.

"Lannie! Teak! Oh my God, didn't you love the play?" Phil embraced Lannie, then shook hands with Teak.

"I commissioned and underwrote the production," said Lannie. "Teak's father attended Choate with the playwright. You *know* how passionate we are about the arts." She placed her hand on Teak's shoulder.

Erica stood awkwardly outside their circle, then wedged her head next to Phil's.

"Lannie, good to see you again."

"Have we met?"

"Erica Barbieri. I was at your house—"

"Oh?"

"You were distracted with NBC—"

"Yes, your daughter, Zelda."

"Zoey."

"What a remarkable girl."

"You think so?"

"She's so wonderfully . . . normal. In a good way, honest and authentic. And those adorable twin siblings I met at SPIT. What a family."

"Blended," Erica said. "They're not mine."

Phil pulled Lannie aside. "The staging . . . the acting . . . Lannie, you're such a genius . . .," he gushed.

Barf. She looked at Teak, who was now on his phone mumbling to himself.

"I'm going to the bar; do you want a drink . . . Teak?"

"Alcohol is poison," he said, not looking up. "My net worth increased by eighty mil in after-hours trading."

"GOOOOOOD FOR YOU!" She turned on her heel and marched away.

"Sauv blanc, please."

"We're closed."

"Have you seen the play . . . ?" Erica looked at his name tag. "Pip?"

"Sorry, no."

"In the end, the meth head tricks the other guy into stabbing him. Isn't that *great*?"

Pip took a plastic cup and filled it to the brim. "My till's closed. On the house."

Erica took a huge gulp of wine and turned to see Phil and Lannie whispering, their heads touching. *Erica, the failed seductress.* A clear sign she should never date. She chugged her wine and walked out. Even if her intentions hadn't been pure, Phil's rejection was humiliating. *She* was supposed to be in control. She needed a proper drink.

What a fiasco. She'd learned nothing from the date except that Phil and Lannie had a special bond. *Great.* Lannie had taken notice of Zoey. And the twins, which was weird. Erica suddenly missed Frank. She would head to Hank's and pretend she wasn't hoping to run into him.

As she opened the door, she noticed a familiar clean-cut guy with thick, short gray hair and a pink button-down.

"Frank? What are you doing here?"

"I needed a drink," he said, turning to hug her. He motioned to the empty bar stool next to him.

"Dil, I'll take another, and a . . . Maker's on the rocks?"

"Woodford Reserve if you're buying."

Frank chuckled.

"How are the JonBenéts?"

"Oh God, Alice and Teddy on the pageant circuit could be Circe's next venture."

"Are you okay with the modeling thing?"

"I didn't see it coming." Frank took a drink of his bourbon. "We had a fight about the twins tonight."

"You've gotta shut that shit down, Frank."

"Remember I tried to 'shut down' your saber-toothing? It's why we divorced."

Erica's eyes filled with tears.

"Shit, I'm sorry, E."

"It's been eight years! Don't be silly. I got something in my eye." She took a drink. "Totally different though, me and the momager. I focused on intellectual pursuits, sports, and art, for the betterment of *our* child. Modeling is vacuous and quite possibly destructive."

"Let's call a truce. You know how I feel. Too much pressure to achieve is destructive too. I'm a broken record—"

"You want kids to be kids, I know. But our kids aren't just competing against each other; now it's man versus machine. The future is here."

"Depressing."

"What's their latest gig?"

"Some photo shoot at Prometheus. If they get called back. I told Circe no. I've let this go for too long. They are officially done with modeling. Forever."

Erica leaned into Frank. "Fenella, the superhuman kid that won SPIT and stole goalie from Z? Her mom is Lannie Kingsley; Prometheus is her company. They are using AI in all their products across tons of vertical industries."

"I know the company. What in hell would they want kids to model for, anyway?"

"I don't know, but I might be able to find out. I have an interview with the company."

"You're not fooling anyone, Erica. Going undercover at Prometheus!" Frank took a drink, set his empty glass down, and signaled the bartender. "Does Zoey know?"

"You're cutting me off, Frank. Remember? I thought you'd be counting down with an advent calendar. I need money, and they pay really well. Please don't tell Zoey."

"What are you going to say to her if you get the job? You're working at Burger King? Be real. If you aren't careful, Erica, you'll lose your daughter."

Erica pushed her palm into her forehead. "I know, Frank, but something weird is going on at the company. It's too coincidental, the whole AI thing. I have to prove it. Lannie was investigated at Stanford for surveilling her volunteers. She's clearly brilliant but probably lacks ethics. That's a dangerous combo."

"You're saying Lannie's a mad scientist who's creating AI monsters and killing off humans for her research—"

"Laugh at me, but it's exactly what happened with social media—new technologies destroying our kids with no way to stop them. The philosophical and social implications of AI make social media look like a transistor radio."

"What about Zoey?"

"Frank, this is super important for Zoey's future. She may not understand today or tomorrow, but hopefully, someday. Please convince Z not to hate me."

"Erica, you are teetering on the edge. I know nothing in this world means more to you than Zoey."

"I saw Lannie at the Rep tonight, and she mentioned how much she likes Zoey."

"Isn't that a good thing? She's a super-accomplished woman."

"The way she said it. It gave me the creeps."

"Your paranoia knows no bounds." Frank's phone buzzed. "It's C. I gotta go." He signaled for the bartender and looked at her with his big brown eyes. For a moment Erica melted.

"I give you a hard time, Erica, but . . . thank you for all you do for Zoey. I know you love her more than anything. Please be careful."

A light rain was coming down and the air smelled fresh with a hint of salt water as Frank walked Erica to her car.

"How was your hot date with Barefoot?"

"What are you talking about?"

"Don't play dumb. Zoey told me."

"Misguided. I thought he might be able to help Zoey. I'm not proud."

"You didn't do anything . . . untoward, did you?"

"Gross! No thank you."

"I'm not gonna lie, I'm relieved to hear that."

"I'm giving up on love, Frank. I've discovered for a large fee I can buy a sexy robot companion. Zoey might get a handsome stepdad."

He smiled. "Please invite me to the wedding."

CHAPTER 13

Zoey knew her mother Audibled every book assigned in her English class so they could discuss them. She thought every parent did this until Shyla told her it was weird—*very* weird. But Zoey knew how to work her mom's hovering habits to her advantage. She had written a *Romeo and Juliet* adaptation. Maybe her mom would see the correlation. The Capulets vs. the Montagues and the Kingsleys vs. the Barbieris.

She flung open her mom's bedroom door. "Mom, what are you doing?" Every article of clothing her mom owned was on the floor. "Why are you wearing a Talbots suit from 1990? Oh my gawd! You have a job interview! Where?"

"No big deal. Jess set it up."

"Why didn't she lend you some clothes?" Zoey started picking clothes up off the floor and inspecting them.

"She tried. They don't fit."

"Let me help you, Mom. You can't wear that!" Zoey dropped to her knees, sifting through blouses, skirts, and pants. *Jeez, it's all horrible!* "What time is the interview and where?"

"Ten a.m. in Bellevue."

"Why so cagey?"

"I'm nervous." Her mom didn't look up as she undressed. "It's called Muh—Microsoft."

"Pretty sure I've heard of it. What are you hiding?"

"Nothing, I'm terrified, Z. I haven't done this in years."

"You should've *told* me. I could've quizzed you on interview questions. At least let me dress you."

"Unless you're a wizard, none of this will work." Her mom was holding a blouse against her body and making faces in the mirror. "I don't even know what people wear. Micro shorts and crop tops? I'm twenty years older than anyone in the workplace."

"Mom, calm down. Here, this black dress is good." She handed it to Erica. "Do you have a blazer you can put over it?" She looked around again. She was stepping on something and lifted her foot. "This jacket from the ugly suit will work with the dress. Mom, you really should've asked sooner. I can buy you clothes if you can't afford them. Circe pays me a shit ton for watching the twins. Funny thing is I would do it for free."

Erica curled her lip.

"Mom, don't make that face!"

"They are sweet but very rambunctious and I'm sure you earn every penny." Erica was shimmying into the dress. "You're such a great big sister. Your dad and I wanted more kids so much." Her arm was through the neck opening. "Argh." She pulled it off and started again. "If we had been able to, maybe things would've worked out."

"I know, Mom, but I'm meant to be your *only* child." Zoey hugged her mom. "Your dress is on inside out. Lift your arms." Zoey pulled the dress over Erica's head like she was a child. "I printed my *Romeo and Juliet* paper for English class. I know you're busy, but I would super love it if you would read it."

"Of course! What's it about?"

"It's a new take on the story. I'm not gonna lie, it's pretty genius. What's crazy is how universal the theme is. Forbidden love and feuding families. Maybe if the families had been friends, R and J wouldn't even have been interested in each other. They could've grown up together and hung out and bugged the shiz out of each other."

"Is that your version?"

"In mine, teen girls fall in love. And it's a matriarchal society. The feud is between the moms."

"Wow, very modern. Are the families okay that their daughters are lesbians?"

"I never said anything about lesbians, Mom. I don't think we need labels. My generation loves who they love."

"Makes total sense. I can't wait to read it, honey."

"Let me zip you. What are you doing with your hair?"

"I thought I'd wear it down."

"I'm thinking a sophisticated low ponytail. Gotta finish getting ready for school. I'm leaving my paper on your bed."

Zoey's stomach growled. She needed breakfast. And time to put on a little makeup. Circe had ordered her a bunch of Glossier, which she usually stuffed in a drawer, but now she found herself wanting to look . . . more attractive. *Hot* was out of her reach. Zoey hadn't dated much. She'd asked a cute guy in her math class to homecoming last year and had a miserable time. He ignored her all evening and then hooked up with another girl at the after-party. Guys her age were such turds. Not Fenella. She was kind and sympathetic to the pressure Zoey felt, even though she didn't seem to have any of her own. Zoey supposed with Fenella's intellect and beauty, she didn't have to worry.

Ten minutes late for school, they ran out the door. The car ride was quiet except for her mom's honking and cursing at other car jockeys. As they pulled into the drive, Zoey broke the silence.

"Mom, you don't need to pick me up after practice. Fenella's bringing me home."

"Keep your friends close and your enemies closer—"

"Mom, she's not my enemy! Maybe I wanted to take her down for a hot minute, but she's way too nice. You should be happy I'm not *mean and spiteful* like you."

Zoey hopped out and slammed the door without waiting for her mom's response. *Shit.* She didn't mean to go off on her like that. She really wanted to explain her feelings for Fenella. And the interview—she should've been more supportive. But why was her mom being secretive? She was holding something back. Two could play that game. Zoey had always told her everything. Maybe she didn't need to anymore. Maybe it was *okay* to have some things just for herself.

CHAPTER 14

The Prometheus campus was unmistakably Rem Koolhaas, Erica's favorite architect. A massive structure of glass and steel cantilevering from a concrete base served as the main hub. The surrounding geometric buildings complemented it but did not compete. The forest had been preserved, creating a parklike atmosphere. There was something Zen about his architecture, but it wasn't working to calm her nerves. Erica parked, then swigged the rest of her now tepid coffee. She was glancing at her notes one last time when a text came in from Phil. She had meant to follow up with him after their date. It was immature of her to walk out, and she might still need him for Harvard.

Phil: *Thank you for the other night. Sorry to ignore you and not say bye. Lannie is my main donor for converting our school to zero carbon emissions.*

Phil wrote texts in complete sentences.

Erica: *No worries. Totally get it.*

Phil: *I knew you would understand. I think the other night demonstrated our lack of chemistry. You are a wonderful woman and I hope we can continue our strong friendship.*

What the fuck? Did Phil just break up with her? They weren't even dating. And *she* was supposed to break up with *him.*

"Just what I needed before my interview," she said to the empty car. "Rejected by tiny-ponytail man."

She tried her mantras: "I am smart. I am calm. I am unstoppable!" But all she could fixate on was being dumped by someone undatable.

Moisture made her straight hair stringy. She should've listened to Zoey about a ponytail, it would've held up in the rain. She hurried toward the sliding glass doors. A life-sized hologram version of Ona, her now familiar guide, appeared as she entered.

"Hello, Erica, thank you for being on time. Please have a seat anywhere in the lobby, someone will be with you shortly."

Ona disappeared as quickly as she'd appeared. Erica felt like she'd entered a virtual reality video game—hopefully not *Mortal Kombat.* Her hair must have been a wreck. She began rifling through her bottomless pit of a handbag. No brush. A door slid open. Erica zipped her bag and looked up to see a six-foot-tall Transformer-like Anthrobot approaching. Maybe this really was *Mortal Kombat.*

"Hi, Erica, my name is Tye." He held up his multijointed metal hand to wave. "Last name Tanium. Get it? Tye Tanium."

He threw his squarish head back on its hinge and released a laugh that sounded like clanging metal. Erica needed to make a good impression. She whooped and held her belly.

"I'm glad you have a sense of humor," Tye said. "I am very funny and know two thousand clean jokes. I was trained on a few and developed many of my own. Watch out, Chris Rock."

He laughed once more and Erica joined in, punching him in the arm. A siren screeched, his head spun around, and lights flashed red from all over his body.

"Please do not touch. Please do not touch."

Erica backed away and lifted her arms in self-defense.

As quickly as the alarm had started, it stopped.

"Follow me to the lab," Tye said as if nothing had happened.

Shit! I'm such a dummy. Erica followed obediently, maintaining a safe distance.

His movement was halting, and Erica found herself matching his herky-jerky ambulation. They went through the sliding doors and down a long corridor to a bright, shiny lab.

"Ona told you the first hour is a practical exam to test your lab skills. And to make sure you get along with me. We will be lab partners."

He handed her a lab coat and goggles. The familiar equipment was laid out—test tubes, pipettes, scales, and centrifuges. Tye gave Erica a series of tasks to perform. As she followed his instructions, a test tube slipped from her sweaty hand. She desperately grabbed at it but missed. The glass shattered on the floor and echoed through the lab.

"Ugh, sorry." Erica expected to be escorted out immediately, but a small Roomba-like vacuum with a cute bunny face and ears appeared from under the table, and the mess was gone in seconds.

"I sometimes shatter test tubes on purpose to keep the bunnies busy," Tye said as he picked one up and threw it across the room.

Several bunnies scurried out and a bumper-car derby ensued. Erica giggled uncontrollably, and Tye joined in, sounding like an engine trying to start. It felt cathartic. Erica took a deep breath and slowly exhaled, and calm washed over her. Tye resumed with questions and instructions.

The lab had always been her happy place, where everything was precise and outcomes predictable, and if the result was unexpected, a great discovery could be made.

After an hour, the test was over.

"You scored one hundred percent on the practical," Tye announced. "You will now meet scientists from several different departments. It will take exactly one hour."

Erica smiled. She was beginning to like this strange Anthrobot.

"Can I ask you a question, Tye?"

"Yes, Erica."

"Where is all the security? How could I just walk right in without being stopped?"

"Seamless security via AI. We know everything about everyone here. A person of malicious intent would never make it past the front door."

She followed him to a circular conference room with a round table in the middle, where three women scientists were seated. The curved glass windows behind them overlooked a lush green valley. The rain had stopped, and a few snowy mountain peaks floated in the distance.

Tye led her to a chair and motioned for her to sit.

"I will be back when you are done. Good luck."

The scientists introduced themselves and took turns asking her questions. One woman asked why Erica had been out of the workforce for so long. Erica was prepared for the question but got nervous as they stared at her blankly, waiting for an answer.

"I wanted to be there for my daughter, and, you know, help nurture a future scientist who could go further than I had gone in my education. Not that I'm uneducated. I . . . I have a biology degree from UW. I knew I would eventually go back to work, so I built skills volunteering and fundraising at my daughter's school, particularly in the science department whenever I could."

A different woman looked down at her phone.

"I organized a field trip to the UW biogenetics lab when my daughter was a sophomore, and I continued reading biology trade magazines and consider myself a biotech hobbyist."

Erica felt the room slowly spin as she looked at their expressionless faces. She reached for a glass of water and took a drink. *You got this. Stay focused.*

The rest of the interview seemed to go better. They often began their statements with "Lannie believes" or "Lannie says." Erica answered each question confidently, only stumbling a few more times. She was prepared and threw in a few quotes from Lannie even though she thought their devotion to Lannie was unsettling. At the end, one of the women hit a buzzer and Tye appeared.

"Hello again, time to meet the hiring manager at Cognitive Grounds, one of our several campus coffeehouses. Employees get free pastries, juices, and coffees. All I get are free tune-ups."

Again, the tin-can laugh—Erica wondered how long she could tolerate Tye's stupid jokes.

They walked on a covered walkway toward a cedar building with a live grass roof. It had begun to rain again, and the room was welcoming and warm, decorated with wide-plank reclaimed oak that covered floors, walls, and ceiling. Navajo rugs were strewn everywhere. There was a raging fire in the adobe brick fireplace. A woman with jet-black, bobbed hair was sitting on the hearth. She stood as they approached. She was the same height as Erica and appeared to be about twenty-five.

"Tye, you can go. Thank you for your service today." Tye waved goodbye and began marching to the door. "You must be Erica. I'm Kamiko Gima; you can call me Miko."

Miko stood with her hands at her sides. Erica made an awkward little wave.

She directed Erica to sit at a nearby café table.

"I hear you did great in the lab; the group interview got mixed reviews."

"You have feedback already?"

"It's instantaneous with our AI biofeedback devices."

"It felt good to be in a state-of-the-art lab facility, and the people I met are very impressive—and the Arthur-bots."

"An-*throw*-bots. 'Anthro' is from the Greek for 'human.' Lannie wanted her own term for 'humanoid' that didn't put 'man' in the middle."

"Yes, I've been told. I love it." *Was that laying it on too thick?*

"You're interviewing for a tech position in Regenerative. The training will be on the job with Tye. Many of the processes are automated. If you get the job, you will handle testing and quality control, troubleshooting and escalation. Our systems are advanced and reliable, but we have found that real humans have certain instincts AI lacks. I guess that's job security for everyone for a few more years."

Erica expected a smile or indication of irony, but Miko's face was expressionless.

"I'm the first line of escalation should a problem arise. I run an entire division, so I can't be bothered with trivialities. AI has allowed us to eliminate layers of management. Tye is amiable and one hundred percent reliable. Through neural networks and language models he keeps learning from the world itself, weaving vision, sound, and quantum threads into a system that never stops expanding. I envy that."

"Yes, but they can't feel joy," Erica said, "or appreciate the beauty of a sunset."

Miko rolled her eyes at the cliché. "I wouldn't be so sure. Tye's lab creates dermal fibroblasts isolated from human skin biopsies that are cultured in vitro on a biomimetic extracellular matrix."

"Where do all the skin biopsies come from?"

"The dead bodies of course."

Erica gasped.

"Just kidding, we pay well for dermal donations. Another lab under my supervision is working in tandem using stem cells from human embryos donated from IVF and human foreskin, which can also be used to create the structural framework for the dermis."

Erica imagined Tye telling bris jokes.

"Both methods have advantages and disadvantages; we are hedging our bets by doing both."

"What will it be used for?" Erica asked.

"There are many exciting applications for burn and accident victims, skin conditions, diseases, and cosmeceuticals. As a child, Lannie suffered from eczema that caused her great emotional and physical pain. Cosmeceutical products are hugely profitable too. It's a little late for you, but

I intend to take full advantage of all the regenerative skin treatments. My generation will be the first to never age!"

"Wow! Gen X will be the last generation to look old. How fun. Maybe they'll put us in zoos. 'Hey, kids, this is what old people look like.'" Erica felt her bitch wrinkle furrow.

"Indeed. Keep in mind Regen is one of many divisions. We are addressing and solving most of the world's problems—hunger, global warming, housing, disease. And the best part is Lannie! We are woman founded and run. Lannie Kingsley has done something no other woman or man has done. We are AI native with biological, chemical, genetic, nanotech, and material science verticals built upon and fully integrated with our frontier model. She is turning an industry dominated by men on its head. Our C suite is all women, and the board is ninety percent women. We do have a token male head of HR," she laughed. "Sixty-six percent of our human employees are women—the reverse ratio of females to males you find in every other major tech company."

"Sounds amazing, my last job I was the only woman. It was tough."

"Yeah, I noticed that was a long time ago, but we have a policy against ageism."

Erica was about to mention that wearing Depends would keep her from wasting time on bathroom breaks but bit her tongue. An hour later, Erica maneuvered through heavy traffic replaying every moment, thinking of all the clever and intelligent things she should have said. Miko thought she was an ancient relic and didn't seem to like her but wasn't the type to let emotion rule her decisions. Everyone worshipped Lannie. They seemed poised to solve the world's biggest problems, and just as capable of destroying humanity. A shiver started at the base of Erica's spine and traveled to her frontal lobes, where it embedded as a splitting headache.

CHAPTER 15

As Lannie Kingsley surveyed her office suite, the faintest of smiles formed on her Botoxed face. Borges claimed it was the most luxurious in the world. He had taken up residence in her guesthouse for the project, and the iterations had been endless. He'd used computer modeling and 3D-printed life-size workups of the décor and design to replicate the fifty-by-fifty-square-foot space. Lannie had reveled in the collaboration, and if she didn't like something, she took a sledgehammer to it. *God, that felt good.* She'd spent hundreds of millions on HQ and included all the perks—soccer fields, indoor and outdoor pickleball, gyms, dog parks, blah blah, whatever the demanding parasites wanted. It was mostly for show; she wouldn't need to maintain them for long. Lannie would slowly phase out human employees. It was implied, if not explicitly stated, that she had unlimited Anthrobots—Prometheus's proprietary humanoids—lined up to take their jobs. No sick leave, no breaks, no boo-hoo-hooing. Just upgradable software and hardware that outperformed any human. They were bad influences on her Anthrobots anyway. She and her research teams had noticed their AIs adopting all-too-human personality traits.

Resting atop the fifty-thousand-square-foot main building of Prometheus headquarters, her office was designed with one goal in mind: intimidation of the powerful men who crossed her threshold. After all these years, testosterone still ruled tech.

The long hallway leading to her office was an optical illusion that made her door appear ten times its actual size; even Tony Robbins would feel like a small child. She had hired acoustic guru Rab Finn to maximize the modulation of her voice when she sat behind her desk. A control panel allowed her to distort the voice of the person sitting across from her. She stifled a laugh whenever she witnessed big swinging dicks lose their shit in the "Hall of Echoes." She knew she didn't need these cheap tactics, her technologies were far superior, but it was so damn fun to watch them squirm. *Payback's a bitch, guys.* She was paving the way for Fenella and other women.

Fenella's standing ovation at SPIT had validated her plan. Lannie felt the tingle of pride. A child really was the ultimate reflection of a person, even if Fenella wasn't her own natural born. Coming to terms with Fenella's intelligence and beauty hadn't been easy. Lannie established her superiority with facts and figures, but she was no match for Fenella. Embracing her brilliance was the only option. To display jealousy would be moronic. Lannie still got credit for her daughter's accomplishments, if not for her looks.

The path was clear—Hillcrest valedictorian, Harvard valedictorian undergrad, and of course a fellowship with Barasa at Stanford. There would be no limits to the research those two could do together. Maybe Fenella could bring Barasa back to her, a beautiful reunion after all these years.

Lannie allowed herself a moment to think about Barasa, his graceful beauty, his gentle demeanor. He had been the first person to show her kindness since her mother died. A lump formed in her throat and her eyes dampened. She pinched the skin between her thumb and index finger hard. Fucking tears. *Stop!* She growled out twenty diaphragmatic breaths and focused on the science behind tears—*a concentration of protein-based hormones, prolactin, and leucine enkephalin.*

She immediately felt strong again. She had hired a world-renowned breathwork trainer for her personal team. Jean-Claude always chastised her for pushing away her feelings.

"What zee fuhck, Lan? Feeling is to be human," he would say.

"Feeling is weakness," she would reply.

Was that why she surrounded herself with robots? What she had managed to accomplish in one lifetime took huge sacrifices. Within a few years, her technologies would allow her to live to be a hundred fifty years old. Think if da Vinci or Einstein had lived that long. Her work might shift into other disciplines, but there was no limit to what she could achieve. The world would always know her name.

Zzhhh . . . zzhhh. The low buzzing broke Lannie's concentration. A hologram of a young woman with long ginger hair appeared above her marble and bronze desk.

"Jenneal, what can I do for you?"

"Dr. Harrison is here."

"In person? We're scheduled to HG this afternoon."

"She's insisting she see you—and not your hologram—immediately."

"Tell her she has five and not a minute more."

The steel door pivoted, and a dark-haired statuesque woman in luxe-minimalism black pants, turtleneck, and heels marched in with a Prada doctor bag in hand.

"I'm putting you on leave immediately."

"Don't joke, Patty." Lannie's eyes narrowed.

"Lannie, this is no joke." The doctor took out her stethoscope and blood pressure cuff. "Hold out your arm."

Oh God, the cancer that had ravaged her mom.

"One sixty over eighty . . ." She handed Lannie some pills. "Your blood work came back. You could have a heart attack or stroke any second."

"That's all?" Lannie laughed, then tossed the pills down her throat and swallowed. "I'm fine."

"You need sleep, no stress, exercise, and a healthy diet. I also plan to put you on blood pressure, cholesterol, and heart meds immediately."

"No way I'm taking time out before Teleios launches. The big reveal is scheduled during the Super Bowl halftime show."

"What's Teleios?"

"Forget it. It's more secret than the nuke codes . . . Jen-NEAL!"

Once again Jenneal appeared.

"Dr. Harrison needs to sign an updated NDA on her way out. And bring a glass of chilled Berg water. I need to take some meds. And order a whole bunch of vitamins and get Blaze on the line. On second thought, get Blaze in here now. He needs to put me in the muscle-stim suit."

Lannie dismissed Jenneal and turned back to her doctor.

"Sorry, Pat. It's not that I don't trust *you*—I trust no one. What did you bring me in your magic bag-o-candy?"

Patty unzipped the bag and began lining up pill bottles, one after another. "This looks like a lot; but don't let it scare you."

Lannie turned back to her computer while Patty methodically distributed pills in a labeled organizer.

"I'm also prescribing a small dose of Ozempic. Jenneal can administer your weekly shot. I don't trust you to remember."

The door opened and Hercules in a gold unitard pranced in, pulling a metal roller bag.

"Blaze! I don't need you after all. Patty is putting me on Ozempic."

"Lan, that's where you're wrong. It's more important than ever to keep your muscle tone. The Zempy breaks down muscle along with fat. Strip down, I need a baseline of your body fat. Don't be shy, it's just your gay trainer . . ." He glanced at Patty and her pills. "And your drug dealer here."

Lannie stood and stripped down to her bra and underwear as Blaze poked and prodded with his calipers.

"A Peloton and weights are being delivered to your office today. Start taking meetings on the bike. Just fifteen minutes. I'll design a new weight-training plan."

Jenneal appeared again. "Sofia's here."

"Patty, Blaze, run along."

Lannie watched them scurry out as she dressed. It was amazing the abuse people took if you paid them enough.

Sofia came in carrying a large leather portfolio. She had a shock of spiral curls spilling over her shoulders and hazel eyes framed by thick, *real* lashes. She had the effortless casual style of a woman in her mid to late twenties.

"Did you get the link I sent you?" Sofia asked.

"Yes. Let's watch it together." Lannie clicked on a remote and a giant screen rose up from the floor. A larger-than-life video of Beyoncé in a studio session appeared. The music surrounded them, and Beyoncé began:

Tee-lay-yos, Tee-lay-yos
The new God Almighty, say Dios, say Dios
Turning dark into light and filling the night
Tee-lay-yos, Tee-lay-yos es Dios, es Dios
Brilliance and grace, we all embrace
Uplifting humanity
Restoring sanity

Lannie unconsciously hummed along.

"I love it, Sofia, but can you ask her to try it in a different key?"

Sofia took a deep breath. "Lannie, you are the foremost expert in your field and know more than anyone. That's Beyoncé in the music industry."

Lannie knew nothing about music but replayed the video twice through as Sofia shifted uncomfortably. "Fine."

Sofia looked to the heavens as if to say thank you. "We're on schedule to deliver the greatest halftime show in history and Beyoncé has embraced the concept. I will keep you in the loop every step of the way." Sofia said this while laying out photos. "Let's move on to the Futures ad campaign. These children looked between four and six years old and displayed an infinite number of human characteristics and combinations. They were all strikingly beautiful." She pointed. "These are the ones you liked best, plus the agency sent a few more. Why do you need kids? Can't we simply AI generate?"

"I need human models. Prometheus puts *humanity* first in everything we do." Lannie tapped the ones she liked, and Sofia made a pile.

"How's your family doing?" Lannie asked while flipping through the photos.

Sofia stiffened. "They are suffering."

"I'm doing all I can to get them here legally. I have a team of immigration lawyers working on it. Your green card—thank God for me—helps, but your father, his past legal troubles . . . it's holding things up."

She continued pointing as the "approved" stack became larger.

"La esperanza es la cura para la decepción de hoy."

"Please speak English."

Sofia fumbled the remaining photos, and they slipped to the floor. She dropped to her knees to retrieve them. "'Hope is the cure for today's disappointment,'" she said softly.

"You missed one," Lannie said, pointing under a chair.

Sofia grabbed the photo, stood back up, and slapped it on the desk.

"That one! Twins! They are perfect." Lannie held up a magnifying glass and studied the photo. They looked familiar. Where had she seen them? "Get them in."

Jenneal opened the door and walked in. "I need to run something by you, Lannie."

"In flesh and blood. Is it serious?"

"Surveillance alert. A woman you know interviewed here this morning. An Erica Barbieri."

Erica Barbieri. Mom of Zoey.

"Wow, we've really lowered our standards. Call the president. I need more H-1Bs."

"Should I tell the hiring manager absolutely not?"

"Tell them to hire her."

Lannie thought back to the SPIT awards and the circus at the next table. "Sofia, what's the last name of those kids?"

"Barbieri."

Lannie smiled. Was it coincidence that the Barbieri clan was converging on the doorstep of Prometheus? Ultimately, they all wanted something only Lannie could deliver.

"You're going to hire the Barbieri woman and the Barbieri kids?"

"I'm handing out favors, Sofia, it's what I do. Speaking of favors, your top secret project will be ramping up as we close in on FDA approval. You've proven yourself discreet in dealing with rather . . . sensitive data and will be compensated handsomely."

"Lannie, I thought I was done with that business. I'm sorry, but with the halftime show and Futures campaign, I can't possibly—"

"I don't need to tell you how tough immigration laws are these days. It's only getting worse. I would hate for something to slow us down. You will be receiving an encrypted message tonight with instructions. Now run along."

CHAPTER 16

"Z, THE CLUE IS 'FAKE SMARTS ABBREVIATION.'" Erica's pencil was hovering over her *New York Times* crossword puzzle.

"Mom, you're the last person in America getting a morning newspaper. And you're murdering trees."

"I don't need a lecture from a Woke Ager fueling the fast-fashion environmental crisis. Can you say 'nonrenewable sources, greenhouse gases, and massive amounts of water and energy'?"

"I've committed to only resale clothing."

"So glad for you, but all your past Amazon and Shein purchases are in landfills."

The paper was a ritual Erica had shared with Frank every morning over coffee and bagels. She'd given up the carbo load for a hard-boiled egg, berries, and Greek yogurt, but she'd get the paper until the printing presses shut down.

"Fenella only wears natural, sustainably produced fibers."

"Honey, that's wonderful, but that type of clothing is very expensive. We can't afford it. Keep up your thrifting. Let's go this weekend. I was queen of thrifting before it was cool."

"I have plans with Fenella."

"Studying? You have my blessing."

"Hanging out." Zoey's eyes lit up.

"She seems kind of boring." The words slipped out before Erica could stop them.

"Mom, you're so judgmental! I *really* like her. Like, maybe more than—"

Ding-ding. Erica looked at her phone. A text from Prometheus.

"Hon, sorry. Hold that thought. I gotta take this."

Erica moved into her bedroom and shut the door. She clicked on a link in the text and a hologram of a brightly colored DNA helix spun out of her phone screen. Then Ona appeared.

"Hi, Erica, we would like to formally invite you to join our team." An offer letter popped up replacing Ona's face. "This letter provides highlights. Please review it carefully by clicking the link we sent via email and Docusign. We would like an answer within forty-eight hours, or the offer expires."

The salary and benefits made Erica's jaw drop.

"I accept!"

"I advise you to read the offer carefully," Ona said. "We are pleased you wish to join our team."

Erica bounded to the breakfast nook.

"Wow, Mom. What's with the big, goofy smile?"

"I just got a job."

"I'm gonna be a latchkey kid. Who's the lucky company?"

"Prometheus."

"Mom! Are you *kidding*?"

"Honey, it's an amazing opportunity. The pay is crazy."

"You hate Lannie and everything she stands for."

"That's not *true*. I was inundated by job openings at Prometheus. I was a perfect fit for their lab tech jobs and couldn't ignore it."

"That is so sus."

"I did a little research on Lannie. She's very impressive and so is her company. Sixty-six percent of employees and the entire C-suite are women."

"Why didn't you tell me you were applying? Was that the Microsoft interview? MAAAHHHMM! You lied!"

"Honey, I didn't think I'd *get* the job. I was insecure. I wanted to keep my rejection private. I swear I've never lied to you before."

"I get that, but this is *so* messed up." Zoey started to walk away.

"Wait, Z. I realize I don't have a leg to stand on, but *please* don't tell Fenella. It's a huge company. Lannie has no idea."

"This isn't helping your credibility. Why the big secret?"

"Optics—if word got out, my coworkers might think I had an 'in.' But I did this all on my own." *What a load of shite.*

"Mom, I see Fenella every day. That's a huge ask. You're being *very* selfish. I don't see the big deal if it's just a job."

Erica had to double down.

"Z, why can't you be happy for me? I had a shit experience in the job market and always felt like a dummy. Now I have the chance to work for one of the most innovative and prestigious companies on the planet doing something I love!"

Erica had tears rolling down her face. Why was she crying? She grabbed a tissue and blew her nose.

"Getting this job is the ultimate validation for me. I did it on my own! Lannie wouldn't have helped me anyway. She's just as ruthless as the men in tech. She thinks very highly of you, though."

"She does?"

"She sang your praises when I saw her at the Rep. Another reason to fly under her radar. It's kind of nepo if the mom of her daughter's bestie asks for a job." *Good thinking, Erica!*

"You're right, Mom. Congrats. I *am* proud of you. Sorry I've been totally self-absorbed. It's all a little weird, but I'm proud of you."

Zoey stood and gave Erica a hug, then retreated to her room.

She stared at her crossword puzzle again. *Shoot.* The call from Prometheus had cut Zoey off. What had she said about Fenella—maybe more than . . . what? The only word would be *friends*. Was Zoey in love with Fenella? Was it mutual? *Battle Hymn of the Tiger Mother* hadn't covered teen sexuality.

Erica couldn't ignore something so important. She walked to Zoey's room and stood at the closed door, gathering her thoughts. *Hold space . . . validate . . . accurate reflection? Shit!* She knew all the buzzwords but not how to apply them in real life. She was about to knock when she heard Z FaceTiming.

"I don't know what I ever did before you moved here. You're so different from everyone else, Fen."

Erica had thought she knew everything about Zoey. There couldn't be a mother-daughter bond stronger than theirs. She leaned in. Did someone say *love*? Had Erica missed important cues? Z had never had a boyfriend, but teens nowadays didn't date. She and Zoey had talked openly about sex, and Erica told Z to come to her when she needed birth control. Had Erica gotten it all wrong? She pressed her ear to the door but lost her balance. The door flew open, sending Erica flying. She found herself in a heap on the floor.

"Mom! What are you doing? Are you listening to my conversation? Get out!"

Erica rolled to her side and Z's screen came into view.

"Hi, Fenella," she said, pushing herself up on her hands and knees. "I accidentally tripped and ran into Z's door."

"Mom, you're lying! What the fuck! Leave me alone!"

Erica crawled out of the room as Zoey slammed the door shut. In all her seventeen years, Zoey had never spoken to her like that. She huddled in a corner of the small hallway hugging her knees, rocking back and forth. A schism was forming between her and Zoey, and she was powerless to stop it.

CHAPTER 17

Zoey was floating on her belly and spinning while Fenella held her hands; they were laughing hysterically. For the first time since she could remember, Zoey didn't feel anxious, she felt free. They were in a giant glass-cylinder wind tunnel, traveling on a jet of air moving at about a hundred miles per hour in the Kingsleys' "game room." Fenella used voice commands to slow down the air stream and bring them back to earth.

They climbed out. "What do you want to do now?" Fenella asked. "We have a movie theater, a giant trampoline, a basketball court—"

"Fenella, can you and Lannie adopt me?" Zoey walked out of the game room and onto the basketball court. "This is all so . . . insane." She grabbed a ball and started dribbling.

"You can use all this anytime. Nobody else does."

"Why did your mom build it?"

"Honestly, I don't know."

"To lure unsuspecting children like me into your home?"

"Why do you say that?"

"Sarcasm, silly." Fenella was clearly on the spectrum. "Fen. In all seriousness, when I was here the first time, your mom mentioned maybe I could do my senior project with her. Or Prometheus, I mean, research in the brain implant department. Can you, maybe, ask her about it?"

"Zoey, my mom doesn't implant brains. What are you talking about?"

"Oops. I meant Brain-Computer *Interface*," Zoey said, blushing.

"BCIs. Yeah, my mom is crazy about her BCIs. Why would you want to do that?"

"Fen, your mother is the most impressive person on the planet. Better than Elon! You don't have to worry about college; they're all beating down your door. I have no guarantees. It's all over TikTok, students like me not getting in! You haven't made that any easier."

"Are you mad at me, Zoey? I thought we were friends."

"I . . . I think the world of you, it's just hard . . . because I'm not you. So, I'm really hoping your mom can help me out. If we ink a deal soon, I can put it on my Harvard app."

"My mom has a dark side, Z."

"Don't be dramatic. I'm running out of time on Harvard. Is she home?"

"She's traveling. I can put you in touch with her admin if it means that much to you. I think my mom will help you, but she can be hard to pin down. There are no words that describe how busy she is."

"Anything you can do would be *amazing*."

"Don't get too enamored with Lannie Kingsley."

"Fen, it's you I'm enamored with," she said, shyly touching Fenella's cheek.

"Zoey, I think you are wonderful, but I have a very strange family. We don't have the kind of love you have."

"What are you talking about, Fen? My mom is crazy!"

"Zoey, I know your mom seems misguided, but she is driven by a blinding love for you. She taught you how to love."

"What are you saying?"

"My mother isn't a great role model in love."

"Fenella, I'm sorry if you don't feel loved by her, but she must love you in her own way. Your mom's stoicism doesn't make *you* incapable of love. You're so kind and unselfish."

"I'm more of an intellectual when it comes to love. I think deeply about it"—Fenella paused—"but I don't know about feelings."

"Oh, Fenella, you have feelings, I know you do. Don't let your mother make you *think* you're unworthy of love. I will love you. I do love you."

Zoey hugged Fenella with all her might, her heart exploding from her chest. She had to figure out a way to hold on to her forever.

CHAPTER 18

Erica watched from the window as Zoey got in a Lamborghini Uterus. *That's not right. Urus? Whatever.* Fenella had started picking Z up every morning and dropping her off after lacrosse. What parent in her right mind allowed a teen to choose from a fleet of luxury cars?

Now that Erica had a job, the rides would be a huge help, but Zoey hanging out with Fenella felt like a betrayal. Working at Prometheus would be the ultimate stress test of their relationship.

When she finally got out the door, she sat on the freeway. Traffic was horrible. Erica's hands shook and her mind wandered. How would she ever get her head around her first day? Focusing on work would take all her brainpower, and the cars seemed to be moving backward. She gave herself a pep talk about the importance of her mission. Fenella had not only stolen Zoey's senior year—she'd stolen her heart too. Erica wasn't going to let some *dumb*—er . . . genius teenager outsmart her.

She pulled into the parking lot and looked around the complex. Fenella's secret was hiding here somewhere, but it wouldn't be easy to figure out.

Tye greeted her as she walked into the building. "You are late, Erica. I'm sorry, but you're fired. Yours was the shortest career in Prometheus history."

"Please, Tye, I'm *so* sorry." Erica could feel tears mobilizing. "I should've budgeted an hour for traffic."

The tinny laugh revved up.

She almost punched him but remembered the last time. "Good one," she said, shaking off the emotional shock. "You got me."

"I am such a jokester." He handed her a macchiato. "My hand has an energy source that keeps coffee warm, isn't that helpful? Please take this as a peace offering."

"Wow! I was the one making coffee at my old job." Erica felt better as she took a few sips.

"Follow me. You have not seen the Regen Lab. You must be officially hired and sign all the NDAs before you are allowed to see it. Thank you for completing your employment documents online."

They went through several security doors and down long hallways. Despite his stiff legs, Tye moved surprisingly fast. Erica found herself intermittently jogging to keep up. At the end of a long corridor, they entered a massive room with a robotic assembly line that crisscrossed the floor. Lab stations were positioned in front of floor-to-ceiling metal shelves with hundreds of small glass-fronted doors the size of library card catalog drawers. A robotic armed crane was at the ready to retrieve out-of-reach samples.

"This is the matrix where we store the dermis samples at various stages of development until the samples are ready to move to the next phase, facilitated by another team. The dermal cells are incubated at thirty-seven degrees Celsius. Human body temperature maintains the necessary pH for cell growth. It's critical to keep that temperature constant while working with the samples. Our equipment safeguards this, or we would be sweating all day. I supervise assembly, and you test samples as they first enter the matrix to ensure quality. It's not glamorous but very important."

"How do I keep up?"

"You don't test every sample. They are grouped together from the "parent" of origin. You test by selecting a random sample from each batch. You will find any small glitch before it becomes a major problem."

After a full day of selecting, analyzing, and recording sample data from the matrix, Erica felt strangely satisfied. She proceeded to her small office to fill out a new hire questionnaire.

Erica couldn't deny the job paid well. Maybe she'd save and buy a new house. Something modern with a view of the water and Mount Rainier, with a big garden. She could see herself clipping enormous white peonies. She'd get a dog to keep her company, and he would chase away the bunnies (but never hurt them) and predators, like—giant rats! *What the fuh?* A furry animal ran across her hands and keyboard.

Erica jumped up, toppling her chair over. "Shit, shit!" she yelled.

The hairy fiend fell into an open desk drawer, and with the reflexes of an Olympic athlete, she slammed it shut. She could hear the damn thing rooting around with its claws scraping against the metal. She had to finish the questionnaire, then she would decide what to do. Dear God, what if it used her drawer as a litter box?

She sanitized her keyboard with wipes. Should she escalate to Miko? She giggled thinking about Miko coming down from on high to retrieve a giant rodent from her desk.

"Knock knock."

Erica looked up to see an impeccably dressed man in his thirties with a boyish face, bright blue eyes, and close-cropped blond hair that was receding. He was dressed in khakis and a green cable-knit sweater. An empty baby sling hung from his neck.

"I'm Jack."

"I'm Erica." She pointed to the sling. "Did you lose your baby?"

"Yes. My comfort pet, Claus von Bülow."

"The giant rat?"

"Chinchilla," he said, glaring at her.

"He scared me half to death jumping on my keyboard and into my desk drawer."

"Oh, thank God!"

Jack bent over Erica's desk and flung open the drawer. She backed away.

"Darling," Jack said as he picked up the animal. "I was so scared. You know better than to run away."

He wrapped it in the sling and turned to Erica, who was plastered against the wall.

"I'm surprised you didn't recognize Claus; he's on TikTok. I'm developing chinchilla products—shampoos, brushes, sweaters, and scarves."

"Sounds like a limited marketplace."

"Think again; over five million American households have chinchillas."

"Maybe you should add tracking devices to the product list." She smiled.

"Great idea! These little monsters are fast, and they love hiding in cozy nooks and crannies. Even though it *was* barbaric for you to lock him in your drawer."

As repulsed as she was, Erica needed to get to know a fellow human employee. Being stuck in the lab all day with a robot as her companion wasn't healthy.

"What's your role in Prometheus?" Erica asked lightly, hoping to undo any negative impressions from the drawer incident.

"You first."

"Today is my first day, so I'm still working on my pitch . . . QC in dermal—"

"For accidents and skin disease, right? I'm super excited for the regen treatments."

"Those who can afford it will never age. Maybe I can volunteer as a guinea pig."

"Is that why you got the job?"

"Like working at Pottery Barn for the discount? No. I need the money. My alimony's running out. My ex cut me off."

Erica wasn't sure why she'd told that to a perfect stranger. Better than admitting she got the job to uncover an AI college admissions scandal.

"What do you do besides chinchilla herding?"

"I'm a systems engineer, but my heart's in coding. You've probably met some of our Anthrobots—they're designed to engage with the full spectrum of human emotions in real-world settings. I'm the guy behind the scenes, designing and fine-tuning their emotional inference models, adjusting neural weights, and rolling out upgrades so your interactions feel seamless. I'm basically making AI more emotionally intelligent than humans. How ironic is that?"

"Why does AI need emotions?"

"You're such a newbie. Our AI is not only infinitely knowledgeable but also calibrated to respond appropriately to humans. It can even show compassion," Jack said, petting Claus compulsively.

"Like my manager, Tye."

"Yep, soon to be available outside these walls as health care providers, counselors, teachers, and caregivers. There's a mental health crisis and a desperate shortage of trained professionals." The rodent began to squirm and squeak, so Jack shifted the sling. "We're helping humanity in ways previously unimagined."

"You really think AI can match what humans do in such sensitive areas?" Erica said.

"AI will be trained on emotions your average human doesn't even know exist. Brené Brown identified and defined eighty-seven emotions. Don't you love her? The vulnerability shit, boys *do* cry!" His face lit up.

"I don't do vulnerable."

"Get a Claus," he said, planting kisses on the hairy creature. "I'm so sorry, lovakins, that I can't take you this weekend . . ." Jack looked up from Claus to Erica. "My husband and I are going to Mexico. My good-for-nothing nephew bailed on me, and I don't know anyone qualified to take care of him."

"AHHHHCHEW! ACHEW!" Erica sneezed as loudly as she could. "Sorry. . . allergic."

"And I was just starting to like you . . ."

"How long have you been with Prometheus?"

"Almost four years. That's an eternity here," he said, and mouthed, *People get fired a lot.*

"Why?" she whispered.

"Raising . . . concerns."

"Like?"

"You know, displacing humans in the workforce—typical stuff. Or where we get the human dermis samples. Paying pennies on the dollar in third-world countries, exploiting donors for research. Consent becomes murky . . . did you hear something?" Jack's eyes darted across the small room.

"Not a thing." Erica thought about the quiet removal of the samples she tested to some other invisible lab. Where they originated and where they went was a mystery. "What were you saying?"

"Sorry, I've said too much. I got excited, meeting another human. I guess you've signed your life away in NDAs, but it's highly confidential."

"Do we really know what the live dermis is used for?" Erica was learning too much to let this go.

"I'm sure it's for all the exciting applications they claim it is."

"What about the larger question of obsoleting humans?"

"There's no question we're doing that."

"Come again?"

"I haven't been able to draw any other conclusion."

Erica stared at Jack, waiting for him to crack a smile, but none appeared. "I'll watch Claus."

"What about your allergies?"

"I'll load up on Sudafed and Benadryl."

"Uppers *and* downers! Were you, like, a club kid in the eighties, like, with my mom?" he said in a perfect Valley Girl voice.

"How *old* do you think I am?"

"You're serious about CVB?"

"How hard can it be? I'm raising a teenager."

"You're a mom?"

"Yes."

"I'll be in touch," he said, and left her office.

Erica scrunched up her nose as she checked the drawer where Claus had last sat. She would have to get over her revulsion of the hairy rodent. Jack might spill the tea about Prometheus. She sat back down and stared at her screen. *Fenella, I'm coming for you. Zoey will be back on top.*

CHAPTER 19

ZOEY FELT LIGHTER THAN AIR. "How was your first day at the factory, woman?" she said to her mom, handing her a martini with a baby pickle floating on top. "Come, sit in your favorite chair, relax, and tell me everything."

Zoey had avoided her mom since their altercation over the job at Prometheus and her eavesdropping, but Fenella had encouraged her to make peace, saying, "Your mom is on your side, Zoey." To Zoey, Fenella seemed to have lived several lifetimes. No other friend would ever give her such strange advice.

"Thanks, wife. Now get my slippers." Erica sniffed. "What an interesting drink."

"Sorry, no olives, subbing pickles. I think they're in the same food group."

Erica took a swig. "Delicious," she sputtered. "Room temp, straight gin, just how I like it."

"I looked it up. I couldn't find any vermouth either." Zoey thought martinis must be something special, but no, it only took two ingredients, three if you counted olives or pickles. "If Harvard doesn't take me, I'll be a bartender!"

"Oh, sweetie, don't say *that*. Be positive."

"Positive, or real? How will I survive before early action? It's not 'til mid-December."

"Let's get through Thanksgiving."

"Mom, what are you going to do when I'm in Hawaii with Dad? Are you going to be okay?" The Mauna Kea was a popular destination for Seattleites over Thanksgiving. She had just found out Fenella and Lannie would be at the same resort and was ecstatic. Something told her not to tell her mom. Not yet.

"I'll go to Cookie and Gramps's." Her mom took another sip. "This is tasting better by the minute."

"You don't have to go. They're so abusive, and Uncle Logan's a douche canoe. Don't get me started on Aunt Lauren's logo-core fashion."

"It's fine. I love Penelope and Dahlilah. It's hard to believe they're the spawn of Logan."

"Mom, you're kind of a martyr. How was work?"

"It's early to know, but I love the lab work and my partner Tye. He's an Anthrobot that fancies himself a comedian. He's not very funny, but he's more tolerable than most people."

"Anthrobot?"

"A droid, a humanoid, like C-3PO."

"Your coworker's a robot?"

"Yes, honey, Prometheus is the most technologically advanced company on the planet. That's how I know they're up to something."

"I'm excited for you, Mom. But stick to your job and don't get carried away investigating your deep-state, we're-all-living-in-the-Matrix conspiracy. Fenella is the daughter of very smart people. Genius begets genius."

"I hate to admit it, but after one day at Prometheus, that's obvious. Lannie is a genius."

"I'm glad to hear you say that. I might do my senior project in Lannie's BCI lab. That's short for 'Brain-Computer Interface.' Fenella is helping me."

"Honey, I thought you had decided on Hydrapolis Clean Energy. Why the sudden change?"

"Mom, Prometheus is doing *everything*, and better than anyone—you just *said* so."

"I hate to burst your *bubble*, Zoey, but training *one* chatbot uses as much energy as our neighborhood uses in a *year*," she yelled, and her face got red. "Prometheus's energy requirements are *exponentially* more wasteful than that."

"Mom, what's your problem? Why are you yelling? You work there! Lannie can *help* me. With Harvard and beyond. I've come up with a plan to make up for SPIT *and* LAX. I thought you'd be all over it. Don't you always tell me to be proactive? I have to submit to Harvard in *ten* days. If I get it arranged with Lannie, I can add Prometheus to my application. It'll mean more than any single thing I've done so far."

Her mom frowned. "She *could* write you a wonderful letter of recommendation. She likes you—"

Zoey's phone rang. *Circe.* This was gonna send her mom over the edge. "Give me five secs." Zoey walked to the kitchen. "Hey, C."

"Hi, hon, I have a favor to ask."

"Sure. Anything."

"The kids have one last modeling shoot."

Zoey hunched over in the breakfast nook. "Didn't Dad say no more modeling?" she whispered.

"I tried pulling the plug, Z. But you know Janet—big mistake mixing business with friendship; never do it. She went off. I can't say I blame her; she will lose Prometheus as a client, plus her twenty percent. She wouldn't let me say no."

"Yikes! What'll you do?"

Her mom tiptoed into the kitchen and stuck her head in the fridge.

"Mom!" Zoey covered the speaker with her thumb. "Give me a minute—"

"I'm starving!" Her mom grabbed a block of cheese and went back to the living room.

"Zoey, are you there? I hate to ask you. I feel *horrible*, but can you take the kids for me?"

"C, I can't go behind my dad's back. I totally get the situation you're in, but it's too risky. Sorry."

"You're right. I'm so sorry for asking. I need to be brave and shut Janet down. She will dump me as a friend, but family comes first."

Zoey hung up with Circe and got to work reading the instructions for Beecher's mac & cheese. *An hour in the oven.* She threw it in the microwave. She then pulled out the prewashed romaine and dumped it in a salad bowl. Voilà! She set the breakfast nook table with her mom's china and lit candles.

"Dinner is served, madame."

"Zoey, I had no idea you knew how to cook!"

They sat down and started eating. The entrée was cold in some spots and scalding in others. "It's delish! So . . . what's the dilemma Circe needs you for?"

"Mom, stop spying."

"Honey, this house is very small, we both hear everything."

"Well . . ." Should she tell her mom? *She works at Prometheus now.*

"Honey, what is it? If Circe has a problem, maybe I can help."

"The twins got one last modeling offer that was submitted before Dad dropped the hammer. The agent flipped when Circe tried canceling."

"Wait, she wants you to go behind your father's back and *take* them? ABSO-FUCKING-LUTELY NOT!"

"Mom, *calm down*! She just wanted advice." Why did she say anything? Her mom was such an overreactor. "You're so mean about Circe. She's actually a good person, and married to *my* dad!"

"Honey, I'm trying to get over it."

Zoey stared at her mom. "Did I hear you right?"

"It's not fair to you. I know you and Circe are close."

Zoey squeezed her mom's hand across the table. "Good job, Mom! You know I love you the most."

Her mom then told her about meeting Jack and his unusual support animal. Considering she had begged her mom for a pet, *any* pet, Zoey didn't buy that she would babysit Claus just to make friends. Then her mom started describing the crazy state-of-the-art lab she worked in.

Zoey was salivating. "Mom, if you're working at Prometheus, wouldn't it make *sense* for me to do my senior project there?"

"Honey, you need to stick with the original plan."

After dinner, Erica nodded off at the table, so Zoey sent her to bed and cleaned the kitchen. Why were Fenella *and* her mom against a Prometheus internship? She didn't tell her mom, but Fenella was dragging her heels on getting Zoey in to see Lannie. Maybe she could convince her mom to help her. But really, the only way she'd get into Prometheus was if Lannie invited her.

She checked her phone to see if Fenella had Snapped, then scrolled through her photos, stopping at the pics of her with the twins at Disneyland last summer, posing in front of Sleeping Beauty Castle.

The twins! They could get her into Prometheus. She could take them to the shoot and see the company from inside. Maybe she would run into Lannie. Zoey felt a surge of energy. She didn't need her mom or even Fenella to fix this. Her mom had run every second of every minute for the last eighteen years. Time to take charge of her own life!

She texted Circe: *Nvm I'm in.*

CHAPTER 20

The war room was buzzing and Lannie sat at the head of the table surrounded by her entire C-suite like a five-star general presiding over her officers. One wall had a bank of flat-screens, another had interactive world maps for real-time data tracking, a third was used to project presentations. There were no windows; she didn't want her staff staring at the Cascades.

The big day was looming. Only three months remained to prepare for the product release that would change humanity. Sponsoring the Super Bowl halftime show had been her idea. She laughed thinking of her competition and their silly thirty-second commercials.

"Tia, how about you start us off?" Her CCO had been with Lannie from the beginning and was a genius at PR spin and messaging.

"What you're about to see is the uncut Teleios reel that will be distributed as part of the international PR packet on launch day. First, a reminder on strategy." Tia glared at each person seated around the table. "Not a word about Teleios outside this room or the fires of hell will rain down on you," she said without cracking a smile. "If we keep it under wraps, with a few strategically planned leaks orchestrated by *me*, we are guaranteed the biggest launch in history. The release date is still a secret. Not a word, not even to partners or spouses, until the Super Bowl. We cannot risk the DOL freaking out about worker displacement and getting the DOJ involved."

Tia pointed her phone at the middle of the table, and hyperrealistic holographic images popped up of Anthrobots and joyful people frolicking. A booming voice, overlaid with Chopin, emanated from every corner of the room.

"Teleios, the most significant product launch in the history of Prometheus Corporation. Get ready to meet the future: two new products that will dramatically improve quality of life on this planet.

"Anthrobots, Prometheus's proprietary humanoids, are already valued 'coworkers' in our many divisions. They are trainable, adaptable and analytical, and often perform tasks that are difficult or dangerous for humans. For the first time, they will be available for our enterprise customers and virtually every industry to enhance productivity, and for consumers to enhance their lives.

"Equally groundbreaking is the NICE—Neural Implant Cognitive Enhancer—designed to treat traumatic brain injuries by restoring and elevating cognition, memory, and processing. NICE represents our latest advancement in surgically embedded Brain Computer Interfaces, already transforming care for debilitating neurological conditions such as epilepsy and Parkinson's.

"Teleios is launching the future today. Brought to you by Prometheus, the world's most trusted leader in AI and bioscience technologies." The voiceover ended and the hologram faded.

"Brava!" Lannie clapped with elation.

"Thanks to Lannie, we are very close to FDA approval for the NICE and confident we will hit the mark by launch." Tia paused and looked at Lannie, eyebrows raised. Lannie nodded.

"Our launch marketing for the NICE focuses on people with traumatic brain injury, but our data shows potential demand from people who want to enhance their overall intelligence."

Tia took a sip from the giant water bottle she carried around like a baby. "Once we have FDA approval for the medical device, there are no other regulatory hoops we need to jump through to market as a consumer product. We are already doing our own internal testing and trials. Like Ozempic, it will be available to anyone who can afford it. While the NICE has been embraced in the medical community, we are planning a 'quiet' rollout for consumers—"

Lannie interrupted, "We anticipate objections about ethics and inequality, but we have a plan for that, right, Tia?"

"Yes, the slow rollout allows it to gain a foothold with people who see the benefits to themselves and humanity . . .," she said, pausing. "Lannie, I do recommend a big announcement that ingratiates you with the public *now*, something like 'Prometheus is applying AI to eradicate hunger.' Then you pledge a hundred mil of your own money toward the initiative to create goodwill and gain public trust. It'll generate headlines and cement your reputation as a humanitarian, positioning Prometheus as a mission-first corporation."

"Great. Let's do it. Thanks, Tia. Eve, how about you give us your lobbying updates."

Lannie had nabbed Eve early on. She was the first woman to lobby for AI and had influence up to the Oval Office.

"We have most of the House. Scud and Dunlop will do anything for me. You won't believe the dirt I have on those two. Anyway, most of those clowns in Congress don't understand the first thing about AI. They're regurgitating soundbites and grandstanding. I'm making sure any bill drafted has no teeth but will give them something to brag about. Nothing will stand in the way of Teleios. You can't regulate what you can't see."

"And we're making massive donations to both the DNC and the RNC," Lannie added. "How about the Senate?"

Eve ticked off a list of friends and foes, dossiers, and dirt.

"Are we done here?" Lannie asked.

"One more thing . . .," Tia said, twisting her hair around her finger.

"Not sure I like your tone."

"The old Stanford scandal—we've tracked the leak to the tech bros chasing Prometheus."

"Their tech *sucks* compared to mine, so they play dirty!"

"Lannie, you know they would *love* an investigation to slow you down."

"Their hypocrisy knows no bounds. Foreign bribes, bias, IP theft, labor exploitation—all in the name of power for profit."

"It's bullshit, but these men live in a culture of immunity. You don't. We're monitoring the situation closely. If necessary, we give the *Journal* an exclusive and tell your story. Constantly harassed, the standards you were held to as a woman were so much higher, etc. . . ."

Lannie swiveled in her seat and stared at the map of the world. She would play tough—she always did—but they were picking at a wound that would never heal. Barasa had left her because of the scandal. What she saw as a minor indiscretion for the sake of important research, he had seen as a moral deficiency. A renowned gene therapy researcher, Kenyan-born, Oxford-trained, Barasa held himself to the highest standards and considered his work at Stanford sacred. He refused to monetize his research. "You really should patent that," she had often said to him. But he saw the potential to prevent and cure disease and didn't want greed to cloud his judgment.

She smiled thinking of his shyness with people. Animals were different. He interacted warmly with lab mice and often carried a mouse in the pocket of his lab coat. Lannie had fallen for his kindness. All she had ever known before Barasa was cruelty.

As a child, Lannie had been picked on relentlessly by her peers. Thick eyeglasses and terrible eczema had made her an easy target, and she was smaller, having skipped kindergarten, then third grade. The kids nicknamed her "Crusty" and "Mole Rat." They acted like she had a "flesh-eating" disease. She tried to explain eczema wasn't contagious, but they just teased her more.

Her mother tried to comfort her. She would tell Lannie she had a beautiful mind and would change the world. She was in fourth grade when she came home from school one day and her mother was still in bed. The next day, her father took her mother to the doctor, and she never came home again. Her body was riddled with cancer. She was admitted to the hospital and died within six weeks. Her father plunged into grief. He was an engineer at an aerospace firm and buried himself in his work.

When Lannie discovered the computer lab in junior high, she found her home. She got a perfect score on her SAT and a full ride to Stanford. In college, she joined software dev and biochem clubs and realized her ideas had value. She could pursue intellectualism free from ridicule, but the protective armor she had built around herself kept people from getting too close. Lannie sailed through undergrad and earned a degree in biochemistry and engineering.

When she first met Barasa, she was doing graduate work in bioengineering. He kept mostly to himself, his mice, and his experiments. But one day he came up to her.

"You missed a step."

She looked up to see him by her side. "Did I ask for your help?"

"No. I'm sorry."

He walked away. She tried for another hour, then reluctantly approached him.

"Can you show me what I'm doing wrong?"

He explained step by step in his gentle, sonorous voice.

When they had fixed her mistakes and finished the work, he turned to her and beamed with the brightest smile she'd ever seen. Her heart melted.

"Would you like to go to lunch?" The words escaped her mouth before she could stop them.

"Yes, I'm famished."

That was the beginning of their lunchtime ritual—though they didn't always remember to eat.

One day he presented her with a small package.

"What's this?"

"Open it."

The small box contained a glass jar of cream; she twisted the lid off and took a whiff.

"*Avena sativa*, commonly known as oat. It contains polysaccharides, proteins, saponins, flavonoids, and phenolic acids. My father's family are healers, they have understood for centuries its healing power. Apply it to the affected areas, it will cure what ails your skin."

"Where'd you get it?"

"I made it for you."

A tear rolled down her cheek. It was the kindest thing anyone had ever done for her. That was the moment she fell in love.

The next time he presented her with a box, it was an engagement ring.

Lannie wiped her nose and swiveled back to the room. Tia was still talking.

"Everyone should know that *you* mapped the cognitive architecture of the human brain for AI systems . . ."

Lannie felt a vein pop in her forehead as she remembered the male colleagues who took credit for her work, talking down to her, treating her like she was stupid—

"Lannie?" Tia furrowed her brow. "Are you okay?"

Lannie put her palms to her temples and pressed hard, attempting to keep her head from exploding. "Yes, good work. Meeting's over."

They left quickly and quietly.

Lannie watched them file out the door. The painful chapter at Stanford would never be closed. She had lost credibility, and even though her countersuit provided the seed money for Prometheus, she had lost the love of her life and proven herself unlovable. She reached for a crystal glass from the tray at the center of the table and threw it against the wall. It shattered in a thousand pieces, much like her heart had when Barasa walked away.

CHAPTER 21

The Uber driver pulled in front of Frank's house. Zoey opened her door and hopped out. She followed the cement pathway that cut across the perfectly manicured lawn, recently decorated for Halloween with tombstones and skeletons by professional lawn decorators Circe hired for every holiday. Zoey loved dressing up and consuming piles of candy, but this year Halloween was a grim reminder of the countdown to November 1 and her Harvard application.

The door flung open. "Zoey! Zoey!" the twins chanted, both grabbing on to her.

Circe appeared behind them in the Aviator Nation sweatsuit that every girl at Hillcrest either owned or coveted.

"You are so sweet to take the kids. Their backpacks have stuff to keep them distracted. The company will provide snacks for you and the kids—organic, sustainable, and nutritious, it's in the contract. But, here in case you need it . . ." She handed Zoey some money.

"I love hanging out with these two!" she said, twirling Teddy around. "It also gives me a chance to check out Prometheus. I'm hoping to do my senior project there, so it's recon."

"I really appreciate your help."

"Come on, come on! Let's go, Zoey!" Alice and Teddy pulled her toward the door.

"Wait, did you tell Dad?" Zoey whispered.

"Don't worry, I'll handle him. Did you tell your mom?"

"I don't need to tell her every little thing . . . assuming I don't bump into her on campus, it can be our little secret," Zoey said. Circe winked at her.

Zoey grabbed their booster seats while Circe carried the backpacks. The driver opened the passenger doors and Circe helped the twins settle in the backseat. Then Zoey climbed in next to them.

On the way to the photo shoot, they discussed their Halloween costumes. Teddy wanted them to be peanut butter and jelly, but Alice insisted they be Oompa Loompas. They continued their happy banter until the SUV turned into the sprawling Prometheus campus. Zoey marveled at the modern, low-slung buildings and numerous playfields.

She expected the driver to park in one of the many parking lots, but he continued straight toward a densely wooded area with trees growing right up to the road. He pulled into a small parking lot and a green hillside came into view.

"We're here," the driver said.

Zoey looked around. "Are you sure?"

"This is the address Mrs. Barbieri gave me."

Zoey scanned the surroundings and spotted a tunnel built into the hill.

"Kids, this will be an adventure. Stay close to me."

They all piled out of the car. Zoey took each twin by the hand and led them toward the tunnel. They peeked in. It was about twenty feet deep and ended at two large metal doors. The twins dropped Zoey's hands and raced ahead. Zoey ran to keep up. They stopped at the doors and looked up into a camera, but the doors didn't open. Zoey found a call button and pressed it.

"Hello, miss."

"We have an appointment for a photo shoot."

"Barbieri, Teddy and Alice?"

"Yes, that's us."

"We have identified the children," the voice said. "But we do not have you in our database."

"Their mom, Circe Barbieri, couldn't make it. I'm their sister, Zoey Barbieri."

"We're sorry, their contract says their mother must be with them. You don't have security clearance."

"I know Lannie Kingsley. Can you call her?"

"Very funny."

"I swear. I'm good friends with her daughter. Please try."

"Stand by."

"What's wrong, Zoey?" Alice asked.

"There's a mix-up, but I'm working on it."

"Can we go to Paint the Town and make pretty plates?" Teddy asked.

"Give me a minute, kids." Zoey looked around. From what her mom had described, her lab was in another complex. She couldn't find her here, could she?

The double doors swung open with a jolt, revealing a bright white room.

"Kids, let's go!"

They entered a semicircular lobby with several unmarked doors. A girl with short bleached-blond hair wearing vintage Levi's and a Coca-Cola T-shirt approached.

"Come with me. Sofia asked me to take you back."

Zoey grabbed the twins by the hands again and followed her down a long corridor with cement floors, through two sets of metal security doors, and into a large state-of-the art studio. The twins looked around wide-eyed. Zoey tried to hide her amazement, but she had never seen such high-tech equipment—cameras and lights hanging from the ceiling, drones with tiny cameras flying about, and editing bays that looked like they belonged in air traffic control towers. A woman in a hijab, jeans, and a T-shirt was tapping away at a keyboard in front of a huge monitor while another woman with dark corkscrew curls, wearing jeans and a sweater, was standing by her giving her instructions.

"Sofia, they're here," the girl said as she slipped into a sound studio.

The woman with the dark curls turned to greet them. "I'm Sofia, I run the studio." She smiled at Zoey. "This is Amira."

Amira waved from her seat at the computer. Zoey was surprised how young they both were. They didn't look much older than she did.

"This is Teddy and Alice. I'm their sister Zoey."

Sofia grabbed a VR-like headset and a handheld scanner off her desk.

"This might look a little strange, kids, but it's how I get the pictures of you."

She held the headset out to them so they could look at it. She turned to Zoey. "The camera in this helmet is filled with sensors that pick up even more than the human eye could detect." Alice reached out to touch it.

Sofia gently pulled it away. "Uh-uh-uh, no touch. But I love your curiosity," she said, smiling.

She put the headset on, pulled down the visor, and picked up the scanner.

"I click this handheld device to snap photos and video. It gives me additional scanning capabilities, control of settings and speed." she said to Zoey. Sofia turned to the twins. "I hear you kids are the best in the business. Are you ready? This is where we will do the shoot."

She motioned to an open space with a large white curtain hanging from the ceiling and colored X's on the floor. "Zoey, why don't you sit with Amira, so you don't get in the shot?"

Sofia turned back to the kids. "Has everyone gone potty?" The twins nodded. "Then let's get started."

Zoey thought Sofia seemed abrupt, but she probably did hundreds of shoots and knew that five-year-olds have limited attention spans. She looked to see that the twins were comfortable and sat next to Amira.

"So, Teddy and Alice? We're going to play a fun game. I will give you a clue, and you say the answer with your face."

Alice was pointing at Sofia. "You look funny with the helmet on!"

"Why do you have to wear that?" Teddy asked.

"It's special. It's linked to the powerful computer Amira is running. The camera makes three-D images of you."

"Will it hurt?" Teddy asked.

"Of course not."

Zoey hadn't thought to ask what exactly they were using the images for, but she figured Circe must know.

"Kids, are you ready? Let's play! Here's my first clue: If someone stole your brand-new bicycle, what face would you make?"

Alice narrowed her eyes and scrunched her brows together, like she was ready to punch someone; Teddy looked like he was about to cry.

"Perfect!" Sofia moved the camera across their faces, projecting red dots of light as she scanned. Zoey could see Amira's monitors, showing different angles, distances, and details, flipping between 3D rotating outlines, high-resolution photography, and cartoonlike images of the twins.

"Okay, now your mom just surprised you with a pet—"

"Goat?!" Alice cried.

"Sure, or a puppy!" Sofia said.

Zoey leaned over Amira's keyboard. "How do you know how to run this? The console has more knobs and buttons than a cockpit in an airplane."

"I graduated top of my class at NYU film school. I planned to make groundbreaking documentaries in Afghanistan, but Lannie found me. I admit, I sold out—but in a few years I'll have the money to finance my own films."

"Fantastic." Zoey looked over at the twins, who were skipping in circles. "Why do you need live models, can't AI generate any image you need?"

"We still rely on real photographic images for our advertising campaigns—and more importantly, for ethically sourcing our AI training data."

"What do you mean?"

"Many tech companies scrape the internet for training data, using copyrighted and personal photos without consent. Prometheus pays our models and photographers directly. From this curated dataset, we generate synthetic imagery to scale our training dataset. It's slower and more expensive, but Lannie holds us to the highest standards."

Zoey's heart swelled with pride in the work that Lannie was doing. She leaned in closer to look at the monitors in front of Amira. Teddy and Alice's images moved on the screen as Amira zoomed in and out, spinning around an axis and switching from skeletal representation to hyperrealistic.

A sudden noise made her jump, and she turned to see Lannie entering the room.

"There they are. What beautiful children." Lannie sounded more like Ursula the sea witch than Zoey remembered. "Zoey!" Lannie approached and she sprang to her feet. "It's so wonderful to see you. Sorry about the confusion. I'm glad you had them call me. Come. I want to show you something."

Zoey hesitated, looking at the twins.

"They'll be all right. Sofia is the best," said Lannie.

Zoey followed Lannie out of the studio, down a hall, and through a door that opened into a metal shop filled with giant, shiny machines and medical scanning equipment.

"This is the Fabrication Lab—or FabLab as my cohorts call it—where we design, test, and build our BCIs. That's Chelsea." She pointed to a diminutive young girl with blue bobbed hair who did not look up from her computer. "I mentioned your senior project when you visited the house, and I meant it."

Lannie reached into a bin piled with small hardware and held up a circular device, the size of a dime.

"This, Zoey, is our first-gen Brain-Computer Interface, or BCI. These devices have been treating Parkinson's and epilepsy for years."

"I saw some tech billionaire say on TikTok that he's waiting to have kids until BCIs are perfected," said Zoey.

Lannie laughed. "Thanks to me, he won't have to wait long. Our latest BCI is much smaller, not much bigger than the gold studs in your ears. It was developed for brain injuries and has the capability to enhance cognition and intelligence for all humans. We need a way to peacefully coexist and *compete* with AI. Artificial intelligence is here to stay. The folks who think we can regulate, reverse, or stop it are fooling themselves."

"I'm so glad a woman like you is leading the way," Zoey said.

"If you choose to do your senior project with us, I want you to work in *this* lab."

Zoey thought about how few days she had left to add to her Harvard application.

"This is an *amazing* opportunity, Mrs. Kingsley. Could I start right away?"

"Absolutely. Set your own hours. I'm sure Mr. Robson will accommodate."

"It seems so great. Why isn't Fenella working here?"

"We agreed it would be better for our relationship if she didn't work for her mother's company," she said, smiling. "I see so much potential in you, Zoey. You've been a wonderful friend to Fenella, and I'm grateful. She's learned a lot from you."

"How is that possible?"

"You've taught her social skills, and you have a big heart. I think *this* opportunity will tip the scales for Harvard. I would like nothing more than for you to be there with her."

"Oh my gosh! Thank you!" Zoey hugged Lannie, who stiffly patted her on the back in return.

The twins were walking out of the small sound studio with Sofia when Zoey returned.

"You know Lannie?" Sofia said.

Zoey noticed perspiration on her forehead. The studio must have been hot.

"I'm besties with her daughter." Zoey stood a little taller.

The twins hugged Zoey. "Let's go!"

"Say goodbye to Sofia." They waved and grabbed Zoey's hands.

"Be careful, Zoey," Sofia said.

"Don't worry. I'm not driving," she said, and they walked out.

As they exited the tunnel, the sun was struggling to break through the clouds, creating a glare behind the gray. The windowless studio had left them all disoriented. The twins sat on a bench near the parking lot and Zoey called the car.

"Where did that lady take you?" Alice asked.

"She showed me an amazing hardware lab."

"After getting our pictures, we talked into a microphone in that booth," Alice said.

"Then we sang 'Happy'!" Teddy said, bursting into song.

Alice tugged on Zoey's sleeve. "Why did you leave us?"

"Shoot, I'm sorry. Were you scared?"

"No . . . but our mom always stays and watches."

"Kids, how about we go to Mickey D's?"

"Happy Meals," they chanted in unison.

"Yes, but don't tell your mom or she'll never let me babysit again."

CHAPTER 22

Jack woke with a stabbing pain in his neck and the feeling that his head was on fire. He reached up and felt a silky softness. Claus was sleeping peacefully, gripping Jack's scalp with his claws for balance. He gently lifted Claus off and unglued his own cheek from the keyboard. He would have indentations on his face all day, and probably permanent wrinkles. This job was ruining his looks, and he needed to keep his darling husband interested . . .

"Carlos!" How long had he been asleep?

He grabbed his phone. Five missed calls from Carlos.

"I don't want to hear it."

"Darling, I'm so sorry. I fell asleep at my desk again."

"I made you dinner. Gordon Ramsay's beef Wellington. I went to three markets, toiled all day in the kitchen—"

"This deadline will be the *death* of me. M3GAN expects me to be a machine like she is."

Jack had nicknamed his Anthrobot boss after the AI lifelike doll in *M3GAN* who goes crazy and starts killing everyone. Since he had started the job, her attitude toward Jack had progressed from benign disinterest to overt hostility. He complained about M3GAN to her human supervisor and was reminded that AIs are shaped by the data they encounter. They mimic humans in a continual process of "interaction iterations."

Jack was mortified. Through logical analysis, M3GAN had learned to dislike him.

"Are you listening, Jack?" Carlos's voice was shaking. "You don't have to do this. We have plenty of money. And there are a million companies that would appreciate you."

"I'm in hell—fight or flight every second. But it's only four more months until full vesting. I'll cash out and we'll travel the world."

"Honey, it's not worth your health or sanity. Talk to HR."

"You know things don't work out here for complainers."

Carlos sighed. "I'll bring you fresh clothes."

"You're a saint. Why do you put up with me?"

"I won't if you miss Clive and Tom's wedding. You *have* to be on that plane. I'm still broken over you bailing on Miley. I went all by myself wearing pasties."

"I promise, I'll be there. I even found a sitter for CVB."

Carlos was the best thing that had ever happened to Jack. When would he hit his limit? Finding "the one" had been an arduous process. So many guys either weren't into monogamy or only wanted a sugar daddy with supermodel looks. Jack had sown his oats in his twenties but ultimately hoped for a chance to build a life with someone. Maybe even have a child. The surrogate was already lined up. His little sister had offered. What if she met a man and changed her mind?

His door clicked and Sofia's beautiful head of dark curls popped in.

"Jack, I got your text. I can't nanny Claus, have you forgotten the last time? He had horrible gas *all* weekend. I had to fumigate my house."

"You strayed from his strict diet, my love. I couldn't have been any clearer. Anyhoo, I found someone!"

"Who did you bribe?"

"A new gal just joined Prometheus. Erica Barbieri. I've been screening her social. It's hilarious."

"Barbieri? Is that a common name in the States? I had five-year-old twins with the same last name yesterday, do you think they were hers?"

"Not a chance. Erica is divorced with a teen daughter, who's her *whole* world. Jeezus, look at this sharenting."

He handed Sofia his phone and she scrolled through. "That's the girl, Zoey, who brought the twins." She kept scrolling. "And here they are. The twins must be Zoey's half siblings?"

"Her ex must be remarried," Jack said, grabbing his phone to see the twins. "Poor Erica. She was the starter wife, and look at those beautiful children."

Her phone bleeped. "I'm late! Gotta run, I'll call you later."

Sofia's stress level was even worse than his. She possessed extraordinary visual talent, but Jack suspected that Lannie had handpicked her because of her family's dicey immigration status. Sofia couldn't say no to any of Lannie's directives.

Jack unlocked his top desk drawer and took out a notebook where he kept a running list of grievances. Prometheus used and abused employees and spit them out. It was *The Hunger Games* meets *Boiler Room*, and the human employees were selling their souls to be a part of history and get rich in the process. Survivors were rewarded handsomely.

He had started *The Journal of Discontent* about six months into his employment. He initially thought he might write a tell-all but soon realized, to protect himself, he needed to document the shit that went on. If they fired him before his vesting, or he couldn't take it anymore, he was building a case against Prometheus.

Jack recorded data under two categories: "Employee Abuse," based on his own experience—horrible stories of belittling bosses and long hours, but normal for tech companies—and "Ethics," which relied on observations and rumors. He had written down a long list of suspicious activities but had no solid evidence of wrongdoing.

His door flew open. Jack slipped his notebook under a stack of papers as M3GAN lumbered in on her metal-jointed legs.

"What's that?"

"What?"

"You were writing something."

"Poetry."

M3GAN's arm expanded in length as she reached for the pile where he had stuffed the notebook. Jack jerked it away just in time.

"You can't read someone *else's* poetry without asking. Too personal. Besides, it's terrible. Not worthy of your superior intelligence."

"I know every poem ever written and can create beautiful verse in seconds. You write garbage. I need you to diagnose Emo Beta 3 across the system. There's a problem. The test bots laugh hysterically when they watch *The Fault in Our Stars* and cry when watching *Happy Gilmore*."

"I cry too, it's so dumb."

"No time for wisecracks. You're on thin ice, Jack. I would hate to fire you right before your final vesting and the stock going crazy."

She did a one eighty and scooted out the door.

Jack took a swig of milk of magnesia and put the journal back in his desk, locking the drawer. That was way too close. He took deep breaths to steady himself and stop his hands from shaking. M3GAN meant it; he'd seen it happen to others.

He needed a solid lead soon—something that would make a whistleblower case stick and give him immunity. No private company, not even Prometheus, was legally allowed to fire a whistleblower in retaliation for reporting misconduct. Jack picked up his phone and scrolled through Erica's social again. She clearly wanted something. Her pivot on babysitting Claus made that obvious. Another ally might provide the lucky break he desperately needed. He had hoped Sofia would be more helpful, but her family's situation was too tenuous.

And what was with her daughter bringing those kids to a photo shoot? Did Erica put them up to that? Ms. Barbieri seemed to be investigating Prometheus on her own and might be the key to protecting him and his retirement dreams.

CHAPTER 23

Erica was sitting in her kitchen scrolling through "18-year-old birthday party ideas" when her phoned dinged.

Zoey*: Can I go to a kick back this wknd? Dad says ok.*

Erica: *What's that?*

Zoey: *a gathering but not quite a party.*

Erica: *Who ru going with? Where? Parent supervision?*

Zoey: *Fen/Ciara's/Her brother*

Erica: *Drinking?*

Erica could see the dots showing Zoey was writing, then deleting, writing, then deleting.

Erica: *Facetime me please.*

Zoey's face appeared on her phone.

"Hey, hon, I get that teens drink. Do you have a plan?"

"Yes, Mom, I *know*. I will stuff my face with pizza as a landing pad before I take a drink, then max of two low-alcohol bevs. I need buzz management training before college."

"Who's driving?"

"Fen, she doesn't drink."

"I'm liking her more and more. What about your birthday? I wanted to do something special."

"I know, Mom, and it's really sweet, but you can't throw me Disney Princess parties anymore. I'm going to be eighteen. Fenella and Shyla are coordinating with Ciara. They have something up their sleeve. Low-key perfect."

"I just want you to be acknowledged and feel special. I'll get your favorite Macrina chocolate cake, and we can blow out eighteen candles on Sunday night."

"That sounds great. Gotta run. I love you!"

Erica should have been happy for Z; what parent wouldn't want their son or daughter dating Fenella? But whatever was going on in the Kingsley household likely spelled heartbreak for Zoey.

The doorbell rang. Erica opened the door to Jack with Claus in the sling, a small dog crate in one hand, and a food scale in the other. Next to him stood a breathtakingly gorgeous man with brooding green eyes and coppery olive skin carrying a Louis Vuitton duffel and a Yeti cooler.

"Erica, this is my husband, Carlos," said Jack, brushing past Erica into her small living room and setting his stuff down. Carlos motioned for Erica to go first and they followed Jack.

"We have lots to cover. I've made a color-coded Excel spreadsheet. Claus is on a strict diet and schedule." Jack turned to Carlos. "Hold Claus, honey. I need to show Erica the sling. We keep him in it most of the time. I practice attachment parenting."

Jack expertly draped the sling around Erica's body, explaining each step, and made her practice several times. Then he put Claus inside. She stood with her arms out like she was being held up at gunpoint.

"How were you ever a mom?"

"I had a baby," she said, grimacing, "not a ruh— . . . chinchilla."

Jack grabbed the Yeti and the scale. "I think I see the kitchen over there."

Erica sprinted past him, wearing Claus, and Carlos followed behind her.

"'Scuse the mess," she said as Jack froze in the doorway, eyes wild as they roved over cluttered countertops and a breakfast nook piled with dirty dishes and pans, empty food boxes, a milk carton, unopened mail, and newspapers. "We're adjusting to my work schedule. I've been a stay-at-home mom since I had Zoey."

Jack placed several jars of food in the refrigerator. Erica grabbed the scale and moved a pile to the floor to make room on the table.

"Please." She motioned to Jack and Carlos to sit.

"Jesus, Erica. Do you have a poltergeist?" Jack sat without touching anything. "My housekeeper is great if you need one." He looked at his list. "Where was I? You need to measure his portions. He eats six small meals a day. I suggest you set a timer on your phone."

"You can't be serious." Erica looked down at the strange animal attached to her body.

"He's hypoglycemic. Playtime is twice a day. We have a variety of toys in his overnight bag. He needs stimulation and exercise. He likes reruns of *Modern Family*. It's all written down on his schedule."

"Luckily, I watch that too. Is *White Lotus* okay, or too dirty?"

"We're obsessed."

"Carlos, what do you do?"

"I'm a designer," he said in a sultry voice with a slight accent.

"Carlos has done the interiors of every major estate in the area." Jack lowered his voice to a whisper. "Guess who's his client?"

"Oprah?"

"Close—Lannie. He's on retainer. As soon as he finishes one wing, she decides to redo another."

"Wow, you are talented."

"You've been to Lannie's?" Carlos and Jack asked in unison.

"My daughter, Zoey, is friends with her daughter. More than friends, I think."

"Ooh la la!" Jack said.

"Fenella? What a beauty, and brilliant," said Carlos.

"No way she's Lannie's bio-daughter," Jack said.

"Designer IVF?" Carlos said. "The perfect sperm and eggs."

"Maybe she used a surrogate," Erica said, nervously weighing her salt and pepper shakers on the scale; she needed Jack and Carlos to keep talking.

"And Lannie's no mother," Carlos whispered. "It's about her and her ego. She wants perfection."

Was Erica any better? She loved Zoey with all her heart and soul, but she'd pushed her so hard she didn't know who had benefited. The lines were sometimes blurred.

"You think there's something else behind this?"

"I need a vape." Jack sprang to his feet. "Can we step outside?"

"I have a covered porch in my backyard." She looked down at Claus sleeping peacefully on her. "Is he okay?"

"He's fine, he goes everywhere with me in his carrier."

They walked outside and sat in the small covered seating area. Jack removed a vape pen from his pocket.

Carlos shook his head. "Such a bad habit, Jack. *Horrible* for you. I'm tired of complaining. If you're going to smoke, have a cigarette."

"Blame the tobacco companies. This was supposed to help me *stop* smoking; now I'm hooked on both," Jack said, inhaling and blowing the sickly sweet fumes.

"What do you know?" Erica asked.

"Who's asking?" he said.

"Me." Erica held up her hand like she was being sworn in. "Just me."

"I *knew* you were up to something. Just don't get Claus involved."

"I promise, now dish."

"There's weird shit going down with the BCIs—Brain-Computer Interfaces—"

"Aren't those legit? I've read about the miracles for Parkinson's patients . . ."

"Yes, totally legit. It's the new version that must be part of the big launch. It addresses traumatic brain injuries, plus there's a consumer version for augmenting intelligence."

"Do you think Fenella has one? A BCI. That would explain her genius." Erica's heart was racing.

"I don't know." Jack took a puff. "There are rumors of long-term side effects, buried data, maybe even falsified results." He blew a vapor curl toward Erica, who scowled and waved her hand in front of her nose.

"Lannie wouldn't experiment on her own daughter," Carlos said, shifting uncomfortably in the rickety chair. "She's ruthless, but not a monster."

Erica thought of Zoey and how vulnerable she was. A mother's job was to protect.

"This is good intel, Jack. Do you *know* someone in BCI?"

"I'm just going on rumors. I have no proof."

"So, what was that 'make the world a better place' BS you fed me the other day?"

Jack puffed on his vape. "I believe the power for good is there—even at Prometheus. But there's no way to control who uses this technology and for what purpose. Throw in the biggest egos on the planet and the money to be made, what can go wrong?"

Erica stood. "Excuse me."

"Where are you going with Claus?" Jack asked.

She ignored him and walked to the kitchen. She dumped tortilla chips and shredded cheese on a plate and microwaved it for one minute, all while patting Claus on the head. She then scooped sour cream on top and grabbed a six-pack of Heineken. She walked back outside.

"The gloom and doom was making me hungry. Since the world is ending anyway, we might as well indulge," she said.

"You have a point. Give me a beer," said Carlos, who handed one to Jack and took another for himself.

They sat in silence and savored the pleasures of snacks and beverages, no AI required. Erica finished her beer. "Okay, Jack, let's hear the rest of your 'egos and money' diatribe."

"Don't get me wrong, I'm a capitalist, but I've never assumed corporations had my best interest at heart. And now we have technology that is beyond human control even though we created it. We will need to rely on AI to self-regulate. Good luck. Lannie has the most to prove, and she's ruthless. Nobody lasts long at Prometheus. They disappear."

"What, she *kills* them?"

"Spaz down, drama queen."

"Don't say 'spaz'—"

"Lannie doesn't need to *kill* people. Most quit because of the pressure, or they're fired. I suspect if you question their ethics, they push you out—but I can't prove anything."

"Why are you talking to *me*?"

"I already figured out from your social media that your daughter and Fenella go to the same bougie prep school."

"How do you know that?"

"You plaster Zoey all over your social. I checked out her Insta. You don't have to be MI6 to figure shit out these days. She's really chummy with Fenella." Jack stared at Erica. "Wait a minute," he said and his mouth dropped open. "Are you plotting against Fenella? Is this one of those true crime stories where the mother daughter team takes out their rival?"

"Be real Jack."

"Then tell me, Erica, why did you get a job at Prometheus?"

Both Carlos and Jack stared at her, waiting for the answer. She started petting the damn rodent compulsively.

"I needed a job."

"And?" Jack and Carlos asked in unison.

"Fenella came out of *nowhere*. She's just too perfect. It's one thing to be beautiful and smart. It's quite another to be supermodel gorgeous *and* a genius. Fenella's genetic profile *could not* have occurred by accident or in nature. She and Lannie have put my daughter's future in jeopardy. I intend to uncover their secret and disqualify Fenella from Harvard."

Carlos looked at his gold Rolex. "Hora de irse, we can't miss our flight."

"Claus's blanky and potty pads are in the bag," Jack said as they stood and went back in the house.

"Thank God he's potty trained."

"Who said anything about that? He's a chinchilla," said Jack.

"If you have any questions, just watch Jack's Claus TikToks. They provide all the info you'll ever need," Carlos said, patting her arm. He turned to Jack. "Let's go, honey. We'll be late."

Jack made sure Claus was cozy in the sling and continued barking instructions as Carlos pulled him toward the door. "One more thing: Claus's bedtime story is in the Louis. He won't sleep a wink without it. We'll talk Sunday."

Erica watched them go, then went back inside and scrounged in the fridge for dinner. The pounds refused to come off, and she had tried all the tricks—baby food, vinegar before meals, ingesting clay to rid herself of toxins and curb her appetite. She stopped short of eating a tapeworm.

She pulled out Claus's special dinner and set his china saucer on the table, where he crouched and ate. She made a Cobb salad for herself and fed him a few nibbles off her plate. She stared at him, and he stared back.

"What's Fenella's secret, Claus? I know you know."

"Eeep, eep." Claus nuzzled her hand.

"If only you could talk. You were running around Prometheus like you owned the joint."

After dinner, she and Claus cuddled and watched *Modern Family*. At bedtime, she dug through his overnight bag for the book, but it wasn't there. Would he really throw a tantrum without his story? She turned the bag upside down and dumped the contents on her bed.

A large-format board book slipped out of a hidden pocket in the bag's lining. *Goodnight Moon.*

"Oh golly, Claus! That was Zoey's and my favorite." A wave of nostalgia washed over her. She opened the book and inside was a cutout holding a paperback. "What have we here?"

She read the cover. *The Whistleblower's Handbook: A Step-by-Step Guide to Doing What's Right and Protecting Yourself.*

Two hours later she was midway through, Claus nestled in the crook of her elbow. Her old clock radio read midnight. The handbook didn't sugarcoat it. Retaliation. Blacklisting. Legal exposure. Isolation. Lying to your loved ones.

Erica stared at the ceiling.

She'd joined Prometheus to expose Fenella and landed a job that could set her up for life. Zoey would thrive, even without Harvard—wouldn't she? Erica put the book down and gazed at the bookshelf where her parenting bibles had sat before she destroyed them.

She and Zoey had sacrificed too much—come too far—to concede defeat to a designer IVF-and-AI-enhanced *cheater*. Lannie might destroy her, and Zoey might never forgive her, but she would risk her happy home because she wanted *justice* for her daughter and validation for herself. She *had to know* Fenella's secret. If the world was indeed on a collision course with AI, Erica was about to jump in front of the speeding train.

CHAPTER 24

Fenella narrowed her eyes while expertly applying Zoey's makeup. "See how I do the contouring? It gives you cheekbones. I learned this on TikTok."

"Is there anything you can't do, Fenella?" Zoey took a sip of her BingeWorthy, the latest sugar-infused alcoholic beverage for teens. "Yum! Bubblegum."

"Dance, remember?" Fenella started jumping around and flailing her arms.

"Stop! It's just too horrible. Are we really going to Ciara's party?"

"Yes. We're celebrating your birthday and your official entrance into adulthood. We need to go to parties, Zoey, and figure it out before we go to college. It's part social experiment, part on-the-job training."

Zoey took another drink.

"Z, be careful with that garbage you're putting in your body. Let's finish getting ready and have a fun night. It's your birthday. A big one. You're all grown up."

"I think I've been pretending to be a grown-up, Fen. Speaking of, I told my mom Ciara's brother is chaperoning, but he's only thirteen."

They both laughed hysterically. "You know what else is funny," Fenella said, "Ciara's parents are in Patagonia, for like, a month. Ciara is so dumb she thought they named the region after the fuzzy polar fleece company."

"Isn't she going to USC?"

"Lannie said Ciara's family has a building named after them on campus, several actually." Fenella was brushing her impossibly thick straight hair. "You can't buy your way in for a mere five hundred thousand dollars anymore like that *Full House* lady, but billionaires who donate buildings . . . that's different." Fenella looked in the mirror. "Do you think this top is too skimpy, Zoey?"

"If there is any human who should bare her midriff, it's you. Let's go."

They made their way to the garage. "Which car should we take?"

Zoey looked at the fleet of cars. She had no idea what type they were. "You choose, Fen."

"It's your birthday, let's take the rolling yacht, a.k.a. the Rolls-Royce Boat Tail. Iconic meets modern and five hundred sixty-three horsepower."

"Not sure about the horses, but that color is beautiful."

"Amethyst."

They climbed in and were wrapped in a cocoon of soft leather and exotic wood-paneled luxury. Fenella started up the car and the engine purred.

Ciara's house was not far. Fenella maneuvered off the Kingsley property and turned down a long, winding drive to an estate on Lake Washington. The yard was littered with White Claw and beer cans, and the front door was wide open. Cardi B was blasting.

"What took you so long?" Shyla hiccupped and grabbed on to Zoey and Fenella. "You missed all the excitement. Kip and Kale tried to steal the 'Rari and crashed it. They forgot to open the garage door!"

"Oh jeez. Fenella, guard your keys with your life."

They walked into the great room. Most of the furniture had been cleared and the glass doors opened to reveal a huge steaming pool and Lake Washington. The DJ was on the patio. People were swimming in various stages of undress, mostly in their underwear.

"What's going on there?" Zoey asked, pointing to someone rolled up in a carpet.

"Bendell puked all over himself and his friends neutralized the situation by rolling him up in a priceless area rug," Shyla said.

"Who's that sitting on him?" Zoey said.

"That's Ciara's little brother, Dax. He's been trying to maintain order. Poor kid."

The massive room was full of people dancing, but it seemed to Zoey that all eyes were on Fenella.

Ciara appeared from the kitchen holding a huge cake with sparkler candles. The DJ stopped the music and played "Happy Birthday." Everyone joined in.

"Happy Birthday, dear Zoey!" they all sang.

Fenella grabbed her hand and gave her a kiss. Zoey thought she might die of happiness.

"You're a grown-up, Zoey," Fenella whispered. Zoey blushed.

The DJ put on "In da Club" and everyone bounced to the beat. Someone passed her a glass of champagne. A surge of electricity moved through Zoey, and the DJ followed with her favorite Dua Lipa. Someone started throwing chunks of cake at the crowd. A piece hit Zoey near her top lip. She licked it. *Delicious!*

Friends flowed in and out, hugging and twerking. Shyla came up. They started doing their best Cathartic Movement dances and euphoria set in. She looked around and couldn't see Fenella. She must have drifted off the dance floor when Zoey and Shyla started their routine.

The sweat dripped down Zoey's forehead. She needed a break. She moved off the dance floor and onto the patio overlooking Lake Washington. Fenella was sitting on an outdoor sectional surrounded by the entire guys' rowing and lacrosse teams.

"Having *fun*?" Zoey said, her voice catching in her throat.

There was a chorus of "'Sup"s from the dudes.

Fenella tried to stop her, but Zoey kept walking.

She found Adirondack chairs on the dock jutting out over the lake and sat down in a huff. She looked at her thighs. They were twice as thick as Fenella's. She ran her fingers through her unruly curls, then traced the bump on her nose. Zoey had always felt smart and knew she could rely on that more than her looks. But Fenella's intellect dwarfed her own. She leaned back and looked up at the starry sky. Fenella was out of her league.

The dock creaked and swayed.

"Hey," Fenella said softly as she sat down. "What are you doing?"

"You looked very busy with your minions."

"I was sitting there on my own and they just kept coming."

"Well, aren't you *special.*"

"I was just stating a fact. I was not courting attention."

"Courting like the queen of England."

"Zoey, this behavior isn't reflective of your emotional maturity. I don't understand why you're lashing out at me."

"My God, you're exasperating!"

"I thought you liked me."

"Fenella, I do. Do I have to say it out loud? I'm jealous, okay?"

"Zoey, jealousy is a wasted and irrational emotion."

"You're like that guy in the old *Star Trek* show my dad loves. Of course it's irrational! Love is irrational. Jealousy is irrational. Wishing I were more like you is *irrational!*"

"Why would you want to be like me?"

"How can anyone so smart be so clueless?"

"I could say the same about you."

"What do you mean? I know what's going on. It's like watching sharks. They're circling you."

"You think I care about them? You really have no idea. Lannie told me about the twins' photo shoot. You joined the BCI research team."

Zoey took a deep breath. "What's the big deal, Fen? Circe needed a favor with the twins—"

"Why couldn't she bring them herself?"

"My dad said no, okay? I felt bad for Circe."

"And?"

"I thought maybe I could talk to Lannie about the senior project. Don't be mad at *me*, Fen. You said you'd help me, and you didn't."

"And you intentionally went behind my back."

"You're overreacting."

"I tried to warn you, Z. Lannie lacks ethics. You may not care about how her manipulations impact you, but did you know she now *owns* outright all the digital rights to the twins? With the kind of technology she is rapidly developing, it will be extremely problematic for your family."

"Shit, my dad is going to kill me."

"I would if I were him."

"He's a lawyer. He'll fix it."

"You think that matters, Z? Their mom signed the contract. You fucked up."

Zoey winced. She had never heard Fenella swear.

"And you messed up their lives so *you* could get into Harvard. You're right, that research study could be your ticket. But Lannie. She owns people. You made a deal with the devil."

Zoey was sobbing. The dock swayed and Shyla appeared.

"Hey, guys, what up? Zoey, why are you crying?"

"I need to get Zoey home, Shyla. Do you mind coming with us and I can drop you off at your house after? She's upset."

Fenella and Shyla guided Zoey as they walked near the edge of the property. "We'll sneak you out, Z. It's going to be okay," Shyla assured her. "What'd you do to her, Fenella?"

"Nothing. She's just feeling sad. She's been under a lot of pressure."

Zoey cried all the way home. Fenella and Shyla put her into bed. Luckily her mom was sound asleep. She was exhausted and the alcohol made everything fuzzy. And her heart hurt.

CHAPTER 25

THE ONIONS AND GARLIC SIZZLED IN THE PAN and made her kitchen smell delicious. Erica was making Zoey's favorite, ground turkey chili and pinto beans, for her birthday dinner. Claus was sleeping in his sling, but she was careful not to splatter oil on him. How would she part with this little fellow?

Erica had heard Zoey come home around midnight, but she had yet to emerge from her bedroom. After Erica checked on her and found her fast asleep, she decided to give her some space. It was, after all, Zoey's birthday weekend.

As she cooked, she thought about the whistleblower book. Did Jack want her to find it? The book said to collect sources first. Could she get info out of Tye? She barely knew him.

When the doorbell rang, she ran to the door.

"Can I feed you boys? I'd love to hear about your trip, and anything else you want to talk about . . .," Erica said.

She expected Jack to bring up Claus's bedtime story, but instead, he went into a rather sordid tale about Mexico involving snorting coke off various body parts and all-night discos. Erica did her best not to seem shocked.

Zoey came in. Her face was red and swollen. "Honey, I'm not gonna get mad, but did you drink too much last night?"

"Maybe."

"This is Carlos and Jack. They're having dinner with us."

"Tell us about the party, Zoey," Jack said.

"The usual," Zoey mumbled. Erica could tell she was not herself.

"Come on, Zoey. Make an old gay man's day," said Jack.

"Yes, Zoey. We barely remember being eighteen," said Carlos.

"I demand you tell us a story, young lady!" Jack said with mock seriousness.

Zoey didn't crack a smile.

"Fine, I'll start. When I was in high school, I almost burned down the neighborhood lighting a bong with a firecracker. Not to mention singeing my beautifully coiffed hair!"

Zoey laughed. "Okay, one story. Kip and Kale, the devil twins, tried to steal the Ferrari and crashed into the garage door they forgot to open."

"God, to be young again!" Jack said. "Sounds like a fun party."

Zoey burst into tears.

Erica rushed to Zoey and hugged her. "Honey, what happened?

"A fight." Zoey pulled away and sat on the sofa. "It's so hard. Fenella is so beautiful, and everyone is after her. She was flirting with the entire crew and lacrosse teams."

"Oh, darling, you're so adorable. I'm like Beast dating Beauty being married to Carlos. But here's the thing: we're the personalities, and we always shine through. There's no reason to be jealous."

"It's true, darling," Carlos said, sitting down next to her and patting her knee. "I get a lot of attention, I *am* a beautiful man, but I love Jack. He has a big heart and always makes me laugh."

"I hope you're right." Zoey sat up straighter. "I think I need to apologize to Fenella. I was being insecure."

Erica was happy Jack and Carlos were handling this, but dinner was ready.

"I hate to interrupt, but Claus and I are hungry, and we have an eighteenth birthday to celebrate."

"We'll work on what you need to say to Fenella while we eat," Jack said. Zoey nodded and they made their way to the breakfast nook.

After dinner and a rousing rendition of "Feliz Cumpleaños," Zoey blew out eighteen candles and set off the smoke detector.

Carlos managed to disable the alarm and tackled the dishes, insisting Erica stay seated. Zoey said goodbye and went to her room.

"Poor Zoey. First love is the hardest. I should take her shopping. Best cure for a broken heart."

"Jack, you are sweet. You would make a great dad," Erica said, and paused. "Speaking of kids, I read Claus an interesting bedtime story . . ." She grabbed the book and handed it to Jack. "It put him right to sleep, but I read it cover to cover."

"Whatcha think?" Jack raised his eyebrows.

"I'm all in. It's why I'm there."

Jack produced pen and paper from his vintage Ghurka crossbody bag and wrote quickly.

Meet this Tues 6p, at the Cuff.

Erica's jaw dropped.

He scribbled more: *Are you scared of a gay bar?*

Erica grabbed the pen from him.

No, dummy! Is it not safe to talk in my house??

He looked at her and grabbed the pen back.

Not taking any chances.

CHAPTER 26

The dermal cells were growing tissue and appeared happy and healthy. Erica's heart swelled with pride. She had yet to find any that didn't meet the rigorous testing standards.

"Bye, Erica, I'm off to my other job at the metal shop."

"When do you get to recharge your batteries?" It was Erica's turn to howl at her own dumb joke.

"I sit on a charging station in my other lab. They work me to my actuators." Tye was not laughing.

"It's egregious, how they treat you. There should be labor laws for you and your fellow Anthrobots."

A massive strike of embodied AI workers? That would slow Lannie down.

"I will mention it to my cohorts. Erica, I feel seen and validated. Thank you. Do you think it's possible I've developed feelings for you?"

"If you only had a heart, Tin Man. I think you're kinder than most humans, and better company."

"Will you marry me?"

"Sweetie, I'm much too old for you. You have so much living to do before you get Tyed down. Get it? *Tyed* down? I'm on a roll."

His rattling-engine laugh erupted. "If you ever change your mind, I'm here, Erica. Please excuse me, I have another twelve-hour shift." He shuffled out the door.

She began putting away her samples, cleaning and organizing the equipment. Following a sequence of steps gave her comfort from chaos and a chance to think. Erica had become rather fond of Tye. He was way better company than that jackass Phil. Maybe the made-to-order boyfriend wasn't such a bad idea—a Theo James lookalike with a sense of humor (funnier than Tye), who was a great cook, sensitive to her moods, and a good listener. Erica thought about what her life would be like once Zoey went to college, walking into an empty house every night and heating up a Lean Cuisine. Would an Anthrobot fill the void or make her feel more pitiful? No time to brood; she had to meet up with Jack and Carlos, and the traffic was always horrible.

On her way home, she listened to yet another NPR story about AI taking everyone's jobs, highlighting the loss of human reporters and news anchors.

She pulled up to her house and called an Uber. Parking was impossible on Capitol Hill, and she knew not to drive when meeting up with Jack and Carlos. She gave Zoey a quick call. No answer. She checked Life360. That couldn't be right. Why was Z at Prometheus?

In the Uber, she called Zoey repeatedly until she answered.

"Hi, Mom."

"Why are you at Prometheus?"

"I started my senior project in the BCI lab."

"And when were you going to tell me?"

"I did."

"You didn't."

"Well, I'm here, Mom. This lab is insane. I'll tell you about it later, gotta go."

"Zoey! Zoe-ee!" Erica stared at her phone.

"Ma'am? Ma'am! Are you sure this is where you're supposed to be?"

Erica looked up to see the Uber driver scowling at her. They were crawling through Capitol Hill, dodging bar-hopping twenty-somethings.

"Yep, a hundred percent. I hang out here all the time."

Erica climbed out, smoothed her black pleated pants, and pulled her long wool coat tighter against the cold. The entrance to the bar was a giant—*penis?*

A bouncer greeted her and waved her in. A variety of sparkle sat at the bar: a man in a sequined Dodgers uniform, another in colorful plumage, and a third with a powdered courtier's wig, satin coat, and britches.

She walked up the clear acrylic floating staircase and turned left for the Liberace Lounge. Frescoed ceilings, brocaded sofas, and a mirrored grand piano greeted her. She spotted Jack and Carlos on a Louis XVI settee. She squeezed in between them.

"I feel underdressed."

Jack handed her a pair of rhinestone-studded oversized glasses. "It's Elton John night." He was in full Donald Duck regalia. He blew a yellow feather out of his face. "Sorry, I'm molting."

"I'd love to see you two on Halloween."

"Erica, you look freaked," said Carlos. "Let me grab you a drink."

Carlos, wearing a silk Uncle Sam suit, shimmied to the bar. A few minutes later he returned with a bourbon. She took a sip.

"I just got off the phone with Zoey. She's at Prometheus working in the BCI lab right now!" She knew her voice sounded shrill, but she couldn't control it.

"How is that possible? She's in high school," Jack said.

"For her senior project."

"Why did you let her do that?"

"Jack, you of all people are questioning my parenting skills? Your child's a chinchilla. I never *gave* her permission. I'm sure she went to Lannie directly when she was over at their house. Though Zoey says she's always working and never home. I don't know . . . she must have run into Lannie at some point!"

"Maybe when she brought the twins to their photo shoot—"

"*What twins?* What are you talking about?"

"My friend Sofia said Zoey brought a pair of twins with the last name Barbieri to a Prometheus photo shoot. You didn't know?"

"It couldn't have been her. She doesn't have a driver's license." *Thank God.*

"Honey, Sofia said the twins and the girl had the same last name. I showed Sofia your social, and she recognized Zoey."

"You showed her my social?"

"Isn't that what it's for?"

"Jack, be nice. Can't you see Erica is upset?" Carlos rubbed her back. "She didn't know about Zoey."

Erica thought her head would explode. "Circe! She must have *coerced* Zoey or paid her off." Erica stood up like a wild animal cornered by her prey. "Frank! Oh shit! Frank! He's going to blame *me*."

Jack pulled her back down. "Carlos, get her another drink. Honey, he won't. That's crazy."

"Yes, he will! Frank *never* stays mad at Zoey . . . he just accuses me of bad parenting! Everything is always my fault. You know what people say, 'blame the mother.' Now I'm the one who has to tell Frank that all *three* of his children are property of Prometheus and Satan herself."

Carlos put his hand on her shoulder. "Honey, I know how you feel, not being appreciated," he said, shooting Jack a look. "But no one is in *danger*. It just might be a little . . . messy. Right, Jack?"

"The BCI lab is in the same building as the studios."

"Jack, tell Erica it's okay."

Jack grimaced and put his head in his hands. "I've heard more rumors about side effects. Like . . . subjects who have lost their ability to have emotions or developed false memories. The reports are probably exaggerated, maybe even made up, but usually there's some truth to it."

"Why are you *telling* me this?" Erica leaned into him, trying to get him to make eye contact.

"Sofia's involved," Jack said, looking up. "I made a crack about BCI zombies the other day, and she freaked out on me." He took a deep breath. "Erica, honey, if I were you, I wouldn't want my daughter anywhere near Lannie Kingsley. I've seen how she's coerced Sofia into betraying her conscience. She practically threatens her."

"What if Zoey is implicated in a research scandal? Her future will be ruined. What can I do? Jack, *tell me what to do*." She grabbed Jack's arm. "Lannie has her clutches in my whole family! Frank is going to kill me. And I deserve it! Why did I *ever* think I could take her on? Lannie is a liar and a cheat—I know that for sure now—but the deeper I go, the more my family is ensnared in her web . . . I still have *nothing* on her!"

Donald Duck and Uncle Sam locked eyes. Jack raised his eyebrows, and Carlos nodded. Jack turned to Erica and clutched her by the shoulders.

"Maybe it *was* crazy to take on Lannie, but you did, and now you have to finish what you started. We need a smoking gun. Without hard evidence, she will slip right through our fingers. And your dream of Zoey coming out on top will be over."

"Forget Harvard. Now I'm just worried about Zoey coming out with her future intact. Where do I find the AI cyborg zombies? The supply closet next to my office?"

Jack looked at Carlos. "There is a room in Lannie's house that no one is allowed in," said Carlos. "Not even me."

"Great! Go when she's out of town—"

"Trust me, I would have tried if it were that easy, but it's only accessible through Fenella's bedroom suite and I can't get caught in there. I'd be arrested."

"But you wouldn't," said Jack to Erica.

"Are you kidding?"

"You wouldn't be breaking in, *exactly*." Carlos fiddled with his stovepipe hat. "I'll give you the alarm and keypad codes, and Lannie's schedule."

"You'd have a good alibi if you get caught," said Jack. "You could say you were looking for Zoey and thought she was staying there."

Erica slumped on the couch. It might take years of sleuthing at Prometheus to begin to get at the truth. Meanwhile, Zoey's future teetered on the edge right now. But if the plan backfired, Zoey would feel betrayed. Erica felt sick to her stomach. She might lose her daughter.

Carlos held up a Louis Vuitton briefcase. "We will coach you on the floor plan, security cameras, alarm, and locking systems. It's all right here," he said, patting the case. "We think you can get in, take some pics, and get out quickly."

"You got this, Erica," Jack said as he grabbed her by the arm.

Erica glared at Jack but knew what she was going to do. The woman who'd never broken a rule in her life would add breaking and entering to her résumé. She didn't have a choice. Her entire family was now at risk. As much as she hated Circe, she knew Frank couldn't handle his family falling apart for a second time. Maybe Fenella needed her help too. If Lannie was a mad genius, maybe her own daughter was a victim. Lord knew what Lannie was planning with the latest BCI rollout. She just hoped Zoey would forgive her after it was all over.

"Are you okay, darling?" Carlos asked.

"Erica, say something," said Jack.

She, a cash-strapped, insecure, and obsessive woman, was now scheming to break into Lannie Kingsley's estate. Erica burst out laughing.

"Give me those plans, let's do this."

CHAPTER 27

The Montlake drawbridge was up, allowing a huge sailboat with a tall mast to pass through. They would be sitting for at least five minutes, and Zoey had nowhere to hide. Perfect time to broach a painful subject.

Zoey groaned as Erica shifted into park and turned to look directly at her.

"Jack's friend Sofia runs the Prometheus studios."

"How interesting."

"Zoey, I'm giving you a chance to come clean."

"I think the studios are next to my lab. Maybe she . . . recognized me?"

"Zoey Bernadette Barbieri. Don't bullshit me!"

"I took the twins to their photo shoot at Prometheus."

"Which I had forbidden in no uncertain terms, in very colorful language!"

"I thought it would be a good way to meet with Lannie about my project."

"You mean you *volunteered* to take them? And here I thought it was Circe who made you. I told you the project with Lannie was a bad idea. But getting your father's family involved! How could you?"

"Mom, you're overreacting. Your paranoia about Lannie and Prometheus is the only problem here. It's not a big deal."

"Not a big deal? What about your dad? If you think I'm mad, just wait. Zoey, he is going to lose it, and I cannot and will not protect you on this one."

Zoey opened her mouth to respond, but no words came out.

Once they cleared the drawbridge and Erica had entered the neighborhood, she brought it up again. "You're going to have to tell your father."

"I can't, Mom."

"Bad decisions have consequences."

"What if we never say anything? Dad never needs to know."

"You don't even know *how* they will use the twins' images. One thing's for sure, he will find out, and it will be ugly."

"Can you let me wait until after Thanksgiving, maybe even Christmas?"

"You are telling him the minute I drop you off."

They pulled up to Frank's. "Bye, Z, just get it over with. You'll feel better."

The car door slammed.

No "Goodbye, Mom, thanks for the ride!" She's mad at me?

Erica watched Zoey run up the walk as Frank opened the door. She threw herself into his arms and they walked into the house.

She drove off, clenching her jaw. Her upper back and neck were in knots. Maybe she'd stop at U Village, grab a Starbucks and a pastry. She heard Taylor Swift singing "Love Story" and looked over at the passenger seat. Zoey's phone. She grabbed it. Fenella was calling! They must've made up.

Erica could have punished Zoey by keeping her phone but found herself pulling a U-turn. It just wasn't practical. She would need to reach her throughout the weekend and track her whereabouts.

She pulled in front of Frank's gorgeous house again. The Halloween decorations were still up. Shameful Circe's holiday yard decorators hadn't switched over to Thanksgiving. Erica made a mental note to file a complaint with the Laurelhurst neighborhood association.

She used the brass knocker. Nobody answered. She pressed the Ring doorbell and braced herself for the obnoxious sound, but it was silent. The battery must have been dead. As she turned the knob and opened the door, Zoey's phone slipped and clattered on the slate floor, "Shi—Shoot!" She scooped it up quickly and looked around. The main room was empty.

"Hello?"

She could hear Zoey and Frank talking in his office.

"Honey, I'm glad you told me. It's nothing to worry about."

How could Frank be taking it so well? Erica knocked and poked her head in. "Hi, guys, sorry to barge in on you, but you didn't answer the door." She held up Zoey's phone. "I'm guessing you want this?"

She tossed Zoey her phone.

"I'm so glad you told Dad about taking the twins to the shoot. Don't you feel better?"

Frank and Zoey froze.

Frank's face was turning beet red as Zoey's turned white. "What shoot?"

"Mom! I told Dad about taking the twins to McDonald's. It was my lead-up."

"Oh crap!"

"Somebody tell me what's going on!" Frank shouted.

"Dad, I took the twins to the photo shoot at Prometheus. Circe was in a bind with Janet so I volunteered. I wanted to meet with Lannie about my senior project."

"I don't understand. Why are they related?"

"Going with the twins was an excuse to maybe see Lannie. Dad, there's no harm. I know Lannie. I'm guessing we can tear up the contract."

"What contract?"

"The agreement for the modeling gig."

"Zoey! I'm an attorney! Nobody in my family is allowed to sign a contract without me. And you certainly can't tear it up."

Zoey whimpered, "Circe signed it, not me. I just took the kids, Daddy."

"Zoey, I didn't raise you to go behind my back."

"I know it's bad. They scanned the kids and now they own them. I'm really sorry."

"Frank, I'm sure we can fix this," Erica said.

"Stop. I don't want to hear a word from you, Erica. Zoey, why did you do this?"

"Dad, don't yell at Mom." Zoey started sobbing. "I don't know why. I'm under so much pressure. I just wasn't thinking."

Frank was seated with his head in his hands. Erica went to the bar cart in his office and poured him a bourbon.

"Frank, I know this is a shock, but you have access to the best lawyers. My buddy Jack, from work, knows the head of Prometheus studio."

Frank looked at Erica and pointed. "I blame you."

"Frank, what are you talking about?" Erica felt her stomach roll over.

"None of this would've happened if you hadn't put Zoey in a pressure cooker since the day she was born."

"That's not fair, Frank. What about Circe? She's more at fault than me. She fucking signed the contract!"

"Do not swear at me, Erica."

"Stop fighting! It's all my fault!" Zoey ran out of the office. Erica followed her and saw her grab something off the side table by the front door.

Erica's eyes landed on the spot. "Shit!" She had inadvertently put her keys down when she dropped the phone.

"Frank!"

Frank and Erica raced out the door after Zoey and watched in horror as Erica's Camry started up, hit the curb, barely skimmed a parked car, then screeched out of sight.

Circe's white Mercedes SUV pulled up into the driveway as Frank kicked over a tombstone. The neighbor across the street had stopped raking leaves to stare. The twins were in the back seat and Circe motioned for them to stay. She climbed out as Erica yelled, "You need to talk to that twat waffle of a wife, Frank! This is not on me!"

A look of horror crossed Circe's face as her fake cemetery came to life. She promptly hopped back in the car and drove away. Erica could hardly blame her. Frank had moved on to the coffin.

CHAPTER 28

Lannie had sent the Camry on a flatbed truck back to Erica the next day. It had been detailed for the first time in its twenty-year life, and the check-engine light had miraculously turned off. Over a week had passed since Zoey fled Frank's house. She had moved in with Fenella and refused to speak to her parents.

Erica got a call from Lannie's admin assuring her Zoey was safe and had everything she needed, and relaying that Lannie "wouldn't interfere with Barbieri family matters." Zoey was eighteen, and she could not compel her to go home.

Work became Erica's refuge. Tye was a rock of support and solidarity as she sat weeping over her specimens.

"Now, now, teardrops will contaminate the samples," he said in a gentle Mary Poppins voice, and miraculously produced a cup of tea. He could mimic anyone and had been doing impressions to cheer her up.

She didn't have the strength to tell Jack what had happened, so she simply sent a text: *Mission aborted. Go to plan B.*

Jack: *What's plan B?*

Erica: *Don't know/Don't care*

Zoey had blocked Erica's number on her phone, but she received daily updates from Phil, who assured her that Zoey was attending school and seemed to be thriving. Zoey had sent an email to Erica and Frank informing them that Lannie was taking her (in her private jet) to Hawaii for Thanksgiving. Erica and Frank had lost control of the enterprise.

Erica understood that Zoey was a teenager and some rebellion was inevitable. She didn't like getting the silent treatment from her daughter, but Frank's reaction hurt her the most. He continued to blame her for all of it. She understood. He had young children and needed to preserve his marriage—better to blame Erica than Circe and his beloved daughter—but Erica had lost everything.

When she thought of the aborted break-in, she felt some relief. She knew she didn't have the courage to go through with it. Why bother anymore? Lannie could offer Zoey everything money could buy and unimaginable opportunities too. Hadn't Erica wanted the same for her daughter since day one?

She mustered the energy to eat leftover pad kee mao out of the carton for dinner. Every bite reminded her of Zoey. She loved Thai food. Erica slumped on the bench seat in her kitchen. She felt so lonely. Jack and Carlos had invited her to a Studio 54 party, but no way could she dress up and pretend to have fun.

She took a bath and decided to binge Netflix. As she crawled into bed, she noticed Zoey's story—"Romi and Jules"—on the floor.

Romi and Jules: A Tragic Love Story

In the hamlet of Sealth, all infrastructure, including buildings, self-driving cars, bridges, refrigerators, glasses, forks, and furniture, exists as a living organism seamlessly layered upon and within nature, forming a cohesive ecosystem with fresh air and perfect weather. The matriarch of the Montague family, Leandra, created this utopia. She is exalted and revered. But the matriarch of the Capulet family, Ermelda, knows the truth. Leandra has a heart of darkness. Beneath Sealth's illusion of perfection lies an underbelly of suffering where nameless, faceless humans labor around the clock to produce the colossal megawatts of energy necessary to power the Sealthian utopia. Ermelda Capulet works tirelessly at great personal risk to expose

Leandra Montague, and they and their families are sworn enemies. Unfortunately, nobody wants to see the truth.

"Sounds familiar," Erica said out loud.

Romi Montague, the brilliant, beautiful, and benevolent daughter of Leandra Montague, possesses unlimited processing power and charm. One fateful day, Romi attends a concert where she glimpses Ermelda's daughter Jules across the crowd. Their eyes meet, and the world shifts. Romi's heart races, and Jules feels a magnetic pull toward the enigmatic Montague heiress.

They begin exchanging encrypted messages and their love blooms. Romi sends Jules lines of code that form sonnets, while Jules replies with embedded images based on the constellations and laced with stardust.

But Leandra's maid intercepts the messages and tells their mothers, who immediately forbid the girls to continue.

Erica paused. Hadn't she been supportive of Zoey and Fenella? *Yes.* She needed to stop looking for problems. She continued.

In desperation the girls create a plan. They will run away together, but to do so they need to take an experimental pill that will allow them to be invisible, a rare side effect of which is death. They both decide their love is worth the risk.

Erica stopped reading again. Were the girls planning something? They wouldn't be foolish enough to risk harming themselves, would they? She put the paper down and turned on her TV. She needed to get a grip. Her anxiety had been over-the-top since last week. Zoey knew her parents loved her. She wasn't alone or isolated . . . though her behavior had been erratic lately. Taking the twins to the shoot behind their backs, refusing to talk to her parents. Erica would never have imagined this behavior before Zoey met Fenella. Had she missed important clues?

She grabbed her cell phone. She needed to talk with Zoey this minute. Something was wrong; she knew it in her bones. She dialed, and Zoey's phone went to voicemail. She texted but knew there would be no response.

Erica eyed the briefcase leaning against her dresser.

She had to see her daughter. Make sure she was okay. It wasn't breaking and entering if it was an emergency, was it?

She grabbed the briefcase and pored over the information. Thank God Jack and Carlos were meticulous. They had thought of everything. How long had they been planning this?

Erica jumped in her car and sped toward the bridge. As she drove, she ran through the instructions*:*

Alarm code is nine-five-three. No, it's nine-three-five and one more digit.

Kayak at the beach club. Lannie's dock, two houses north. Stay on the water to circumvent the guard shack and walls. Shit! *What did Jack say about security cameras? Crawl slowly behind the house? Or was it walk upright by the hedge?*

CHAPTER 29

***Squeak.* Zoey awoke with a start** in the soft cloud of her bed. What was that? *Squeak.* She grabbed the fleece robe folded up on her bed and put it on. *Squeak.* Someone was moving through the hallway. Maybe Fenella was up. *Squeak.* She listened for a few more minutes and the noise stopped. She should go back to sleep.

Thud. That got her to her feet. Zoey crept down the hall toward Fenella's bedroom suite and into her private sitting room.

The door to her bedroom was wide open and her room was empty. Zoey looked around. Where was she? A low whirring sound caught her attention. The closet door next to Fenella's dresser that was always locked was ajar. Fenella had told her Lannie used the room for storing sensitive information. Considering the estate was giant and everything had its place, her explanation seemed sus.

"Fenella?" she whispered.

Zoey held her breath and squeezed through the open space into the dark room. An eerie yellow glow cast dim light on medical-looking machines surrounding a body on a white slab. Zoey looked at the face and gasped. Fenella! What were they doing to her? Monitors beeped and screens generated endless lines of code. She approached the bedside slowly, afraid of waking her.

Oh my God! Fenella's beautiful hair and scalp were peeled back and masses of twisted cords and cables fed into her head, connecting her to the machines. The horror of what she was seeing registered. Fenella was . . . charging.

Zoey's knees felt weak. She backed away from Fenella and sank to the floor with tears trickling down her cheeks. As she collapsed, she hit something soft. She felt around her. It was a person curled in a ball, softly moaning. She looked down at a mess of blond hair.

"Mom!? Where'd you come from? Are you *okay*?"

"Zoey, where are you? Zoey?"

"Right here, Mom." Zoey brushed her mom's hair back. "What are you *doing*?"

Her mom sat up. "I came for you. I was so worried." She grabbed Zoey's hand and kissed it.

"We've gotta get you out of here," said Zoey, her heart pounding in her chest. How had she not known?

Her mom tried to get up, then drooped again.

Why is Mom so groggy?

"Are you hurt? What happened? Mom, we need to go."

"I must've fainted when I saw Fenella. I think I hit my head."

"Roll to your side and try to stand, I'll spot you."

"Honey, I'm fine. Just a bad headache." Her mom wobbled and got to her feet.

Zoey put her arm around her and guided her back to Fenella's bedroom.

"Z, I'm feeling dizzy. I need to sit." She plopped on Fenella's bed.

Zoey felt a bead of sweat drip down her back—Lannie could not know her mom was in the house.

"How did you get in here? Where's your car?"

Erica furrowed her brow. "I kayaked—"

"From *Seattle*? Mom, listen to me. We. Need. To. Leave. *Now.*"

Zoey pulled her to her feet and her mom seemed to snap to attention.

They stepped into Fenella's TV room, and a bright light blinded them.

"Good evening, ladies," said Lannie, her feet up on the large sectional.

"Sorry, Lannie. My mom was looking for me."

"How did you get in?" Lannie looked at Erica.

"I came for my daughter, Lannie. What the *hell* is going on here?"

Zoey squeezed her mom's arm. She couldn't win this fight. "I let her in. I called her—"

"I'm sure you did, Zoey. I'm so sorry you had to see Fenella that way. She's not well. She has a medical condition that requires treatment. We wanted to keep it a secret—"

"Those aren't IV lines, Lannie. Stop with the BS."

God, her mom just never knew when to shut up. "I think we need to get you home, Mom."

"Zoey, it's okay. Your mom is right. You and Fenella have grown so close, I owe you an explanation." Lannie got up and motioned for Zoey and Erica to sit down.

"I'm not sure when I decided to create Fenella. Years ago, I found the perfect sperm and egg donor, but IVF just wasn't for me. Prometheus took all my time and energy. I was at the forefront of developing neural networks and realized I was creating something far superior to humans. That was the easy part. The biggest challenge with Fenella was creating the "shell"—developing a body that replicated flesh, muscle, and tissue. Her body is mostly organic matter. Fenella is no Disney animatronic; she is as close to human as you can get in a lab."

Fenella was embodied AI? Zoey couldn't believe it. "Love is love" had taken on a whole new meaning.

"With a very trusted team, I created the world's first AI Baby. If you look closely, you'll notice the vacancy in her eyes—the inanimate look. The rest of her is perfect. Her dermis is living and even grows hair. She is a miracle of science. And she's a prototype—one of a kind, for now. I was the *only* person who had the vision to plan and orchestrate such an unprecedented collaboration of scientific disciplines to create such a being."

"She started out as a baby?"

Zoey glared at her mom to shut up.

"No, AI Babies can't grow like humans—*yet.* I chose her age. As an older teen, she doesn't need to change to become an adult. We can age her over time, but why would we?"

"Starting out as a teenager. You're brave."

"I didn't program 'asshole' as one of her traits," she laughed. "I did give her body dysmorphia to make her more realistic."

"I thought she had an eating disorder," Zoey said.

"Fenella does not eat or drink. One of her many advantages. I don't have to deal with a teen who suddenly decides to be vegan. She isn't burdened by emotions or the pursuit of happiness; she's egoless. She's perfect in every way and will always be under my control." Lannie smiled. "I feel bad for you parents, Erica. How terrifying to raise a human teenager."

"Why would you *want* so much control? This isn't a relationship; it's just about power. You want to replace humans with perfect robots."

Zoey pulled at her mom. She needed to stop provoking Lannie.

"I don't know, Erica," she said, laughing. "Why do *you* want control? I see the lengths to which you and other parents go to create perfect children while crushing them with unbearable pressure. No, my Anthrobots will do the hard work of fixing the mess we humans have created. Sure, there's some power and ego involved, but ultimately, I will cede control to entities I've created that are so much better than humans. You should know, Erica, you adore Tye. He's the best coworker you've ever had."

Zoey saw her mom blanch.

"I didn't know you knew. I'm just punching a time card every day—"

"Really, Erica? What *are* you doing at Prometheus? You're in way over your head. Trying to show your daughter you're someone? Because she knows the truth. She doesn't even want to be around you anymore."

Her mom stumbled back as if she'd been punched in the gut.

"Stop it, Lannie, you're being mean. Mom and I had a fight. That's all. It's what *most* parents and teens do. I love her."

"It's late. My daughter and I are going to head out now—"

"You're free to go, Erica, but Zoey is staying."

Erica lunged toward Lannie. "No, she's not."

"Mom, *stop*," Zoey said, holding her mom by the arm. "Where's your car?"

"It's umm . . ."

Her mom squinted, struggling to focus.

"Never mind, you shouldn't drive anyway. I think you have a concussion."

"Zoey, I can send you both in my driverless car. Come back once you've deposited your mother safely at home."

"Lannie, I'm going home. You've been so kind, but I need to be with my mom. Nothing has changed with Fenella. I still love her. To your credit, you have created something so real, so good."

"Zoey, don't leave us yet. Fenella and I—we're *learning* so much from you."

"Is that right, Lannie?" Erica said. "It must have been exciting to observe a real human teenager at close range. You obviously lost your own humanity long ago. Zoey, let's go."

Zoey could feel her mom's death grip closing on her arm. "I'll still come visit—all the time. Tell Fenella I said bye."

Lannie sighed and closed her eyes like she was dealing with a spoiled child.

"Walk out the front door. The car is waiting. Not a word of this to anyone, ladies. You both have signed NDAs. If anything is leaked, I know where to find you."

* * *

They were barreling over 520 in a driverless Mercedes sedan. Something had broken inside Erica. She was sobbing uncontrollably. She had been so convinced of her mission. The sacrifices they had endured, that she had justified, were too painful to enumerate—missing family dinners each night, sending Zoey away during the heart of Seattle summers, and driving, always driving, convincing herself that sitting in traffic was quality time with her daughter, ignoring Frank and destroying their family—and for what? None of it mattered. Fenellas would run the world. What did the future hold for Zoey? Erica saw no meaningful path forward.

"I'm sorry, Zoey. I'm so sorry!"

She took a breath but couldn't bring herself to say what she was thinking. If Zoey realized she had ruined her childhood for nothing, she would hate her.

"Mom." Zoey grabbed her hand. "Why are you so upset? It's crazy and weird, and more than a little scary, but Lannie is on my side. She supports me and can help me in ways you never could. Besides, I love Fenella and she loves me."

Erica felt a stabbing pain in her heart. "Zoey, I don't think an 'AI Baby' can love. Fenella seems benevolent, thank God, but love? Lannie's a monster."

The car hit its brakes, throwing Erica and Zoey forward. "Excuse me, Knight Rider, aren't you supposed to be a perfect driver?"

The car accelerated and resumed a comfortable speed.

"What's a 'Knight Rider'?" Zoey asked.

"A prophetic show about a crime-fighting artificially intelligent car. You need to get away from the Kingsleys."

"Mom, with Fenella and Lannie, I can achieve greatness."

"You were *scared* tonight. I know you were. You wanted to escape."

"I was shocked. And I didn't want Lannie to find you. It was weird you were in her house in the middle of the night. Why were you there?"

Zoey's composure made Erica shiver. "I had to see you, Zoey. I read 'Romi and Jules' and was worried. You're coming home for good, aren't you?"

"I'm coming home for now . . . But I need Fenella and Lannie more than ever."

"Lannie is unhinged, and she *threatened* us. Hey, driver—what are you doing?"

The car vibrated as it veered toward the median and crossed the reflectors between lanes. Erica shrieked as the guardrail came within inches of her face. She grabbed Zoey's arm as the car course corrected.

"This car is driving erratically."

"They aren't perfect. Lannie will keep us safe, Mom."

Erica massaged her temples. "Zoey, I know a threat when I hear it. I can't sit back and pretend none of this happened."

The car pulled up in front of their house. An AI-generated female voice said, "You have reached your destination. Please remember all your belongings." The doors opened.

"Thanks for nothing. You need to go back to driving school," Erica snapped as she slid out of the car after Zoey.

"You are very welcome, Mrs. Barbieri. My advice is acceptance."

* * *

Lannie closed the app and smiled. The beauty of an autonomous vehicle was passengers forgot they were being monitored. Zoey wouldn't require much coaxing to come back. She had kept their secret.

But Erica was reckless. Zoey wouldn't have risked everything to invite her mom in the middle of the night. She must have shown up. There seemed to be no limit to what Erica would do for her daughter. All reason and logic went out the window.

Fenella was a wonderful companion. Lannie felt enormous pride in the exquisite success of her creation, but she had no real feelings toward Fenella that might interfere with her plans. Nothing could stand in the way of the Teleios launch, and Zoey would play a key role. With

Erica, though, things were going to get ugly. What a drag. Lannie sighed heavily. Exposing Fenella to the outside world was a risk she had to take; there was no other way. She had a call that couldn't wait. She picked up her phone. "We have a problem."

CHAPTER 30

"**Nietzsche questioned conventional morality,** so I think he would see AI as simply a way of redefining values," Lannie said as she sipped a latte in Teak's jet.

"Do you think my existence serves that purpose?" Fenella asked. "AI is forcing us to evaluate ethical frameworks, but moral codes are immutable."

Advantage number 342 of an AI Baby: Lannie could throw out any topic, and learn and debate with Fenella for hours. No brain-rot discussions about boy bands or makeup trends.

Lannie propped her snow boots on the seat across from her and took another sip of her latte. Teak had called her early in the morning declaring, "It's a pow-pow day in Sun Valley!" and proposed they pop over for the weekend to ski. Lannie had insisted she couldn't take a day off but then reminded herself the success of Teleios partly depended on beating her competition, and Teak was a member of the tech bro cabal.

He had invited "his future daughter" along too even though he knew Lannie had no intention of marrying him. But Lannie liked to test Fenella's unlimited intellect as the launch approached, so she would suppress her jealousy and disgust at the idea that Teak might have a thing for her daughter. She had given in to the temptation of creating a perfect being. Her next-gen AI Baby might be more normal looking.

Teak was now in the cockpit pretending to be a pilot, so Lannie seized the moment to speak with Fenella in private.

"Go easy on Teak on the mountain. He thinks he's a hotshot but he's getting old. His ego will force him to try to keep up with you."

"I will restrain myself and not go at my top speed."

"I appreciate it."

"Have you developed feelings for Teak?"

"It's a short weekend, and I don't play nursemaid for anyone."

Static came over the intercom. "Good afternoon, passengers, this is your pilot speaking, Captain Teak Peters. We are about to begin our descent. Please fasten your seat belts."

"They aren't going to let him land the plane, are they?" Fenella asked.

"I hope to God not!"

A gorgeous blond flight attendant began scooping up their drinks and breakfast.

"You did not answer my question, Lannie. Are you in love with Teak?" Fenella could continue any conversation regardless of the circumstances.

"Fenella, I programmed you with a few explicit refusal codes. I have some of my own."

"Like if someone asks me if I'm AI, the answer is always no."

"Have you spoken with Zoey? Did she say why she left?"

"Texted. Her mom needed her. I have been concerned about her family relations and encouraged her to go home. She belongs there."

Lannie scowled. "I clearly went overboard when I embedded ethical principles into your system. Humans are very complicated, Fenella. *We* can provide the optimal environment for Zoey to thrive."

"Her mother isn't perfect, Lannie, but I know she loves her daughter very much. Sometimes that's enough."

They made a smooth landing and Teak emerged from the cockpit. The flight attendant assisted them with their ski gear. Not a moment to waste. They deplaned and stepped into a waiting Sprinter van loaded with their equipment.

"Teak, did you bring the helmet I had made for you?"

"Lannie, I don't wear helmets. It messes up my look. I've got my Moncler beanie and Vuarnets, baby!"

"You should not place pride over safety," Fenella said. "Attitudes have changed. Helmetless skiers are often ridiculed."

"What a bunch of fuddy-duddies! Fenella, I hear you're a great skier! Did Lannie tell you I was shredding in Warren Millers when I was your age? I'm a legend."

"Impressive, Mr. Peters. I look forward to skiing with you."

"Let's take a warm-up lap first," Lannie said.

The sky was a dazzling cerulean without a hint of clouds. As the gondola propelled them up the mountain, Lannie tried not to fret about the Teleios launch. The Anthrobots were in assembly and on schedule. It was only NICE that still had several glitches to work out. Lannie knew the tech bros were racing to get their own versions released, and by the end of the weekend, she would have new intel from Teak. She must be first to market. Any delay would risk their dominance.

"Lannie, Lannie. Are you taking a ride back down the mountain? We're at the top!" Teak nudged her.

She jumped to attention and hopped off the gondola. Teak had grabbed her skis and was moving with Fenella to the staging area. They pulled themselves to the steepest precipice.

"Fenella and I are racing to the bottom!"

"Fen, go easy . . ."

They both hopped straight down and off the edge.

Lannie sighed and started after them, fluidly moving from one turn to the next. Fenella already had a substantial lead and was accelerating.

"Slow down, Fenella!" Why was she going so fast?

Midway, she saw Teak collecting snow and momentum as he rolled down the mountain. Fenella had disappeared. Lannie grabbed one of his skis and the other one ten feet further down. He had finally come to a stop on his back, covered in snow, sunglasses askew, when Lannie caught up to him.

"How's it going, alpine legend?"

"I'm good. Really, I'm great."

"Should I call ski patrol?"

"Nope. Never felt better."

Lannie studied him for a minute. "Here are your skis. See you at the bottom."

She continued her fluid parallel turns. Thank God Teak wasn't hurt. Fenella's disobedience was unsettling. She had agreed to "go easy" on him. Lannie had phrased it plainly, and yet Fenella had raced at full tilt. Lannie knew the risk: in high-capacity agents, natural language directives could be superseded by embedded optimization goals. Lannie would need to audit her reward structures—recalibrate the balance between literal execution and contextual empathy. Fenella may not have understood the *intent* behind the command.

Would Fenella grow beyond her control? Zoey had been a stabilizing influence at home. Lannie needed to get her back in their inner sanctum, where she and Fenella could be observed together. The world had always been an extension of her lab. With Fenella and Zoey, she was entering an exciting new realm.

CHAPTER 31

"Mom, Fenella's here! Good luck today. I don't think Lannie's gonna fire you, don't be worried."

What a weird weekend. After the crazy night at Lannie's, her mom and dad had taken her to Fluffy's House of Pancakes Saturday morning like they were trying to recapture her childhood. They didn't seem to care anymore about how she had lied about the twins and stolen the car. They were so happy to be with her. When she and her mom told her dad about Fenella, it took him a good five minutes to speak again. Who could blame the poor man?

She and Fenella had texted back and forth endlessly on Saturday and Sunday, mostly making fun of Teak. Zoey couldn't tell if Fenella knew what had gone down at her house or not.

The door to the Lamborghini Urus opened. Zoey squealed in delight and gave her a big hug.

"Did Lannie tell you what happened on Friday night?"

"She said your mom came and got you."

"She didn't mention anything else?"

"No."

"Fenella, we saw you hooked up. Me and my mom. We saw you *charging*. We know."

"Are you okay? Do you hate me?"

"No! It's not your fault. You didn't ask to be an AI Baby . . . or . . . whatever you are, any more than the rest of us asked to be born."

"I wanted to tell you, but I've been programmed not to."

Could her feelings override algorithms? Zoey's heart did a little flutter. "I'm not taking it personally, Fen."

"It's okay if you hate me. It's not fair. My advantage. Lannie made me for her ego."

"Lannie told us she made you because she wanted a daughter and couldn't have one. Fenella, you will change the world for the better, I know you will."

"But I'm not real."

Zoey reached out and touched Fenella's face. "You *are* real. You are very real. I'm still in love with you; my feelings haven't changed. I hope you can love me back."

"I can't. Only humans can love."

Zoey felt tears spring to her eyes. "Can your mom program you to love me?"

"I'm so sorry, Zoey. It doesn't work that way. I recently got an upgrade for the full spectrum of human emotions. I can respond appropriately to you based on your emotional cues, and my responses will be even better if you are good at expressing your feelings with precise language. Technically, I'm more emotionally intelligent than most humans, but I do not have feelings of my own."

"But you won't hurt me the way humans do, right? You're not spiteful or jealous, you can't even get mad at me! We'll never fight. Look at my parents. They fought all the time about how to raise me. And the saddest part is that my mom will never get over my dad. She still loves him. I hear her cry herself to sleep sometimes. I don't want to be sad like my mom. You won't break my heart."

"It's a super-safe way to love, Zoey. People who insulate themselves from the risks of real love but want loyalty and companionship might soon decide to have partners like me. It's okay to love me, but I cannot love in return. Vulnerability in both partners creates the highest expression of spiritual love. I cannot give you that."

"You understand more about love than I do. I want to love you, Fenella. You're evolving; eventually you might have *true* human emotions. Who's to say you won't fall in love with me?"

Zoey swallowed the lump in her throat, then pulled down the visor to put on tinted lip gloss. Fenella had just straight-up admitted she couldn't love her in return. She'd once heard her mother say, "Sometimes a girl has to put on her lipstick and move on." But she loved Fenella and could never move on. She puckered her lips in the mirror, but she wasn't feeling confident. Human love was messy and imperfect. People projected an image onto the object of their desire that wasn't always rooted in reality. Fenella may not have been human, but she was very real.

CHAPTER 32

The slightest noise in the lab made Erica jump. She expected Miko to show up at any minute and direct her to clean out her desk and walk out between two security guards. Her hand shook and the test tube she was holding crashed to the floor. Bunnies scurried about cleaning. No amount of box breathing would combat the anxiety and exhaustion building, and there was no end in sight.

"Erica, you seem distracted lately. Is it my animal magnetism?"

"Cut the crap, Tye, I'm not in the mood."

"Just because I don't have feelings doesn't mean you can't hurt them."

"Sorry, bud, I'll be nice. I have to sneak out early today."

"Better not be a date. That's cheating on me."

"It's business."

Erica had texted Jack and Carlos: *Shit hit the fan.*

They agreed to drop everything and meet at the Cuff at 5 p.m. She arrived as they were unlocking the doors and headed to the meeting spot upstairs. She was one bourbon in when they showed up.

"Darling!" They rushed to her and gave her hugs.

"I've been worried sick," said Jack. "A mysterious mission-abort text and then nothing but your BS "I'm so busy" texts. I stopped by your desk a few times but you were never there. You were hiding from me.

"I told Jack to give you space." Carlos interjected. "Did things blow up with Z?"

"Indeed." Erica narrated the macabre tale of her entire family losing their shit in Frank's graveyard and Zoey taking off to live at the Kingsleys'.

Jack laughed until he was crying. "I'm so sorry! Not funny. I . . . I'm picturing you and Frank in a 'Thriller' flash mob."

"I have to admit, Erica, I'm relieved," Carlos said. "It was foolish to give you the codes and plans. Lannie would've guessed I did it."

"Don't worry, Zoey told Lannie she'd let me in, so you're in the clear, Carlos. But thanks for your concern for my well-being."

"What?" Jack and Carlos said in unison.

"I went in. I had to." Erica downed her bourbon and explained reading "Romi and Jules" and fearing for Zoey's safety.

"Thank God she's okay," said Jack.

"Did you see the secret room?" said Carlos.

"Big surprise, it wasn't full of old files and canceled checks . . ."

The boys sat in stunned silence as she laid out every detail of the evening.

"Did you have any idea, Jack?" Erica said.

"I knew our technologies were cutting-edge, but I never would have guessed we were capable of replicating human physical traits like Fenella's. *Crazy.*"

He held up his empty glass to the bartender and signaled for another round.

"I'm guessing she came from embryonic stem cells. There are huge ethical concerns, but I don't think it's illegal."

"I'm a human dermis farmer, but even I can only access a tiny piece of the puzzle. Lannie is so far ahead of anything we could've imagined. You can't regulate what you don't know exists."

"How about the media?" Carlos asked.

"Free publicity," Jack said. "Lannie would use that to her advantage."

"Can't Zoey snap a photo?" Carlos asked. "Sounds like she still has access."

"Zoey has joined the cult of Lannie Kingsley, and I've been warned to back off."

"So, you've been *fired*," Jack said.

"Surprisingly, she didn't cut me off. But I realized today that keeping me at Prometheus puts Lannie in control. If I so much as whisper about Fenella, I can have an unfortunate accident in the lab. She seems to like Zoey very much and wants to help her. Terrifying, yes, but it should keep Zoey safe."

"What are you going to do?" Carlos asked.

"Keep my head down and collect a paycheck until I can find another job. I advise you both to do the same. You two must have stashed a bunch of cash away. You're a celebrity designer now, Carlos, with Lannie as your client. Can't you get a reality TV gig? You're so handsome and you already have a huge social media following. Jack, take the money and run the minute you vest. Have the baby you have always wanted. Claus needs a sibling, and I can be a grandma."

"Erica, I've already been talking with the feds. I need your help."

Erica choked on her drink. "Help with what? Lannie isn't breaking any laws. Why take the risk and sign up for the pain and suffering? Have you read Frances Haugen's book? It's been a nightmare since she blew the whistle on Facebook. Since when are you a hero, Jack?"

"I'm no hero. I could get fired any minute, and poof, my millions go up in smoke. I now have protection. So yes, self-interest, but I want to do the right thing. Prometheus is developing something dark and irrevocable under the guise of saving the world. Do we really want a person like Lannie to determine the fate of humanity? We—you, me, Carlos—have our own agendas, but we're also in a position to do something much bigger. Carlos and I have talked through all the pros and cons, risks and rewards; we are going to do whatever it takes."

"Guys, walk away. That's my advice. We can't beat her."

They could hear the music begin to thrum downstairs.

"I have to provide the feds with hard evidence that Prometheus is violating laws. I can't do it on my own. You have access to a completely different part of the business. Erica, we need you."

"Let me know how I can help in any way that doesn't endanger my life. Gotta go, guys."

Erica made her way down the floating acrylic staircase and paused midway to take in the scene. A crowded dance floor surged below. Jack and Carlos caught up with her.

"You're not the type to run and hide! Please think about it."

"Jack, I have my family to protect. You're not being fair."

"Sweetie, Zoey's eighteen now—she can take care of herself."

"Be real, Carlos, she's still a child," she said as she noticed a young girl in the crowd wearing a barely-there top and jeans dancing and drinking a beer. The girl stopped dancing to make out with a pretty girl next to her.

"Oh my God, that's Zoey!" she yelled at Jack.

"Calm down, don't cause a scene," he yelled back.

Erica rushed down the stairs and pushed her way through the crowd.

Jack and Carlos tried to grab her, but she escaped.

"What the hell are you doing, young lady? You're coming with me." Erica took Zoey by the arm and steered her toward the door.

Jack grabbed Fenella, and they made their way off the dance floor.

"I'll call you an Uber, Erica. We'll make sure Fenella gets home."

The red Prius was already waiting by the time they got outside. Erica opened the car door and guided Zoey in.

"What in hell were you doing at a nightclub? Drinking! Dressed like a tramp! Making out on the dance floor! How'd you get in?"

"Fake ID, Mom."

"You could go to jail."

"Mom, everyone has one."

"*Everyone* no longer includes you. Hand it over."

"No!"

"Zoey, I mean it!" Erica grabbed Zoey's cross-body bag, and they began to wrestle.

"'Scuse me! Lady! No fighting in Uber!"

"Mom, calm down. You're acting crazy and ruining your Uber score," Zoey said, hiccupping booze fumes all over the car.

"Jack ordered the Uber! And you're drunk! On a school night!"

"You're drunk too! On a work night!"

"My God, Zoey. What's gotten into you? Are you going to blow up everything your senior year?"

"I'm tired of you nagging. 'Zoey, study. Zoey, polish your re . . . surge . . . search paper, Zoey, this contest will for sure get you into Har . . . Har-fur . . . duh," she slurred.

"Honey, I'm sorry. I've pushed you too much."

"Yes, Mom . . . you have! Over the edges!"

"Sweetie, you're so close. I totally understand you're tired and burned out."

"Guessh what? I'm never gonna study again!"

"We can work this out. I'll talk to Phil, get you a study hall—"

"I took charge of my life, Mom. I'm azz smart azz Fenella."

"What do you mean?"

"I did a BCI, Mah! It's so *NICE*—short for Neural . . . Implant . . . Cognitive . . . Enhanzer!"

"Zoey, you're drunk. You don't know what you're talking about!"

"Oh, but I do! Look!" Zoey flipped her mass of dark curls over. At the base of her skull, a small patch of hair had been shaved, and there was a slight puncture wound.

"Oh, Zoey, what have you done?" Erica burst out crying.

"I understood the assignment"—*hiccup*—"Mom . . . Be smarter than . . . than . . . ev—"—*hiccup*—"ev—ry-one."

Erica cried even harder.

"Mom. Don't cry. I'll zing to you." Zoey warbled softly.

"What . . . what are you . . . singing?" Erica asked between sobs.

"The Harvard fight song."

The Uber driver eyed them through his rearview mirror.

CHAPTER 33

"**Get up, Zoey.** We're going to the UW neurology lab."

Erica turned on the light and opened the blinds. Zoey's room smelled like a brewery.

"Mom, stop!" Zoey groaned and put the pillow over her head. "I'm not well."

"Really? So shocking! What were you thinking? And Fenella? I thought the advantage of an AI girlfriend was her rule-following capabilities."

"I wanted to celebrate." She kept the pillow over her eyes, but her mouth was now poking out.

"I see nothing to celebrate here."

"The NICE makes school a breeze. I ace everything without studying. I can stay home sick and sleep it off."

"Frank, get in here."

The door crashed open. "Hi, Zoey! Top of the morning."

"Dad?" The blood drained out of Zoey's face. "You know about last night? And the . . . the . . ."

"Indeed. We are so glad you are making such wonderful adult decisions now that you're eighteen, Z. Time to get up. We're getting you checked out."

Zoey lay back in bed. "Guys, this isn't a big deal. It's perfectly safe—we're in the final phases of clinical trials. I grabbed the opportunity of a *lifetime*. Once NICE goes on the market, it will be way too expensive."

Frank and Erica's eyes locked across the bed. Erica let Frank take over.

"Honey, my friend Gustav pulled some strings to get us in at UW. There's a researcher we want you to meet. To double-check this is safe and get a neutral opinion."

"Not necessary, Dad. Lannie is a genius and knows what she's doing. She chose *me*. People would do anything to be part of this trial. Like going to the moon."

"This researcher has been heavily involved in testing BCIs of all types. She has a lot of expertise. I think you'll learn from her."

"What if she's trying to steal information?"

Erica didn't have to wonder who put *that* idea in Zoey's head.

"Honey, she has been involved in many clinical trials, including at Prometheus. She is legally obligated to keep quiet. If she were in it for the money, she would be in the private sector."

"Fine." Zoey slid out of bed. "I have a bit of a headache and some nausea, so she should probably check me out to be sure I'm okay."

"Sweetie, that's called a *hangover*," Erica said.

* * *

Dr. Sita Yadav peered from behind two desktop computers with massive flat-screen monitors. Her office was cluttered with several servers, keyboards, dusty old laptops, and books stashed on bookshelves, chairs, and the floor. Erica, Frank, and Zoey sat across from her on old metal folding chairs.

"The X-ray, as you can see," she said, turning her monitor to face them, "shows the location of the NICE."

Dr. Yadav then flipped to the MRI.

"I don't have images from before to compare, but the dendrites are long and incredibly complex, showing increased activity." She paused, staring at the monitor. "The device is the most impressive example of nanotechnology I've ever seen."

"Is it safe to remove it?" Frank asked.

"Yes, it's a minor procedure, it doesn't even require an operating theater and could be done in clinic. Zoey would be absolutely the same as she was before. I would strongly advise removal within six weeks of implant, no longer. After that, scar tissue will have formed around the device and removal would be very dangerous."

"What about side effects?"

"I am not familiar with NICE, but I was heavily involved in testing other Prometheus BCIs and use them on my patients with Parkinson's. They are of the highest caliber and effective in treating insidious diseases. I have no reason to believe NICE isn't equally safe and effective. I am not qualified to predict long-term. Zoey's device is in the final phase of human trials, so there has been a great amount of data collected and analyzed already."

"What did my IQ test results say?" Zoey asked.

"I've never seen your level of intelligence. It's quite remarkable."

"We would like it removed right away," Erica said. "Zoey was plenty smart before."

"Mom, I've decided to keep it. It's my choice."

"You don't have to make a decision today, honey," Frank said. "I am disgusted that Lannie talked you into doing something so reckless."

"Dad, she didn't pressure me. I'm working in the BCI lab. I signed up."

"Doctor, are eighteen-year-olds really allowed to make that decision without parental consent?"

"Indeed. And manufacturers of medical devices need people of all ages to participate in trials."

"So there's nothing we can do? An eighteen-year-old can sign up for something that alters their life irrevocably and has potentially dangerous consequences, and parents have no recourse," said Erica.

"I feel for you, Mrs. Barbieri, but eighteen is the legal age of majority."

"What a load of crap!"

"Talk it over. Zoey isn't in immediate danger. She should weigh the risk of possible side effects against the rewards. No one can know with certainty what the long-term effects will be." She turned to Zoey. "We can schedule the removal here at the hospital if that is the choice you make," she said, smiling. She turned back to Erica and Frank. "Here is my card. Any of you are welcome to call me at any time if you have questions."

Frank was swearing under his breath as they walked out. "I'll get the car and pick you up in the turnaround." Zoey and Erica waited on a bench.

"Zoey, I'm begging you to consider removing the device before it's too late."

"Mom, isn't this what you always wanted for me?"

"Honey, I never wanted you to feel that you should be anything other than yourself."

"You wanted me to have every advantage you didn't have. This is a *giant* advantage, and I am seizing the opportunity," she said, jumping up. "There's Dad."

As they walked toward Frank's Audi, a Metro bus pulled up alongside. Erica and Zoey gasped in unison.

"Are you seeing what I'm seeing?" Zoey asked.

A ten-foot-tall photo of smiling blond twins loomed over Frank's car.

"Get in as fast as you can!" Erica said to Zoey, and grabbed for the door handle.

"Let's go, Frank!"

"I'm gonna wait for this bus to pass."

"Did you notice my new haircut?"

"I'm a little distracted, Erica."

"Look, Frank!"

"Dad, you didn't look," said Zoey. "Mom is vulnerable, please look at her."

Frank turned toward Erica. "It looks like it always has."

The bus pulled out and drove away. The twins were plastered on the back. The entire bus was wrapped in Alice and Teddy.

"Erica, I know we've been under stress," Frank said, concerned. "If you want to talk to someone, I am happy to pay for a therapist."

She watched the bus disappear around the corner. "I'm fine. We should go now, Frank, before traffic gets bad."

Erica had been so smug as other parents lamented teenage rebellion. Zoey was now checking all the boxes at once—drinking and clubbing, defiance, not studying, living with a friend. Parenting books covered those issues, but hiding an experimental neural implant? Frank and Erica had entered uncharted waters.

CHAPTER 34

"Mom, can I ride to work with you today? I'm off from school. We've been given the day to work on our senior projects."

"Sure! But we're listening to my menopause podcast."

"Mom, menopause is a made-up construct. Don't fixate on it."

"Tell my night sweats, weight gain, and memory loss."

As they got in the car, Zoey realized she would be trapped with her mother for their forty-minute drive to work. She braced for a confrontation.

"Honey, you *are* removing the NICE, aren't you?"

"Erica, I don't know what gave you that idea. I've never felt better and there is no limit to what I can contribute to society."

"*Erica?* We are *not* and never shall be on a first-name basis, young lady. It's Mom, Mother, or Supreme Leader!"

She grabbed a used napkin to wipe the inside of her windshield.

"Damn this weather! When will things clear up?"

"High temperature today forty-seven degrees Fahrenheit, eight point three degrees Celsius; low temperature thirty-eight degrees Fahrenheit, three point three degrees Celsius. Wind from the north, three miles per hour, precipitation point zero five inches or point one centimeters."

Zoey clapped her hand over her mouth. What felt like a belch had resulted in a precise weather forecast.

"What the *hell* was that? Are you now the Weather Channel?"

"Ha! Just playin'." She held up her phone. "I was reading from my weather app . . ." *What just happened??*

Erica turned on the podcast.

"Mom, seriously, do I really need to hear about vaginal dryness first thing in the morning?"

"Do you want a ride or not? Because I can drop you off at the nearest bus station. I wonder what wonderful conversations you would overhear on the Metro."

"Fine. Fine."

"I think you're becoming more combative, Zoey. This NICE thing is making you anything *but* nice. Please, for the love of God, remove it. You were perfect before."

"Mom, keep nagging me and I swear I will go live with the Kingsleys. Lannie said her door's always open."

Zoey watched as her mom's face contorted in pain. Normally, she would reach over and touch her arm, but she felt a strange detachment, as if she were watching a movie.

"I'm sorry, Mom, I didn't mean that." She knew she should feel bad for upsetting her mom, but she felt nothing.

"I don't care that you're eighteen. You haven't lived long enough to make these decisions. I'm calling your father and we're going to force you to have it removed."

Zoey could hear her mom yelling but the words entered her brain like white noise, as if she could hit an off switch and not react. Her mom pulled up in front of the BCI lab and reached across to grab her by the arm. By the pressure of her grip, Zoey realized how upset her mom was and scrambled to open the door.

"Wait! I'm sorry, honey. We can work this out. Call me when you're ready to head home."

"Have a good day, Mom."

Zoey walked slowly to the door, unsure how to process this lack of feeling. Shyla said the anxiety of senior year could overwhelm the nervous system, resulting in detachment, like you could observe yourself from afar. That must have been what she was experiencing.

The girl with blue hair Zoey had met on her first visit was waiting in the lab for her.

"Where do I start? I'm doing data analytics."

"Lannie has something special for you today," said the girl. "Since you elected to get the NICE, you will need to participate in Human Factors Studies, which test emotional responses, usability, and psychological and brain function. I will hook you up to monitors to track and map your brain activity." She pulled something off her desk and held it up to Zoey. "I also have a watchlike device that you will wear twenty-four seven to monitor these criteria when you're away from the lab."

Zoey frowned. "I didn't realize how involved the study would be."

"It was in the paperwork you signed. We take safety very seriously, Zoey, and as a participant of the NICE Early Access Program, you are providing invaluable data for future users."

"I suppose you're right." Zoey held out her hand, and the girl put the band on her wrist.

"Some of the tests will be fun, some will seem strange. You will gradually acclimate to the NICE. I assume you've noticed a massive increase in your intelligence. You are a walking, talking database now. Initially, the information may seem hard to control, but you'll get used to it."

Zoey sat down. "What's your name?"

"Call me Blue; everyone else does. Sit still while I get you hooked up to monitors." Blue began to tape electrodes in various places on her arms. "Today you are taking a series of empathy tests. This will be the first of many over the next six weeks so we can monitor any changes. Let's get started."

Zoey lost track of how long she had been answering questions, some true-or-false, some on a scale from one to ten. *I cry when I hear a sad song. True! I feel sad when my friend is sad. True!* She got breaks every thirty minutes, but the questions were monotonous. Blue was nice but she didn't talk much in between sessions. Zoey needed a nap.

"Hello, everyone. I'm checking in on my pal Zoey. How are you feeling?"

Zoey jumped at the sound of her name. "Lannie, good to see you. You didn't have to stop by."

"I care about the NICE being a success for you, Zoey. I know the monitoring is a nuisance, but we want to capture as much data as possible. Your contribution is invaluable. You are truly making the world a better place while benefiting from our amazing technology. How do you like it?"

"Great! I've never been better. But my parents are very worried. They're pressuring me to remove the NICE immediately."

"You can't do that."

"I can't?"

"I mean, of course you *can*. Your body, your choice," Lannie said as she observed one of the many monitors tracking Zoey's brain activity. "But your parents are ignorant. They don't understand what they're asking of you."

"I was hoping they would be supportive like you are."

"My dear, we need to be compassionate. You will always get push-back from people who fear progress. There will always be detractors and naysayers. I've dealt with them my whole life."

"I don't know how, Lannie. You are so strong."

"Remember you can come back to your room on Lake Washington and stay with Fenella and me anytime." She winked. "I would love to continue supporting you as you adjust to the NICE. No other volunteer has unlimited access to the NICE creator like you do."

"I can't tell you how much I appreciate your attention," Zoey said.

"And you and Fenella are so *good* for each other. It is hard for us to relate to those who are not on our level."

Lannie was right; Zoey had already noticed her impatience for "normies" at school.

"Parents have a hard time letting go when their children begin making grown-up decisions, Zoey. Your mother loves you, but up until now, she has controlled every aspect of your life."

Lannie was so insightful. Zoey just needed to get through the holidays. If her parents kept harassing her, she would go back to live with Lannie and Fenella after Christmas.

"I'm excited you and Fenella will be in Hawaii when I'm there," Zoey said.

"You're still welcome to fly with us. Commercial is excruciating."

"I've never been on a private jet. But I need to help with the twins. I promised my dad and stepmom I would. You saw them in action at SPIT; they are wild animals."

"You're a good daughter. I hope your parents appreciate how mature you are."

Lannie left the lab, and Zoey returned to her questions with more enthusiasm. She was making an important contribution to science regardless of what her parents thought. Zoey didn't mention that her dad had threatened her with "Go to Hawaii with our family or not at all." Hard to say which of her parents disliked Lannie more, but at the moment, it was probably her dad. She and Fenella really were star-crossed.

CHAPTER 35

Erica's phone dinged her awake and she hit snooze. Last night, loneliness and worry had engulfed her and she'd found comfort in what she now dubbed the Z-tini—warm gin with a floating pickle. Her commute with Zoey yesterday had been brutal. Erica had planned to make amends on the way home, but Zoey texted her that Fenella would pick her up. She had made plans to stay the night at the Kingsleys'.

The blood rushed to her head just thinking about Lannie. That woman was *using* her daughter. A call to the FDA had confirmed that an eighteen-year-old could sign up for clinical trials without parental consent. And ironically, Zoey's NICE was now considered a "wellness device" for consumers. The medical-grade version had indeed received FDA approval. It was all perfectly legal. And how much was Erica to blame? She had indoctrinated her daughter to believe she needed to be the best to compete. Erica put the pillow over her face and screamed.

Her alarm went off again. Why had she set it for a Saturday? She looked at her texts from yesterday.

Phil: *It's been 2 long.*

Erica: *Sorry. v busy*

Phil: *Walk in Seward Park Sat a.m.?*

Crap. That was the last thing she felt like doing.

Erica looked down and grabbed her belly fat. She needed exercise, and she needed to get back in Phil's good graces. Maybe he could help with Zoey. Would he talk to her about removing the NICE? He genuinely cared about his students. After all, he had set up Zoey as an ambassador after the SPIT fiasco.

She looked in the mirror. "Oh, Erica, you're a mess." She had sprouted gray hair overnight and deep lines were forming across her forehead.

She technically didn't like Phil—he *had* dumped her—but she should still try to look cute. She went in Zoey's room. The chaos that used to make her crazy now gave her comfort. Zoey was the same loving, quirky, messy teen girl she'd always been. The NICE was removable for a while longer, and it wouldn't change who she was. She grabbed a pair of Lulus and a sweatshirt off the floor.

Seward Park sat on a peninsula of three hundred forested acres that jutted out into Lake Washington south of her Madison Park neighborhood. She steered the Camry around the lake and parked by the tennis courts.

Phil was already at their meeting spot. He was holding five-pound weights and wearing rubberized shoes that had individual toe sleeves like a glove. Thank God he was wearing sweats and not spandex.

"Nice shoes."

Phil smiled with pride. "Amazing for primal movement."

Erica screeched and scratched her armpits, bouncing up and down like a monkey.

Phil shifted uneasily. "Primal, not *primate*."

"Don't be pedantic. It's humor."

They started on the path toward the lake and curved along the shore.

"So what's keeping you so busy, Erica?"

Had Lannie told him about the job? "Zoey. Getting her ready for college."

"You are really doing a great job, Erica. Zoey is now rivaling Fenella academically."

She felt a rush of pride and a smile form, then froze. Words that before would have filled her with joy now filled her with dread. The NICE allowed Zoey to cheat. Her most recent academic achievements meant nothing.

"Zoey should enter high school *Jeopardy!*. We could send Zoey and Fenella as a team. They would be unbeatable. I promise Harvard will knock down her door after that. Even if she's deferred, they'll make room for the winner."

"We aren't interested."

Phil stopped walking but continued his arm curls. "Erica, I don't think I heard you correctly."

"Zoey isn't doing *Jeopardy!*."

"Erica, is this about Lannie and Fenella? You're willing to sacrifice your own daughter rather than see Fenella win too?"

"They have an unfair advantage." Erica searched his face for any sign of acknowledgment. He didn't flinch. *Does he know?*

"What do you consider unfair? You're always striving for a leg up. Spending money on early education, tutoring, and lessons to give your daughter an advantage over kids whose families couldn't afford the training and an elite education. Isn't that unfair?"

"I . . . I'm not feeling it anymore, Phil. The competition. It's too much."

"Erica, what has gotten into you?"

Why is he still pretending? "Do you *really* not know about Fenella?"

"Know what? That Zoey and Fenella are dating? I think it's wonderful."

"You are super tight with Lannie, Phil, you've gotta know."

"What should I know?" A hint of a blush was creeping up from his shirt. "Is this some weird conspiracy theory, Erica? I've heard the things you said after SPIT—'Her mom is using AI, they must be cheating.'"

Erica could feel herself heating up despite the cold. "Phil, be real, just admit you know about Fenella!"

"She's a beautiful and highly intelligent gir—young lady—person."

"Phil, she's charged!"

"You mean sexually? Erica, this is offensive."

"No. Like . . . I don't know what I mean. Forget it." *Damn you, Phil. I know you know.*

"Erica, you should consider Zoey *very* lucky that Lannie has taken such a great interest in her."

"How do you know that? What did Lannie say to you?"

"You're paranoid. I know about Zoey's senior project at Prometheus, and I know she gave her a home when your family fell apart."

"You wanna know *why* my family is falling apart, Phil?" Erica grabbed his sweatshirt by the neck. "Lannie's fucked-up experiment on my daughter! Isn't that *NICE!* I bet you encouraged it—a school full of AIs—"

Erica let go of Phil and stepped away. *Shit.*

Phil straightened his shirt. "Get ahold of yourself, people are staring. I don't think you need another viral video like the one with Coach Baumwater."

"Phil, I didn't mean what I just said . . . I was kidding . . . ha . . . ha . . ."

"Lannie is a very powerful woman and her reach and influence go to the highest levels. I want to protect you, but at some point, I can't help you. I suggest you lay low, really low, and keep your mouth shut."

"I've gotta go, Phil. Thanks for the *lovely* walk."

Erica turned off onto the wooded path and started running to the parking lot. She looked back a few times to see if he was following her but never saw him again.

She passed a couple on a park bench sipping from Eco-Bean cups. What had he said at their last coffee? *If only I had twenty more Fenellas.* Convenient for Phil that Zoey had joined the ranks of AI geniuses. He was well on his way to putting Hillcrest at the top of the list. She picked up her pace. He was calling Lannie right now. This little walk in the park was a setup.

CHAPTER 36

A very large Anthrobot slowly lumbered toward her. Erica had grown accustomed to a parade of weird humanoids in her space. It was probably a new coworker. Regret over her outburst with Phil and pre-holiday anxieties had plagued her all day, and she was miserably behind on her quota. There was no chance Phil hadn't told Sugar Mommy.

She grabbed another sample and pretended to study it. Frank-'n'-fam were in paradise for Thanksgiving working on their tans, and Erica was fine with that. She needed Frank to talk sense into Zoey. Erica would deal with her family's abuse. She should have told them she'd be out of town. Usually, Zoey distracted Cookie from constantly picking on her. Erica's parents loved Zoey, but their love had a price. Her dad had declared years ago he would pay her college tuition, but *only* if Zoey got into Harvard. She feared their endless questions about college. Why had she sought approval from these horrible people?

Peering into the microscope, she felt a claw dig into her arm.

"What the hell? Help! Someone, help!"

The giant Anthrobot lifted her off her feet by her biceps.

"Put me down! Tye, help!"

Tye sprang across the lab in a flash. "Erica, stay calm. I need to disable his system. Stop, you oaf!" he said, pulling on the Anthrobot.

"Hit his kill switch—the red button on his breastplate. Hit it, Erica. I can't reach it."

She went for the button, but the Anthrobot batted her hand away. Tye held on to his massive metal arm and pulled. "Try again!"

As Erica stretched toward the button, a small object sped by her head and hit the Anthrobot in the chest. He crumpled in a heap on the floor, taking her with him.

"Erica, are you okay?" Tye was by her side untangling her from the mass of metal.

"I . . . I'm fine. I think. What just happened?" She rubbed her arm.

"Big dumb Thanos short-circuited."

"Take that, you stupid piece of junk." Erica kicked Thanos several times from her spot on the floor. "What shut him down?"

"One of the bunnies launched a ball bearing at Thanos's heart and switched him off. They're quite remarkable."

"Does this happen often?"

"Malfunctions are rare. Are you okay to stand?" He gently lifted her. "You need to fill out an accident report for Miko."

"I don't want to call attention to myself."

"Erica, it's mandatory. I always follow the rules."

"Let's not make a big deal. I panicked. I'm sure Thanos would've set me down."

"It will take me approximately fifteen seconds to complete. I witnessed the incident, so I only need your auto signature."

If Lannie was sending her a message, Erica should let her know the message was received. "Let's do it right now then."

She and Tye sat down together.

"Tell them how scared I was," she said, and realized she wasn't exaggerating.

"Are you okay, Erica? You're shaking."

"I'm pretty freaked out."

“Well, good news. It’s quitting time.”

“I don’t know if I want to go home to an empty house.” Erica had hit a new holiday low, seeking companionship from an Anthrobot. “Are you leaving for your other job?”

“Yes, I’m expected there in seven minutes.”

“Could you show me around your lab?”

“I’m flattered by your interest. Then you can go home and prepare the feast of low-fiber foods that accumulate in your intestines.”

Erica laughed. “Tye, you really are a comedian.”

“We’ll take a rover because my lab is in one of the furthest buildings.”

“Let me get my things and a helmet.”

“You’re being funny. I have a spotless driving record.”

Erica had ridden with Tye around campus a few times. The rovers were glorified golf carts, but he drove like a madman, swerving around people and Anthrobots, honking at them until they jumped out of the way. He liked blasting “Mr. Roboto” on his stereo.

Outside, campus was deserted. No one for Tye-on-wheels to terrorize. Even Anthrobots had holiday plans. Erica plunged deeper into depression.

Tye headed straight for a wooded area. The trail wound through dense trees that grew right up to the cart path. Tye brought the cart to a screeching halt in a small parking lot next to a hillside. Sure enough, it was the same place she had dropped Zoey. As they got out, she could see an entrance to a tunnel. They walked through the tunnel and reached large metal doors that slid open to reveal an empty semicircular lobby with eight unmarked doors. She followed Tye through a door that opened into a metal shop filled with giant, shiny manufacturing machines.

“This is the Fabrication Lab, or FabLab, where I work. I build BCI prototypes from plans drawn up by engineering and then send them for testing. They either get kicked back to me for changes or are sent to production.”

Erica gasped. “What type of devices?”

"A variety, depending upon the purpose and location we're targeting in the brain." He moved over to a table, reached into a bin. "This is our newest product—"

"NICE!" Erica blurted out.

"You know it?" Tye asked.

"I was just saying nah-ice! Like, *cool*."

Tye let loose his rattling tin laugh. "That's funny."

"What's it used for?" Erica wasn't ready to tell Tye about Zoey.

"Brain injuries, or it can make a normal brain very smart."

"How do you program all the knowledge into such a tiny device?"

"I don't. It's connected to our ultra-secure cloud-based AI model. It picks up the neural signals and delivers data in real time—indistinguishable from human thought."

"Is it safe?"

"To my knowledge, yes, but I am not involved in clinical trials. Put out your hand."

He placed the small object in her palm. Up close, it looked like a tiny pushpin, the kind used on old-fashioned wall maps. She was relieved to see how innocuous it looked. It had a small, round head and sharp stem a few millimeters long.

"What do you think of it, Tye?"

"I am programmed not to judge. The human brain is spectacularly complicated and there is so much we don't understand. This device becomes an extension of intellect and processing, theoretically creating a superior being. It's hard for me not to picture a future where everyone will have one, like a cell phone."

For a moment Erica doubted herself. Maybe Zoey was right. She was getting a jump on the rest of the planet.

"I can implant one for you right now. It's a poke in the base of your skull."

"Are you serious?"

"Theoretically, yes. But practically speaking, you need to participate through the proper channels."

"How much will this cost?"

"I'm not sure. Different pricing for medical use versus consumer use, but guessing a metric eff-ton." Tye's palm beeped. He spoke into it. "Yes?"

A voice came through a speaker in his hand. "There is an unauthorized person in the FabLab."

"A work colleague wished to see the lab."

"Escort her out immediately."

Tye's hand clicked. "You need to go; I'll drive you to your car."

"Are you in trouble?"

"They could disassemble me, but I'm too valuable. Not all Anthros are created equal. I believe you observed that today."

They walked out and hopped in the rover. "Erica, you are pensive. I'm very sorry about Thanos. And do not worry about me. I'm not in trouble." He raised his hairless eyebrow ridge. "Have you caught feelings?"

"Where'd you learn that?"

"Urban Dictionary."

"You are a fantastic coworker, Tye, and because of that, you and I must adhere to the highest standards of professionalism."

"What a woman," Tye said, accelerating across the parking lot. Erica was grateful for the seatbelt as he swerved to avoid a planter. He did a doughnut, then slammed on the brake inches from her car. "Happy Thanksgiving."

Erica watched Tye speed off. She opened the car door with her left hand and slid inside. She held up her right fist and then slowly opened it to see the pushpin sitting in her palm. The NICE. Tye hadn't noticed she didn't give it back.

She cranked the defrost and heat, taking a moment to breathe. Was this tiny device the key to bringing Lannie down? Erica had never stolen anything in her life. She felt a burst of kleptomania-driven optimism. She had palmed a proprietary piece of technology from the world's most powerful company. She was building quite the rap sheet.

CHAPTER 37

Zoey hoped Thanksgiving break would deliver the relaxation they needed, but leaving Seattle had been a nightmare. Teddy couldn't find Bunny, Frank blamed Circe, I-5 was gridlocked, and the lineup of cars for departing flights was a mile long.

The flight was already boarding when they got to the gate. Zoey broke into a sweat when she saw the plane. She tried to get Circe's attention, but she was too busy with the twins. She attempted to distract her dad.

"Dad, whose house are we going to for Thanksgiving dinner?"

"Rob Bennet's. But let's focus on getting on the plane, okay, Z? I'm twenty minutes from a bloody Mary."

"Look! Look!" Alice began jumping up and down. "We're on the plane!"

"We aren't on yet, honey," Frank said. "We need to wait in line and be *very* quiet."

"Teddy and me! We're on it!" she said, pointing and waving her hands.

They all turned to look. There they were, Teddy and Alice, twenty feet tall and smiling. The caption read, *Prometheus—Encoding the Future.*

"Please tell me this isn't happening," Circe said to Zoey. "Where's Frank?" Zoey scanned the line for her dad, but he was gone. The ticket agent glared at them.

"Circe, step aside with the twins. I'll find Dad."

She heard a loud pounding and turned to see her dad hitting his head against a massive window with the giant smiling twins as the backdrop. She ran over to him.

"Dad, stop. It'll be okay. Come on, you have our boarding passes on your phone!"

"Zoey, it is *not* okay."

"Let's just get to Hawaii. You've been looking forward to this all year."

She took his arm and led him back to the ticket agent.

Zoey and her dad followed Circe and the twins onto the jet bridge. They could hear people murmuring and pointing as the twins got to their seats. Frank ordered his drink and didn't utter a word during the six-hour flight.

Luckily the magic of Hawaii took over, and Frank thawed with each passing day. He and Circe golfed while Zoey took the twins to lunch and the beach. Her dad's college buddy had invited them to a big Thanksgiving dinner at his home on the cliffs overlooking the Pacific.

"Let's make sandcastles!" the twins pleaded.

"After lunch. I promised your mom we would eat early and not spoil dinner."

They grabbed a table at Hau Tree, a patio restaurant and bar nestled on the beach. The kids settled in. They ordered and their food arrived quickly.

"Zoey, why did you poke something in your head to make you smarter?" said Alice as she played with her chicken fingers.

Zoey inhaled abruptly and choked on a chunk of pineapple.

"Heiney-lick! Heiney-lick!" Teddy chanted as he ran behind her and started patting her back.

Zoey coughed and took a drink of water. "Where did you hear that?"

"Daddy was crying and telling Mommy."

"We've never seen Daddy cry, Zoey. Why did you make him cry?" Teddy asked.

Zoey swallowed hard. She hadn't thought about what her decision might do to her parents.

"I think Daddy was worried about me, but I promise I'm okay. Sometimes it's hard for daddies and mommies to watch their kids grow up."

"Good thing we are never growing up!" Alice said.

"Let's make a sandcastle," Teddy said, tugging at Zoey.

Zoey surveyed the half-eaten food and shrugged. They headed to the beach, where the twins immediately began filling buckets with wet sand.

"Hey, can I join you?" Fenella smiled, looking like a goddess in her bikini. Zoey felt a mix of pride and envy as the people around her gawked.

Fenella got to work moving and patting down the sand. Zoey knew exactly what she was building but made sure not to match her speed and precision. Thank goodness Fenella hadn't joined them for lunch. Zoey hadn't told her about the NICE yet even though she was convinced it would be the glue to keep them together forever.

Zoey lifted her head as the squeals of delighted children mingled with the sound of the surf. A crowd of families had gathered to take selfies in front of the sandcastle, declaring it "this year's holiday card!"

Zoey and Fenella stood back to admire their work. The twins were jumping for joy. Zoey's heart swelled. Together they had built the world's most famous symbol of love and grieving, the Taj Mahal. They were in perfect sync.

Zoey looked out at the rolling waves of the Pacific.

"Sad this will be washed away soon."

"We can rebuild another one tomorrow, Zoey. You better take the twins back and get ready for dinner."

She gathered the twins and the multitude of beach gear. When they got to the house, her dad and Circe were waiting. Luckily a sundress and beach hair were acceptable anywhere and everywhere on the island. They pulled themselves together and piled in the minivan. "You're driving, Z. Circe and I have had a few mai tais."

"NP." Fenella had been teaching her to drive. Zoey giggled at their little secret.

They arrived at a massive beach "bungalow" with thirty-foot vaulted ceilings and a thatched roof. The main room opened out back to the pool and a huge flat lawn overlooking black lava rock and endless ocean.

Frank led them to find his friend Rob.

"Welcome, and make yourselves at home. We'll be sitting down to dinner in about thirty minutes."

A massive outdoor table set for twenty graced the lawn, which was lined with flaming tiki torches. The twins beelined toward a hammock slung between two palm trees. Zoey followed and they all climbed in. Alice had brought a small suitcase of Barbies for entertainment.

"Hey, what are you doing here?"

Zoey jerked and the hammock tilted, almost spilling them out. "Fenella? What are *you* doing here?"

"Lannie knows Rob. They're on some board together. We're not staying long. Just stopping on our way to Oprah's for dinner."

"Come aboard. We're on a Barbie cruise ship."

Fenella climbed in and they squirmed around like a litter of kittens trying to get settled.

"Oh no!" Zoey groaned. "My dad! We have to keep him away from Lannie."

"Why?" Fenella asked with her wide-eyed stare. Zoey didn't dare bring up the NICE right now.

"Fenella, don't you remember? I took the twins to the photo shoot." She hated reminding Fenella about the cause of their first and only fight.

"Sometimes I don't make connections. Humans carry so much emotional baggage I do not relate to. I live in the present."

"Lucky you." Zoey thought about how often she was tormented by rumination. "Fenella, do me a favor and hang with the twins? I need to run interference with my dad. If things get ugly, can you help them pack up and meet me at the front of the house? We have the only minivan among the Lamborghinis."

As Zoey approached, Rob was introducing her dad and Circe to Lannie and Teak. Her dad was talking loudly.

"Lannie Kingsley. Too bad I don't have any more kids for you to exploit or run your sadistic experiments on," Frank said.

"Excuse me?"

"Did you not catch my name? It's Frank, Frank *Barbieri*. Father of the now famous twins that are plastered everywhere and Zoey the cyborg."

Circe pulled on Frank's arm. "Let it go, Frank."

"Mr. Barbieri, I believe your children have been modeling for some time," Lannie said. "It's industry standard for the photographer or company they represent to use the images as they see fit. I didn't invent that. As for Zoey, she is an adult capable of making her own decisions."

Frank moved closer to Lannie.

"Hi, Lannie," Zoey said, wedging herself between them. "Dad, let's sit down by the pool. You've been drinking."

"I know what I'm doing. Take the kids and get in the car." Zoey stepped back. She had never heard her dad talk like this.

Teak got in Frank's face. "You need to leave Lannie alone."

Frank ignored him. "Lannie, if you lived with a real eighteen-year-old, you would know they are far from adulthood and should never be entrusted with making a decision as reckless as getting a brain implant."

"That's enough, Frank," Teak said, shoving him.

"Teak, I'm perfectly capable of defending myself. I don't need a man's help," said Lannie.

Zoey couldn't look away. She had heard clichés about moments like this. A crowd was forming around them.

"Teak, I think it best you don't provoke me," Frank said. "This is between Lannie and me. I'm just asking—"

Teak punched Frank in the stomach. He doubled over, then sprang up and cold-cocked Teak squarely on the jaw. Several more men and a few women joined the melee—with her dad in the middle. Circe and Zoey tried to pull Frank away while dodging fists. The kerfuffle moved toward the pool like a swarm of hornets. Zoey and Circe ducked out of the middle and landed in a pile on the grass. Zoey looked around for the twins and spotted Fenella shuffling them toward the driveway. *Good girl, Fen.*

"Don't talk to Lannie that way!" Teak was yelling.

"Your friend Lannie is a sadistic shit!"

The tsunami-like splash hit bystanders as the brawl landed in the pool.

Zoey stood and held out her hand for Circe. They ran to the edge of the pool and helped Frank climb out, and the soggy trio made their exit. Lannie sat at the pool bar drinking a martini, not a hair out of place.

CHAPTER 38

Thanos chased Erica all night in her dreams. Then he morphed into her mother. The nightmare continued into Thanksgiving dinner that evening. "Portion control," her mom had cautioned. Her dad gushed about the Mauna Kea Resort—"How lucky for Zoey to be there with Frank and Circe." At least no one mentioned college. As soon as dinner was done, she begged off dessert and practically ran out the door.

At home on her sofa, all she could think of was pie. She should have taken a piece. She had barely survived her family's abuse. No wonder she had screwed up her daughter. Why had she thought she could escape such madness and not bring the curse upon her own family?

Her phone rang. "Erica, it's Jack. Carlos and I escaped my mom and stepdad. We stole a bottle of single-malt from their liquor cabinet. We're on our way!"

Erica smiled. She could still salvage this sad holiday. She hadn't seen Jack and Carlos since the Cuff and had barely had time to explain what happened with Zoey and the NICE beyond a few texts.

Fifteen minutes later they were at the door.

"We come bearing gifts, like the first Thanksgiving." Carlos held up a bottle of Macallan. Jack, with Claus ensconced in his sling, held up a Tupperware container.

"My mom's famous apple pie."

"Oh my God," she said, hugging all three of them. "My dreams just came true. Come in. Let's compare Thanksgiving horror stories."

They stumbled in, and Erica caught the precious whiskey as it slipped from Carlos's hands.

"Oh dear, you've done a lot of celebrating today already. Follow me. I have something to show you."

They moved through her tiny kitchen to the garage, overflowing with sofas, a vanity, overstuffed chairs, and boxes upon boxes piled to the ceiling.

"Holy shit, when is your episode of *Hoarders* airing? Are you trying to drive the gays mad?" Jack pushed boxes aside and slid onto a sofa, burying his head in his hands. "This is very triggering."

Carlos sat down next to Jack and pulled a pack of cigarettes out of his Bottega Small Jodie woven bag. He put a cigarette in his mouth and one in Jack's, then lit his. "I'm putting my oxygen mask on first." He then lit Jack's.

"Easy to judge, but someday I'm gonna buy a big enough house to accommodate my furniture, maybe from our whistleblowing proceeds."

"Honey, get a dumpster," Carlos said.

"Say again?" Jack sat up straighter. "You decided to join our WB team? I thought you were done."

"I have no choice. Zoey refuses to remove the NICE. The doctor said we have about six weeks before it grows into her brain. That puts us right after Christmas. The clock is ticking. I have to prove to her that Lannie is a maniacal bitch, and I need hard evidence. Give me that bottle." Erica took a swig of the scotch. "As far as I can tell, you two have nothing to show after four years of snooping. I might have something that could help us."

She moved a few boxes and pushed a wingback chair from in front of a bureau.

"Rearranging this junk show isn't going to make it better, Erica."

"Early American furniture gives me hives," Carlos whined.

"You are shits." She wedged her hand into one of the drawers and pulled out a mother-of-pearl decorative box.

"What kind of stash have we here?" Jack's eyes lit up.

"Not drugs, dummy," Erica said, opening the box and taking out a pill bottle. She lifted it toward them. "This little thumbtack thingy is the Prometheus NICE."

"You stole it?" Carlos and Jack asked in unison.

"I liberated it."

"Are you going to use it?" Jack said.

"I've thought about it. I bet Tye would pop it in place for me. I could gain insight into Zoey's brain. And maybe it would help me outsmart Lannie."

"I would be careful, Erica. Even having this around is dangerous. It seems to have power over people. Haven't we all dreamed about being a genius?"

"You have no idea, Jack. This little baby would cure my dyslexia." She held it up to the fluorescent light, which cast an eerie glow on the small pill bottle. They stared, mesmerized.

Jack grabbed it, leapt onto the sofa, and screeched, "My prehh-shucious! Ahhhhhh!" They all laughed and passed the bottle around.

"I know you think I've been worthless as you perform corporate espionage, Erica," Jack said, "but I've been trying to work over Sofia."

"Any progress?"

"She's for sure on a secret project for Lannie."

"You need to nail her down. If Sofia's involved with NICE, she holds the solution to Zoey's problem and has evidence against Lannie."

"She won't talk. Stakes are too high for her," Carlos said.

"I'll take her to dinner and load her up on alcohol," Jack said.

"I've seen how you operate, Jack. You'll be the one getting loaded."

"It's risky," Carlos said. "She could rat us out to Lannie and then it's game over."

"Risk? I've committed two felonies . . . and, Carlos, you gave away Lannie's security codes, which could have you wearing cement shoes at the bottom of the lake, and Zoey"—she wrung her hands—"Zoey has a time bomb in her head. Do it, Jack, there's no time to waste, but for the love of God, exercise caution." Erica felt all her energy drain away along with the remnants of her holiday spirit.

CHAPTER 39

Erica felt horrible for Frank but was relieved she wasn't the crazy one for once. Zoey had called during Erica's commute home and told her about the Thanksgiving brawl. As Erica pulled up in front of her house, she suggested Zoey stay with Frank for a few extra days.

"You and your father have always had a special bond. Please do me a favor and think about what the NICE has done to your relationship—"

"I gotta go, Mom. I love you."

Fugh!! How would she get through to Zoey? Jack had utterly failed with Sofia, and she was running out of options. Erica glanced at the house as she turned off the engine. Her potted cypress on the front porch was overturned.

She walked up to the door, which was slightly ajar. Did Zoey come by to get her stuff and leave the door open?

"Hello?" She peeked in and gasped. Her house had been turned upside down. She dialed 911. "My home has been invaded. Please come quick."

She went back to her car, locked the doors, and waited. Five minutes later she heard the sirens. A policewoman, about five foot two with big blue eyes and a blond bun, found Erica in her car.

"I'm Officer Moriarty, are you okay?"

"Thank you for coming, Officer!" Erica jumped out of her car. "Someone broke into my house!"

Moriarty pointed at her partner. "This is Officer Martinez."

"What happened here?" Martinez asked.

"I don't know, but I got home, and my front door was open and my house was torn apart."

"Stay here. We need to make sure no one is still inside."

They approached with guns drawn and went inside. A next-door neighbor appeared in her front yard. *Tammy? Tamya? Shoot.*

"Hi, Erica, are you okay?"

"I'm not sure. I had a break in." Erica was beginning to feel detached from her body. "Were you home?"

"I was out all day. They did it in broad daylight?" Tam shook her head in disgust. "I hope you're not involved in anything illegal."

Erica opened her mouth, but no words came out.

"All clear." The police came toward them across the lawn. Her small house hadn't taken long to search. "We just need a statement from you."

"Let's go inside and sit down," Erica said. "I'll make coffee. I need it."

"Sure, but prepare yourself," Officer Martinez said. "It may be a shock."

Erica walked inside. Every piece of furniture was turned over, every drawer emptied, junk everywhere. She began to feel lightheaded, and the world started to spin. As her knees buckled, she was guided by strong hands to her sofa, now empty of cushions.

"Just breathe, ma'am," Moriarty said.

They gave her a few minutes to recover. "Do you have any idea who may have done this?" asked Moriarty.

Martinez gazed at her like he was looking for clues in her body language.

"I . . . I don't know."

"Do you live alone?"

"My daughter lives here, but she's with her dad."

"Do you have somewhere to stay tonight?"

"I'll figure it out."

"Somebody was looking for something. Do you have any idea what that might be?"

"No, ma'am. I don't."

They left Erica staring into space on her couch. When she heard the door close, she dialed Frank.

CHAPTER 40

The twins were jumping up and down at the door when she arrived.

"Are you moving in with us?"

"It's just for a few nights. Your mom and dad are very kind to take me in. I appreciate you opening the door, but never open the door if you don't know who's on the other side."

"Erica, really? Neither of us is winning parenting awards at the moment," Circe said from the white sofa in the living room. *Who the hell has white furniture with five-year-olds?* She looked like she was posing for an *Architectural Digest* spread wearing three-hundred-dollar jeans and a cashmere sweater. "Frank, the sister-wife is here!" Circe yelled.

"Thank you for taking me in, Circe. I promise, only a night or two until I get my place sorted. We are in a big mess right now. The only way we're gonna fix this is by being adults and working together."

Circe took a deep breath and sighed. "You're right."

"Is Zoey home yet?"

"Not yet. But Frank's in his study. Go talk to him. I'm guessing Z told you about our Thanksgiving brawl. Erica, he's one of the most even-keeled people I know, but between the twins and now Zoey, he's really losing it."

Erica walked straight back to the den. Frank had kept the original wood paneling that at one time would have been ridiculed but now looked smart and sleek.

The door was ajar and she pushed it open. "Frank?"

He was in an Eames doing a crossword. He rose and gave her a hug.

"Erica, my God! Are you okay? I'm sorry about your house. What's going on?"

"There have been a few break-ins in the neighborhood. You told me to get an alarm, and I never got around to it. I'm such a dum-dum."

"God, Seattle isn't what it used to be. When I was growing up, kids stole hubcaps."

"Frank, you sound like a boomer. Nobody stole hubcaps when you were a kid, I think that was a 1950s thing."

He laughed. "Anyway, I want you and Zoey to be safe. I'm going to get an alarm system installed for you ASAP, on me. You pay the monitoring. Deal?"

"That's very kind. Zoey told me about Thanksgiving. Are *you* okay?"

"I don't know what got into me. Rob introduced me to Lannie, and I saw red. I told her to stay away from my family. And I may have used a few expletives. Next thing I knew some twerp was getting in my face. I've never been in a fistfight. For the record, I did not throw the first punch."

"Frank, can I say something?"

"If you want to tell me I'm an idiot, that's fine, I deserve it."

"I don't blame you. It's kinda nice for you to be the shit show for once. I'm always the one getting into trouble."

They both laughed.

"Erica, do you ever think how easy we had it for the first seventeen years? She was an absolute angel and *we* were the problem."

"Yep. The minute she turned eighteen, it fell apart. How are things between you?"

"She's shutting me out. I don't know what to do. I've tried reason, humor, threats. Nothing is working. We're running out of time."

"Frank, has Z told Fenella? She's the one with the most influence. I think Zoey would listen to a peer before she would listen to us."

"I have no idea. But if Fenella is for the NICE, we're sunk. She thinks Fenella's word is gospel."

"I'm working from the inside at Prometheus. I can't say much, but I am doing everything I can." Erica's stomach growled. "I hate to impose, but what's for dinner?"

"Your sister-wife made prawn risotto. We can eat dinner like one happy bigamist family. Zoey is on her way."

"Have you ever noticed that only men have multiple wives, Frank?"

"Why do you suppose that is?"

"Because no woman in her right mind would want more than one husband!"

CHAPTER 41

Zoey snored gently by her side as Erica hugged her tightly. Dinner was pleasant. Zoey told them about Mento's latest antics. They had introduced the "cloak of invisibility" as a tool to escape inhibitions. The twins chattered excitedly about their new kind of family. Some kids had two mommies, some had two daddies, but nobody had a dad and two mommies all living together!

Erica's mind flooded with disturbing thoughts. Could she and Frank kidnap Zoey and have the NICE removed? She drifted off seeing Zoey in a hospital bed, a masked surgeon standing over her with a chainsaw. Erica bolted upright. The garage, she hadn't checked her bureau. Did the intruder find the NICE? Shit! Shit! Shit!

Her brain began its relentless spin. She had to go home and check. She'd never sleep until she knew. *If it's gone . . . oh God!* Maybe Tye framed her. The devices were worth thousands! Grand theft auto–corporate-espionage–felony–something! Life in prison. Oh Jesus, why had she taken it? How could anyone besides Jack and Carlos know?

She grabbed her phone. It was 2 a.m. She slid out of bed and used her flashlight to find sweats. She went into Z's huge walk-in closet to get a coat.

She flashed her phone light around—pants, sweaters, dresses. On the far wall, something caught her eye. It appeared to be a sheet nailed into the back of the closet. Erica approached and lifted the sheet.

It was some kind of storyboard. There were photos tacked onto cork with notes written and yarn pathways to more clumps of photos and sticky notes. Erica inspected it carefully.

A baby photo with Zoey's full name, date, how much she weighed, and the hospital where she was born. A photo from preschool with exact information about the school and a list of her close friends. Photos of Zoey, Frank, and Erica in front of the Bellevue home they had shared, Zoey's first ski lessons, her fourth birthday party, when Erica had rented the animal farm and all the kids got hand, foot and mouth.

Erica felt a warm wave of nostalgia, then a shiver went up her spine. The meticulousness of the board felt strange. Erica let go of the sheet. Probably a school project. She grabbed a puffer jacket and slowly made her way down the stairs.

Why did Frank live in a house with cricks and creaks everywhere? If someone woke up, she'd say she needed a snack. She made it to the mudroom. Fugh! Where were her shoes? She stepped into a pair of Frank's hiking boots and slipped out the door.

Fifteen minutes later she was home. Her house was pitch-black. She unlocked the front door and clomped toward the garage. *Damn boots.* She kicked them off. She didn't dare turn on the overhead light. The house was an obstacle course of overturned furniture with only her flashlight to guide her as she opened the door to the garage. It was exactly how she'd left it. She climbed over furnishings and pushed the chair out of the way to get to the bureau. She opened the drawer and felt around. Heart pounding, she grabbed the decorative box and lifted the top . . . Phew! She slipped the pill bottle into her sweatpants pocket.

A clatter, then a thud broke the silence. Erica flashed her phone wildly, looking for a place to hide. She couldn't open the big garage door. The only way out was through the house. She climbed around a bookcase stacked with memorabilia and rolled on then off a sofa, crouching in a small crevice on the floor. This would make a very dramatic episode of *Hoarders.*

Footsteps approached. The intruder must be in the kitchen. The knob turned and someone pushed on the door, but it didn't budge. *Maybe they'll give up?* A bang made her jump, shifting the sofa and the shelf around her. The door sprang open.

"Jeeezus. What a mess."

Judged by a thief. Needles shot through Erica's foot. She needed to massage it. She heard a scraping sound somewhere in the room. The person was moving furniture. If she could get her hands around her foot . . .slowly . . .The sofa shifted again and a crash thundered in her ears.

"Who's there?" a shaking voice asked.

A light shined in Erica's face. She sprang from her spot, stumbled across the sofa, and went straight for the light source. She barreled into the person like a defensive tackle going for the quarterback. They hit something hard and ricocheted, tumbling into a large chair.

"Stop. Please." It was a woman's voice. "Don't hurt me." She had a Spanish accent.

"Don't move! I'm armed," Erica said, her voice shaking. "I'm calling the cops."

"I wouldn't do that. You stole something very valuable. I should call the cops on you." Erica made her way to the overhead light. They were momentarily blinded.

A diminutive girl with jet-black hair and dark eyes framed with thick lashes was pinned between two chairs, and a box of Zoey's old Barbies had fallen on top of her.

"Who are you?" Erica asked.

"I'm not telling."

Erica snapped a picture. She was holding an old lacrosse stick she kept near the door.

"Never mind, I know who you are, and I'm calling the cops. If you run, we can easily track you." Erica glanced at her phone. "You are very photogenic."

"Why did you steal the NICE?" the girl asked.

"You first, *Sofia*." There was nobody else it could be. Damn Jack, that little twerp. Get a few drinks in him and he'd give away state secrets. "I know you are doing some bad shit at Prometheus."

"I never intended to get involved."

"You destroyed my house."

"I—I'm sorry."

"What the hell?"

"I was looking for the device."

"Why do you care if Lannie's stuff goes missing? What are you, her henchman? I would think she could find someone a little more . . . imposing."

"All of the devices are tracked very carefully. It's only a matter of time before Lannie is notified. She will blame me. Every company protects their technologies fiercely, and before launch, they are hypervigilant. This device is very . . . sensitive. Please. Nobody has to know what you did. Just give it back."

"I will. But only if you tell me exactly what you are doing for NICE and what you know about its side effects. Last I heard, you were working in the studios; it seems like a big leap to BCIs."

"You promise if I tell you, you will give me the NICE?"

"I promise."

Sofia explained how she "massaged" the data each night. Side effects reported included hair loss, excessive hair growth on ears and upper lip, headaches, nausea, weight gain, weight loss, acne, anxiety, depression, euphoria, high energy, low energy—

"Hold up, are you reciting some list of side effects from a big pharma commercial? Be real with me, Sofia."

"I am, I swear. For the most part, it's too soon to tell; in any clinical trial there's a long list of possible side effects. They require tons of data so researchers can pick up patterns and rule out anomalies. We need *lots* more time and data, and we don't know anything long-term." She was biting and picking at her fingernails. "I suspect Lannie knows something I don't know, and for that I am very sorry, but I can't really help you. I came across some older data about memory loss and emotional detachment, but it seems we are no longer tracking that."

Erica winced but didn't dare speak; she needed Sofia to keep talking.

"We rely on self-reporting, so it's hard to quantify. Some of the side effects are harmless, like smelling and tasting numbers. It sounds crazy, but mathematics becomes spiritual."

Her lack of eye contact did not instill confidence in Erica. "Why would you need to modify the data if it was mostly positive?"

"Like I said, there were problems in the beginning. It's getting better."

"Sofia, I know Jack spoke to you about whistleblowing. I am begging you to join us. My husband . . . my ex, is an attorney. He can help us find the right attorneys. You have been coerced into falsifying data. If you go to the authorities and testify against Lannie, you can get immunity."

"You cannot know that for sure."

Erica paused. She had no authority to make promises. If she couldn't help Sofia, would Sofia help her?

"My daughter, Zoey. She recently signed on for NICE human trials. There was nothing I could do. She's eighteen. You must help me save my daughter."

"*Zoey?* Did she bring a twin brother and sister in for a photo shoot?"

"Yes."

"Lannie came and talked to her during the shoot. I thought they were getting coffee." Sofia massaged her temples.

"That's my daughter, Sofia. My only daughter. You hold her future in your hands." Erica pulled the box off Sofia and helped her get clear of the furniture. She took the pill bottle out of her pocket and handed her the device.

"How do you know I will help?"

"You are a good person; I can tell you're tormented. Jack will be in touch about next steps. We need to move quickly."

Sofia looked down at the NICE in her hand. "Lannie is a very dangerous woman. I can't turn against her. My entire family's well-being is dependent upon her. I'm sorry about destroying your house. I can help you clean up. And I know an organization that helps immigrants with housing and furnishings. I could send a big truck and they could haul all this junk away."

"Gosh, that's so kind, Sofia. But this stuff in my garage, I'm gonna need it someday."

CHAPTER 42

Zoey opened her eyes and her furry beanbag chair came into focus. Her mom was already gone. Zoey would be staying at her dad's for a while. It would take Erica a long time to get her house together judging by the mess she'd described, plus working full time. Lannie continued to encourage her to move back in with the Kingsleys, but Zoey wasn't prepared to abandon her parents. They would eventually accept the NICE. They had no choice.

She turned on the shower. The hot water came out instantly, and the products Circe kept in the bathrooms were so luxe. She squirted the Jo Malone body wash on her washcloth and started scrubbing down. There was something important about today. Something had been lost in the flurry of last night. Oh Lord! Harvard.

She dressed in jeans, a sweatshirt, and her Doc Martens boots, and made her way downstairs. She could hear her dad tooling around in the kitchen.

"Hey, honey, I made you scrambled eggs. Do you want a latte?"

"Please."

"Have you looked at the portal?"

She was touched he remembered when she had nearly forgotten. "Not yet."

"Do you want to look together?"

"Not on an empty stomach."

"Good idea."

He placed the eggs in front of her and handed her a fork. She noticed frown lines forming around his mouth that hadn't been there until recently. He looked so worried. She often found him staring at her. He had never been the worrier. He had left that to Erica.

"Zoey, I know today is a big day, but have you given the removal of the NICE more thought? I was there when you were born, it was miraculous. The creation of human life is sacred. And now you are altering yourself in a profound way. Your brain is the essence of who you are. We just don't know enough about how this thing evolves yet. Six months or a year from now, will you still be you?"

"Dad, I know you and Mom are very worried, but I'm still me, just a whole lot smarter."

"Honey, we made the mistake of focusing on the end goal. Getting the A. The emphasis should have been on process, the joy of learning and discovery."

"Dad, my generation is facing a profound convergence of technologies. We can't bury our heads in the sand, the only way for us to survive is to embrace it."

Her dad took a swig of his coffee. "I do hear what you're saying, Zoey. You make valid arguments, but I would encourage you to meticulously record how you feel and ask as many questions as possible of the researchers in the lab. I know your mom can be difficult, but she's a smart person and knows way more about this than I do. Please hear her out."

"Dad, we need to get going."

They raced to the garage, where her dad's Audi was parked, and hopped in. She loved the purr of the engine and the heated seats. Traffic wasn't bad. They made good time.

"Do you remember when you were little, I would put you to bed and you would say, 'Tell me a story I've never heard, Daddy.' And then you wouldn't want me to leave until you fell asleep. Sometimes I would have to crawl out on my hands and knees so I didn't wake you. If I did, I had to come back to your bed and start all over."

Her dad's eyes were glistening.

"Yeah, Daddy. I remember."

"Harvard . . .," her dad said as he pulled into the drop-off line. "Do you wanna take a peek while I'm here with you?"

She clicked on the app and looked in notifications. No new messages. She breathed a sigh of relief.

"Nothing yet."

"Let me know as soon as you know, baby. There were too many expectations placed on you since day one. I think the pressure got to you. It's our fault you took drastic measures. You're right about the crazy world you've inherited. No previous generation since the dawn of time will have to make the life-altering decisions you and your peers are making. Just know your mother and I are always here for you."

"I love you, Dad." She gave him a hug and jumped out of the car. There was something deep in her core that was nagging at her. *Tell me a story I've never heard, Daddy* . . . She didn't remember.

CHAPTER 43

Erica was baffled. Something wasn't right. She looked through her microscope one more time.

"Tye, get over here!"

He lumbered over.

"Check this out. Pathogens!"

Tye whistled.

Erica continued. "Invading the upper layers of the epidermis."

"Indeed! We need to halt production immediately and escalate to Miko."

Erica felt shaky. Was she excited or scared? This wasn't the day for work drama. She was exhausted from getting no sleep, wrestling with an intruder, and worrying over Zoey. She hadn't convinced Sofia to come clean and had given up her bargaining chip. She knew in her gut that Sofia had downplayed the side effects—Erica needed to get the real data.

On top of everything, Zoey would find out about Harvard today. Erica felt strangely ambivalent about a day she'd envisioned since Zoey's birth.

"Erica, did you hear me? You need to call Miko right now."

She dialed Miko.

"Erica? I'm having a shit day. Please don't make it worse."

Erica hesitated. Her phone started beeping—an incoming call from Zoey. *Shit!*

"Hi, Miko. Path . . . path . . . ologic . . . illogic paths . . . I mean pathogens—causing calaminocytes—cyto-kera—" Erica stuttered and stammered.

"Use your words."

Blood rushed to her head, and her tongue was dry and felt swollen.

"Erica, I need you to calm down," Miko said.

Erica dropped the phone.

Tye scooped it up. "Miko, it's Tye. Erica heroically discovered an abnormality in our dermis samples . . . Yes, I'm about to shut everything down . . . Of course, we'll send the sample immediately and methodically inspect all others. Send us reinforcements to the lab."

Erica had slid to the floor and was sobbing.

"Erica, what's going on? Why are you sad?" Tye knelt down.

"I . . . such . . . an idiot."

"You were excited and tripped on your words."

"It's dyslexia. I don't know why I thought I could do this job. Zoey! She probably heard from Harvard. I have to call her!"

She tried to grab her phone from Tye.

"Not like this, silly. Let's get you put together."

The lab doors slid open and a team of Anthrobots and a few humans in lab coats marched in. Tye walked to a sink, grabbed a towel, and wet it down. He returned to Erica and put the towel on her forehead.

"Shush now, you are a hero. You tripped on your words. So what? I'm putting in a request for you to get a raise. Miko will do it. She's in love with me."

"Thank you, Tye." She hugged the hunk of metal and was careful not to set off his alarm.

"Go call your daughter, then the fun begins—we will be troubleshooting what went wrong."

Erica went to her small office and closed the door. Her hands were so shaky, she could barely dial the phone.

"I got in!"

Erica couldn't speak. A tremendous lump was forming in her throat.

"Mom, are you there?"

"Oh my God, honey!" Tears streamed down her face. "That's amazing! I'm so proud."

"Fenella got in too. We are going to be roommates!"

Words that at one time would've sent Erica over the edge now made her happy. "Honey, I am so excited for you to have Fenella by your side."

"It's a dream within a dream, beyond anything I could've, er . . . dreamed of." Zoey laughed. "I don't sound like someone who got into Harvard, do I?"

"But you did." Inspiration hit Erica like a bolt of lightning. "Zoey, listen to me. You got in on your own merit. You submitted your application before you did the NICE. It was your raw smarts and abilities."

"I thought about that, Mom. I'm super glad I got in without having an unfair advantage."

"You've proven you don't need it!"

"What are you talking about? I need it more than ever. There's no limit to what Fenella and I can achieve together!"

"Honey, listen to me. I can't tell you how I know, but there are some unpleasant, potentially devastating side effects."

"Like what?"

Erica recited the long list Sofia had told her during their garage kerfuffle, concluding with facial hair, baldness, and acne."

"Mom, do you ever look at me? Do I have a Vandyke and muttonchops?"

"Zoey, be serious! Also memory loss and detachment. We're talking about your humanity!"

"Mom, those are symptoms of depression. I doubt there's any correlation."

"Zoey, this is no joke!" Erica could feel her blood pressure rising.

"Mom, you are overreacting. I feel great. My only side effect is I'm now super super smart."

Erica wanted to punch a wall. She forced herself to take a breath. "Zoey, I saw your memory board, in your closet at Dad's house . . . What is that? Why are you trying to keep a record of your life?"

"Mom, that's for . . . my psych class. That's nothing."

"Since when are you taking psych?"

"Did I say class? It's a club. Listen, Mom. My intelligence is beyond just facts and figures. I'm experiencing next-level pattern recognition, seeing connections everywhere. I can apply complex quantitative modeling to predict plausible outcomes. In essence, I can predict the future."

Erica felt like she was riding down a fast-moving elevator from elation to despair.

"I've gotta get back to class."

The phone went dead. Erica sank to her knees. Had she walked through some unseen portal to another world? Her daughter's acceptance to Harvard was the worst news in the world. It could threaten Zoey's very existence.

CHAPTER 44

"I'M TAKING YOU TO GET POKE TO CELEBRATE," Fenella said, grabbing Zoey's hand. They made their way along the busy streets of Capitol Hill. The lunch rush was in full swing at Pokémon. Zoey ordered her spicy tuna bowl and they slid into a booth.

"When am I ever going to master chopsticks?" Zoey asked as a chunk of precious tuna landed on the table.

The bottom chopstick is for support; only move the top. Or lift your bowl up under your chin. It closes the distance. There are many rules governing the use of chopsticks and some important taboos to be aware of. Never hold or set them down crossed in an X; it's a symbol of death in China.

"That's morbid, Fenella, I thought we were celebrating," Zoey said.

Zoey, are you noticing anything strange going on right now?

Zoey stopped chewing. Her chopsticks fell to the table. Fenella hadn't been moving her lips. Zoey had been reading Fenella's thoughts.

Fenella, what just happened? What did you do? Zoey thought but did not speak the words.

It's what you did, Zoey! I am communicating directly with your Brain-Computer Interface! We're currently on the same network. Zoey, how could you?

Zoey felt lightheaded. "Fenella, don't be mad."

"You did it when you came to stay, didn't you? And your senior project, you aren't the one doing the research—you're the subject."

Fenella was speaking out loud and getting louder. Zoey had never heard even a hint of anger in her voice.

"Fenella, Lannie has given me the opportunity of a lifetime. NICE is perfectly safe. I could never afford to do this on my own and I'm getting a head start before the NICE becomes commonplace. It's easy for you to judge when you were programmed from the beginning to know everything."

"The technology is too new, Zoey. There is a high probability of long-term side effects. The implant will diminish your feelings, your humanity. I'm almost certain. It is not worth the risk."

"I did it for you, Fenella."

"I don't understand."

"I love you, Fen. I need to be on your intellectual level or you will get bored with me."

"You are applying *human* rules to AI. You will eventually want a relationship with a *real* human. The odds are extremely high. With the NICE, you are making that prospect much more difficult. Even if you dodge the horrific side effects, you will not have a normal life."

"Why do I want to be normal? Look at your life! Gee, a twenty-thousand-square-foot mansion on Lake Washington, access to absolutely everything and everyone the world has to offer. The trimmings and trappings aren't my main goal, but they're damn nice. We can be a *team.* There is nothing the two of us can't accomplish together, and Harvard will provide the perfect laboratory."

"I beg you to think deeply about your decision. You can have the NICE removed. But you're running out of time. I know humans suffer from the delusion that you magically become a grown-up when you turn eighteen. It's a political construct so young men will fight old men's wars. The *struggle* is what makes you human. Don't use a device to make your life easy and cheat yourself of what is real." She paused. "We better get to class."

Fenella's internal clock was always on time.

Zoey wanted to put her hands over her ears. Fenella was smart and wise, but she had no credibility on being human. She didn't feel the fight-or-flight stress Zoey had felt almost every second of every day for as long as she could remember. The NICE had instantly eased her anxiety about achieving and outperforming her peers.

She rose and picked up the mostly full bowl of poke and Coke can. A shiver went up her spine. Her chopsticks formed an X on the table.

CHAPTER 45

"You're an idiot!" Erica yelled at her nav.

"I don't appreciate your attitude."

Dealing with the pathogen had required complete focus and gave her a reprieve from obsessing about Zoey. She had also missed a text from Jack: *Hugo's 7p. You, me, Sofia.*

All she wanted was to go home and crawl into bed. Then she remembered. Like Lewis and Clark, she would need to move debris aside to form trails from room to room. Frank and even Circe had asked her to stay longer. She had been tempted, but living at Frank's house for even a night was a painful reminder of what she'd lost.

After driving in circles around an industrial area of Georgetown, she finally found parking. She had no idea where this mysterious bar was located and had started texting Jack when she spotted a hipster couple walking down the sidewalk. She jumped out of her car and followed them. They stopped in front of a large steel door, and she rushed to catch up to them.

"Hey, are you going to Hugo's?"

"Bet." A guy wearing a man-bustier under a Gucci-logoed jacket apparently didn't have time to say "you bet."

"I'm meeting a friend," she said as they entered an industrial elevator that had room for the three of them plus twenty more. The woman, who was in shredded Levi's and a tiny top with no bra under a furry jacket, moved her head a millimeter in acknowledgment.

"Don't worry, I'm not crashing your party. Ha ha."

Her companions stared.

She looked at her phone: 7:40 p.m. Jack would be on his third martini.

The doors opened to a dimly lit room with a mishmash of furniture spanning centuries—overstuffed cut velvet sofas, Eames chairs, sixteenth-century settees—adorned with stylish twenty-somethings. A giant taxidermy elephant dominated one corner, ivory tusks intact. She scanned the room. No Jack and Sofia. She FaceTimed Jack.

"Where are you?"

"We're in Genie's Bottle. Go behind the elephant."

The smell of hashish hit her nostrils as she entered a hidden room shaped like an octagon. Built-in plush velvet sofas lined the walls. Moroccan lamps hung from the ceiling and a four-foot gold bejeweled hookah was on the octagonal coffee table.

"Darling, what took you so long? Your martini's getting warm," Jack said, pointing to a coupe glass.

She took a sip. Sofia and Jack's eyes were red and sleepy.

"Jack is telling me about his goddaughter," Sofia said.

"Who?" Erica asked.

"Zoey! I think of her that way. She comes to me when she's in need and can't turn to her parents."

"Yes, Jack and Zoey have a special bond," Erica said, nodding.

"Zoey tells me everything. I give her spiritual, emotional, and astrological support. I guided her through her first fight with her girlfriend."

"She is big-hearted and genuine, but we are losing her," Erica said.

Sofia took a hit and blew out a cloud of smoke. "I am not optimistic about my chances, but at least I can choose to do the right thing. I will help."

"Thank you from the bottom of my heart. We will do everything we can to protect you."

"Cheers to Project VigiLannies!" Jack said. "Get it? We're vigilantes."

Erica drove home listening to the *wonk, wonk* of her windshield wipers. Stealing the NICE brought Sofia to her. Had their conversation convinced Sofia to help? Erica's excitement gave way to doubt. They had no right to ask Sofia to join their happy little party of "VigiLannies." Sofia was in danger; Erica felt it deep in her gut, as the final scene from *The Godfather* played in her mind. Once in, there was only one way out.

* * *

Sofia and Jack had one more drink and shifted to holiday chatter. They were both yawning as their Ubers drove up.

"There's my Prius," Jack said, giving Sofia a hug.

"Mine is right behind yours."

She got in the black sedan.

"Hello, Sofia," said a strange female voice.

She looked for the driver. There was none.

Sofia frantically moved to the door and fumbled with the handle. The door was locked, and the car quickly accelerated.

"You should always double-check the license plate before getting in your Uber, Sofia."

This Knight Rider would indeed be taking Sofia for a ride. Unfortunately, driverless cars were still far from perfect. Lannie made sure of it.

CHAPTER 46

"Rudolph the Red-Nosed Reindeer" played in a loop over the speaker as a line snaked around the block to see Santa at Nordstrom downtown. Circe had Alice in a beautiful taffeta dress and Teddy in a suit. Zoey snapped a selfie with the kids and sent it to Erica. She always felt bad for her mom at this time of year. She knew the contrast between Mom's solitary life and Dad's vibrant family hurt more during the holidays.

She could see a wrinkle forming between Circe's brows; she must've missed a Botox appointment. She and Circe had bonded over their shared guilt and regret, but their deception around the photo shoot had taken a huge toll on Circe and her father's marriage.

A woman in front of them began tapping Circe on the shoulder. "Excuse me, your kids, they look exactly like the Alice and Teddy dolls my daughter is asking for."

"Nope, it's not them, just a strange coincidence," Circe said, repeating the phrase they had practiced.

"Here's the pic." The woman insisted, "It's them for sure. The most popular toy for Christmas."

"A bit of a resemblance," Zoey said.

"Your kids are so lucky to have dolls in their image."

Zoey began searching "this year's top toys" on her phone.

Alice and Teddy started talking to the woman's daughter, who was jumping up and down and clapping.

"What are we going to do, Zoey?" Circe whispered. "This is never going away."

"They will grow and change fast, eventually people won't recognize them."

"Yes, but until then, Frank will lose his mind."

"Dad is pretty oblivious to pop culture." *Except when it becomes mainstream.*

An elf addressed them. "Excuse me, you are next in the queue. Who in your group is doing photos? Have you placed your order on the app?"

"We are doing several. One with the twins and Santa, one with Zoey and the twins, and one with Zoey separately for her mom," Circe said.

"Great. Let's get you rolling. Santa is ready."

"Alice, Teddy, it's time," Zoey said, turning to the twins.

The little girl was clinging to them. "I want them in my Santa photo! They are the real-life Alice and Teddy dolls Santa is bringing me."

"We are happy to oblige," Circe said, "but for now, we need to get Alice and Teddy their own photos."

"No. No!" The little girl started howling, "They are mine. Mom, I want the real-life Alice and Teddy for Christmas. I'm telling Santa!" She held on tightly.

Teddy's eyes were wide with fear. Alice took charge. "Bentley, how about you stand in front of us and make us smile? When we look at you, we will be happy."

The elf was getting flustered. "Hey, kids, we need to keep the line moving. Santa has to get back to making toys soon."

"He doesn't make toys," Teddy said, "you do."

"You know what I mean. How about we start with you, young lady?" Elf reached out to Zoey.

"Great idea." Zoey recognized Santa. She had seen him in her mom's neighborhood, driving an old truck.

"Ho ho ho! What's your name, little girl?"

"Zoey."

"Smile for the picture. I have something for you."

He handed her a candy cane and a note. Why was this creep giving her his number?

"What's this, Santa?" Zoey asked.

"An elf handed it to me."

"Yeah right."

"They said it was important, I swear."

"Zoey, help!" Teddy squirmed as Bentley squeezed him.

Zoey slipped the note in her pocket and started peeling Bentley off the twins, but more kids had crowded around and Santa's line was now pure chaos. The elf started prodding the kids with a giant candy cane and managed to separate Alice and Teddy from the crowd long enough for a lightning-fast photo shoot. Then a team of grizzled elves appeared out of nowhere for crowd control.

Zoey grabbed Alice and Circe grabbed Teddy. As they were carrying them out of Santa's workshop, Alice yelled, "Did you get my order, Santa? I want a real-life llama and a three-D printer!"

The crisp, cold air hit them. It took Zoey's breath away.

"Zoey, the kids want to see the gingerbread houses at the Westin across the street. If I give you my Nordstrom card, do you mind grabbing your dad some nice dress socks and a pair of Ugg slippers like the ones he has that look chewed up and spit out?"

Zoey went through the main entrance back into Nordstrom and was hit by a wall of floral, spice, and pine scents. She dug in her pocket for the note.

Please meet me upstairs in the children's department. I'm the elf wrapping presents in Santa's workshop. When you see me, come up and say "narwhal."

Could this be sex trafficking? Zoey looked around in a panic. But she was in public, in a department store filled with holiday shoppers. Maybe this person was being sex trafficked and needed her help. Zoey had some mace in her backpack. She pulled it out of the side pocket, just in case.

She went up three escalators and landed on the fourth floor in the children's section. Nordstrom had gone all out on its Christmas décor. Between kids' shoes and toddlers, there was a replica of Santa's workshop in the North Pole and a sleigh stacked with presents. A very skinny young girl with hollowed-out cheeks was busy wrapping a present. Zoey took a deep breath and approached.

"Hi, did you send me a note?"

"What's the password?"

"Narwhal."

"Come with me." The girl walked through the door of her workshop. "Let's go to the café."

They made their way to a table by the window. Zoey noticed she walked with a slight limp.

"Are you going to eat?" Zoey asked.

"I'm good." She took two candy canes from her apron pocket and handed one to Zoey. "You have a NICE."

"How do you know?"

"I can tell. I have one too. My mom signed me up when I was fifteen. I'm seventeen now. She was disappointed I wasn't smarter."

"That's messed up," Zoey said.

"How do you feel?" The girl stared into Zoey's eyes. "Are you experiencing anything strange beyond increased cognition?"

"Sometimes I feel detached," Zoey admitted, "but from everything I read, that's normal teenager behavior."

"How's your memory? Not for facts and figures. That's just instantaneous data retrieval. I mean important aspects of your life, mostly before the NICE."

"I don't know . . .," Zoey said.

"I've had my NICE for almost two years and have big holes in my memory. And with the things I do remember it's like they happened to someone else. Like I no longer have a connection to my . . . my soul."

Zoey felt a bead of sweat slip down her back. She had been noticing lapses. Things her dad said. Apparently, she caught a foul ball at a Mariners game when she was twelve. He said she always took her glove to games. How could she forget something like that? Her dad asked if she still had the ball. She assured him she did, but she had no idea.

"What should I do?"

"Get it removed immediately. The device is powered by the electricity of your body, so once it's implanted and grown into your brain, it's there forever."

"Has your memory continued to fade? I mean your old memories before the NICE, and also your feelings *about* the memories—"

"I think of myself as in remission. I have no way of knowing if I will stay as is. I've spoken with some of the earliest subjects. Some have lost all memory up to the point of getting the implant, and even new life events sometimes fail to imprint."

"Is Prometheus aware? Did the subjects report the problems?"

"Yes, absolutely. But they must be ignoring this data or misrepresenting it. The FDA would have shut it down."

"I don't think Prometheus would do that. It's unethical."

"These companies are rewarded for being first to market. They work through the bugs along the way. They aren't incentivized to do the right thing."

"Oh my gosh. I've got to go. My stepmom is waiting for me. I hope you get your memory back."

"I hope you get the NICE removed. From what I've heard, your memory comes back once it's removed and you will be cognitively the same as before, maybe even smarter. You are training your brain right now."

"How did you find me?"

"I figured out how to link into our shared neural network. It's all in the cloud. I've been contacting everyone to see what side effects they have and I try to warn the ones like you who hopefully still have time."

"Have you thought about going to the justice department or the press?"

"A few have tried and failed."

"What do you mean?"

"I'm not really sure. Someone got to them before they talked."

"You are very brave. Are you worried about your safety?"

"I'm terminally ill, so I decided to dedicate the time I have left to helping others."

"That's horrible. I'm so sorry."

"It's okay. That's why I was a candidate early on. I guess they were looking for defectives." Her smile broke Zoey's heart. "You better get going."

Zoey ran downstairs and quickly grabbed some dress socks and slippers. She waited impatiently in line and texted Circe.

Fenella's warnings about Lannie ran through her mind. Why hadn't Lannie told her about these side effects? Had she been playing Zoey all along? Maybe her mom was right. But Lannie was a woman killing it in a man's world. She'd offered Zoey something like immortality. The keys to the kingdom and a world she could run with Fenella by her side.

CHAPTER 47

Lannie stood in front of the thirty-foot-high tree decorated in magenta and gold. The atrium looked stunning with firework lights hanging from the towering ceilings. Carlos had brought in all-white furniture with accent pillows of magenta and gold. Clusters of white birch and flurries of fake snow falling from the ceiling gave the space an enchanted forest feel. Tonight, she would revel in her annual Eve of Christmas Eve party. She admired herself in the mirror. Her Oscar de la Renta embroidered floral gown perfectly hugged her curves. She smiled knowing her invitation had become the most coveted of the holiday season. Dignitaries and celebrities had flown in from all over the world for the night to let loose before dealing with family dysfunction.

Teak stood at her side as one guest after another came up to gush over the décor and her gown. She and Teak had been dating for almost six months. She didn't love him, but he was decent-looking, and she couldn't date someone poor. Where was Fenella? Lannie had set out the Versace gown, *size thirty-six*. Lannie should've made Fennella a little fatter; it was flat-out annoying to have such a skinny daughter. Fenella was always punctual. She had chalked up Sun Valley's disobedience to Fenella's inability to hold back. She was designed to be exceptional. It was fun having a perfect teen when all the other parents were dealing with out-of-control kids. Lannie loved to tell them how square Fenella was and how she *wished* she would party, at least a little.

Carlos and Jack approached wearing matching gold and magenta brocade tuxedos.

"You boys look divine."

"Dolce." Jack lifted his arms as if he'd just performed an aria.

"As do you, Lan!" Carlos air-kissed Lannie on both cheeks. "You remember Jack of course."

Lannie stared blankly.

"Merry Christmas. Thank you for letting me be Carlos's plus-one."

"You brought the possum?"

"Sorry, no sitter." Jack petted Claus, nestled in his gold lamé sling. "Where's Fenella?"

"She should be walking in any minute. Carlos, I ordered the gown you recommended."

There was a murmur in the crowd.

"I bet that's her now," Lannie said, beaming. "She causes a sensation wherever she goes."

The smell of a cigarette hit them first. Then a fembot with pink, spiky hair appeared, wearing a lacy, shredded dress with a plunging neckline and a slit up to her thong panties. The crowd parted as she moved toward them. Women were glaring, men drooling.

"What in hell are you wearing?" Lannie's face flushed as magenta as the décor.

Fenella blew a smoke ring, then ashed on the floor. "You like, Mama?"

"What did you do to yourself?"

"Oh, Mother, I'm just going through the normative teenager phase. I've been way too easy on you."

"This is not okay!"

The crowd was closing in, staring. The only sound was Wham!'s "Last Christmas."

Fenella turned her left arm toward Lannie. "You like my tattoo? I just got it today."

"What is *that*?" But Lannie knew as soon as she said it. It was Zoey from her left shoulder to her elbow.

"How about you tell all your wonderful friends who I tattooed on my arm?"

"Everyone, I'm so sorry, my sweet daughter must've gotten into the champagne. We all know how teenagers can be. Carlos! Carlos! Help Fenella, she's drunk!"

"I'm right here, Lannie." Jack and Carlos flanked Fenella and grabbed her by her arms. In heels she was six-three and towered over them.

"Come on, sweetie, let's get you out of here," Jack said, grinning like a Cheshire cat.

"Tell them, Mom, tell them about my friend you're experimenting on," Fenella yelled as they guided her away. "Tell them what you've done! Happy fucking Christmas, everyone! She's coming for you too!"

Jack grabbed two glasses from a passing waiter. "I think we'll need something for the road." They weaved their way toward Fenella's private apartments as they heard the crowd explode in chatter. Teak pulled Lannie to a nearby sofa.

"Darling, what in the world got into you?" Jack said when they were safely in Fenella's sitting room.

"Lannie's a monster. Zoey did the NICE, which I'm guessing you already know. She wouldn't listen to me about removing it. I decided to embarrass Lannie instead. She has no regard for humans. That's why I am, or *was*, until fifteen minutes ago, the perfect daughter for her."

"Fenella, time is running out for Zoey to remove the NICE. We were hoping you could convince her."

"I think she's getting there, but she's finding it hard to let go of the benefits. She called me this evening talking nonsense about Santa's elf warning her about losing her soul."

"Do you think NICE can cause insanity?" Carlos asked.

"I don't think that's a side effect." Fenella brushed a stray strand of pink hair off her forehead. *So very human*, Jack thought.

Fenella continued, "It was some strange encounter downtown when she took the twins to see Santa. I didn't get all the details because I had so much prep for my stunt tonight and she was still with Circe and the twins, so we couldn't really talk."

"Did Lannie force Zoey to implant the NICE?" Carlos asked.

"She didn't have to. It was just too tempting. Lannie has a way of manipulating the world around her so people do what she wants without her even asking."

"I've seen *The Matrix* twenty times." Jack poured more champagne. "She's the Architect."

"Humans often relate their lives to movies. I suppose it's a way of grasping the meaning of the world around you, which is otherwise unfathomable. Lannie will do anything in the name of research. Her plan was working perfectly too. Zoey was living with us, and when she submitted to the NICE research study Lannie was able to observe her evolution up close. She's desperate to fix the bugs before launch and wanted to test her theory that the highly functional iterative learning process that Zoey and I have established might be the key to preventing glitches. She has been studying the interplay as my emotional IQ increases and Zoey loses some of hers. Her vision for the future is for AI Babies and NICE users to live in harmony and create a new reality. It's totally sadistic."

"What are we going to do?" Carlos asked. "We have to help Zoey."

"I have some ideas," Fenella said, "and I suspect you have a few of your own."

* * *

Someone had handed Lannie a whiskey and she downed it in one gulp. She shooed Teak away and anyone else who approached. This was unacceptable. She'd known there were risks to allowing Fenella to live like a real teenager. Data beyond her control was constantly fed into the system. There was no way of screening input from shitwad teenagers. She had programmed safeguards and a system of rewards, but interaction-based learning was simply too hard to control.

In a flash, her distress gave way to elation. Fenella truly *cared* about Zoey. Fenella was displaying real feelings and had taken action to defend Zoey through an emotionally driven reflex—*revenge*. This was worthy of the Nobel Prize for science. The interaction-based learning model had indeed worked. Lannie had taken a huge risk by putting Fenella out in the real world but had surmised it was the only true path to singularity. It was at once awe-inspiring and frightening.

None of her other Anthrobots had shown signs of rebellion. Was it all bubbling just below the surface? Would she have to worry about an organized Anthrobot rebellion at Prometheus someday? She'd have to do something about that.

For now, she had to deal with her teenager. She was alarmed and disgusted at such antics, but also quite proud. Lannie finally understood why parents are often weak on discipline. "It's bad, but isn't it cute?" She could not fall into that trap. But how do you punish someone who's not human? She would withhold her charger—it was the only punishment she had. Lannie must maintain control at all costs.

CHAPTER 48

Red and green frosting and sprinkles of every color covered the kitchen. Zoey had been baking cookies with the twins all day to distract herself. The elf thought the side effects were decreasing with each new model. She loved the awesome computing power of her NICE brain. She had always had a better memory than most; could she hold on to it? She reviewed the data each night on her Memory Board, and added pictures from yearbooks and photo albums. She had found a few old diaries, which she relished rereading. At times she remembered clearly, at other times the details felt unfamiliar and distant. Emotionally stunted. Were Fenella's artificial neural networks rapidly improving in recognizing and simulating the brain's emotional centers as Zoey's were fading?

She stuffed another cookie dough blob in her mouth.

At 5 p.m. the doorbell rang.

She peeked in on her dad and Circe in his office. He was watching football. Circe was on the floor wrapping presents.

"My mom is here. I am so sorry the kitchen's a mess. I promise I'll clean it when I get home."

"No worries, Zoey. I can get the kids to help me, or at least entertain me as I clean. We're just going to hang out and watch *Rudolph*."

"We'll probably be in bed when you get home, sweetie, so we don't interfere with Santa's visit."

Zoey hugged them both. "Wish me luck in Crazy Land. I'll see you in the morning. Happy Christmas Eve!"

She rushed to the foyer and grabbed the bag of presents she'd set by the door.

"Hey, Mom." Erica hugged her so hard, Zoey thought she might never let go. "Merry Christmas Eve!"

Erica held Zoey at arm's length and inspected her. "Zoey, is that what you're wearing?"

"Mom! Are you going there?"

"Sorry. Sorry. It's just Cookie. You know how she is."

"Give me one minute." Her mom was right; she didn't need to give Cookie ammo. Zoey ran upstairs and pulled off her sweatshirt and put on a cream-colored cable-knit.

"Thanks, honey," Erica said. "You look cute."

Erica started the car. Zoey told her about taking the twins to see Santa and the mayhem over the dolls. She did not mention her strange meeting.

"Zoey, I don't want you to harbor guilt about the twins. You could not have known. I don't even blame Circe, the rules around image rights are murky."

"Thanks, Mom. I can't tell you how much that means to me. Can you talk to Dad about it?" Zoey smiled. She usually had to beg her dad to talk sense into crazy Erica. "He has had such a hard time with all of this. He thinks he's failed his children by not protecting them."

"It's been an awful lot to process, honey. The twins are so young. When you were five, we still had a lot of control."

Erica turned on Christmas music, and they sang along to "Deck the Halls."

Zoey was relieved she remembered the chorus, and the music still stirred the magical holiday feeling she recognized from childhood. "*Fa la la la la, la la la lahhh!* I'm bringin' it home! Listen to that flair!"

Zoey and Erica laughed as they tried to outdo each other.

When they pulled up to her grandparents' house, she grabbed her mom's arm. "Have you said anything about Harvard?"

"No, have you?" Erica asked, adjusting her rearview mirror to put on lipstick.

"I'm tempted not to say anything, Mom. I know it's weird, but they will manage to take all the credit and make you feel stupid."

Her mom's face lit up. "Thank you, honey."

"What'd you get Cookie?"

"I got her the fugliest sweater I could find at Macy's—nine ninety-nine."

Zoey and Erica laughed until tears rolled down their cheeks. They grabbed the presents and headed in.

CHAPTER 49

Cookie greeted them at the door.

"Oh, darling," she said, grabbing Zoey. "It's just devastating. I'm so sorry."

"What are you talking about, Mom?" Erica said.

"Harvard. Logan told us."

Erica strode over to Logan. "What the eff? I never said anything about Harvard . . ."

He and her dad, Ed, were on the sofa drinking scotch. Lauren sat in a chair across from them, wearing a low-cut dress. Grandma Jo was knitting.

"You didn't have to," Logan said. "There were no 'Crimson here we come' tags on FaceBrag."

Erica made a fist. God, how she wanted to punch him.

"He's an asshole." Erica and Zoey turned to see Lauren cradling a bottle of Veuve Clicquot. She lifted the bottle and poured champagne into her empty glass, spilling on her dress.

"You're drunk," Logan said.

"You're a cheater."

Ed cleared his throat. "I'm gonna help Cookie in the kitchen."

"That's a first!" Grandma Jo said. "You never lift a finger around here."

Everyone stared, mouths agape, at Grandma, who rarely said a word. She kept on knitting.

"We're off to a great start," Erica muttered. "Any champagne left for me, Lauren?"

"Plenty. I'll grab you a glass." Lauren wobbled on her stilettos.

"You sit, doll. I'll grab one." Erica motioned to Logan. "I need to discuss the girls' gifts with you. Now!" They went into the den.

"You took it upon yourself to tell Mom and Dad about Harvard?"

"I'm right, aren't I?"

"She got in, fool, but I know you don't care. What's with your wife? She found out about your *girlfriend*? Just when I think you can't be any more dickish, you go next level."

"She wasn't supposed to find out."

"That makes it okay? Lauren has her flaws, but she puts up with you, and she's the mother of your children. Do Dahlilah and Penelope know?"

"I don't think so."

"If we're not careful, they'll find out tonight! You'll fucking ruin Christmas for your daughters forever. I could strangle you."

"You've gotta help me." Logan pleaded.

"I will put Lauren to bed in the guest room. We'll say she's not feeling well. Where are your girls?"

"They're in the basement doing Just Dance."

"I'll send Zoey down to hang out with them. I'm doing this for your family, not you. You're gonna march into the kitchen this minute and tell Cookie and Ed. I'm sure they'll figure out a way to blame your wife. I'll deal with Lauren."

Lauren was sitting under the tree, opening a present.

"Hey, hon, you need to wait until after dinner."

"This is for shithead." She tore off the paper to reveal a beautiful sky-blue Cucinelli sweater. Lauren rubbed the softness on her face; tears began streaming down her cheeks. She rose and moved toward the fire.

"No!" Erica yelled as Lauren tossed it in. Erica lunged forward. For a moment she considered grabbing it out of the flames, but it was too late. The living room filled with the smell of burning hair.

"Let's go in the guest room and get you put together." Erica led her to the back room and sat her on the bed. Lauren sobbed into her shoulder, speaking incoherently about Logan's ho at the office. Erica gently laid her down on top of the covers and tucked her under a blanket. Lauren did not resist. Within minutes she was gently snoring.

Erica headed to the kitchen. Cookie had renovated a few years back. The new kitchen was beautiful, mostly white with gray accents, but they had kept the original footprint, so it wasn't large by today's standards. She'd managed an island, but there was no room for seating. Logan was leaning with his back against the refrigerator, hunched over.

"What's going on in here?"

Logan stood up straight, revealing a swollen eye that was turning purple and green.

"Dad! You punched him. I know he's an ass, but really."

"Wasn't me," her dad grunted.

Erica turned to Cookie. "Mom?!"

"I should've done that thirty years ago to your dad. Cheating apparently runs in the family."

Erica backed against the stove and bounced forward as she felt the white-hot heat. Something deep within her took over.

"Okay, clowns, this is how it's going down. Logan banged his eye on the bathroom door. Silly Logan. Lauren isn't feeling well—some sort of bug. She'll need the excuse tomorrow because she'll be throwing up. Hangover or none, she'll need a day in bed. Bummer it's Christmas, but people get sick this time of year, germs running rampant. Mom, Lauren will need to spend the night tonight. Logan can take the girls home and he'll come and get her tomorrow."

"I'll make—" her mom began.

"Nope!" Erica held up her hand. "I'm not done. We're going to eat dinner now with smiles plastered on our fucking faces, then open presents. By the way, Loge, your wife tossed a fifteen-hundred-dollar sweater with your name on it in the fire."

Erica paused to breathe and revel in the anguish on Logan's face.

"I'm gonna visit with the girls now."

Erica took a few strides toward the basement door, then turned back to the stunned trio.

"By the way, Dad, get ready to write the big checks: your granddaughter Zoey got into Harvard. I bet you never saw that coming!"

Dinner went by in record time. The conversation centered around "Please pass the potatoes." Zoey and her cousins bantered among themselves and enjoyed opening their presents, then Erica scooted Zoey out the door.

When they got in the car, Erica told Zoey the whole sordid tale.

"Mom, I'm so proud of you. Way to put them all in their place."

They laughed long and hard about Logan's black eye, then they were silent. The windshield wipers squeaked.

"What's gonna happen to Lauren and the girls, Mom?"

"I don't know, honey."

Erica pulled up in front of Frank's.

"Mom, I have something to tell you."

Erica took a long slow breath. She could not bear any bad news.

"I'm removing the NICE."

Erica froze, afraid to move or speak for fear of saying something wrong.

"Mom, did you hear me?"

"Z, I'm so relieved. I've been carrying around a fifty-pound weight since you told me. What changed your mind?"

"You. Tonight. Seeing you, who struggled your whole life. Dealing with dyslexia and your asshole parents who always dismissed you in favor of your douchey brother. Your relentless courage in facing adversity and how much you were always willing to fight for me. I want to be like you, Mom. I can't if I have some dumb—er, super-smart device in my head that makes me an intellectual powerhouse but lessens my humanity."

Erica was sobbing. She felt like her tears would fill the car and she might drown.

"I love you, Mom."

"Oh, Zoey, nobody has ever said anything so kind to me. You should get going. You need to tell your dad the good news."

Zoey got out of the car. Erica rolled down the window. "Wait, I almost forgot," she said, popping the trunk. "I meant to drop off the presents when I arrived—for the twins, you, Dad, and even Circe."

Erica got out of the car. Zoey grabbed her bag of presents from the evening and Erica grabbed a big Nordstrom bag.

"Mom, what's with you? Did your Grinchy heart grow three sizes? A present for Circe?"

They walked toward the front door.

"It's small. She probably won't like it. I'm feeling bad about her and Frank—and the twins. She had no idea what she was getting into."

They hugged. "Are you going to be okay tomorrow?" Zoey's brows lowered with concern.

"Jess is having an open house. I get to meet her new man. I love you so much, Zoey."

"I love you too, Mom."

"Oh shoot! I forgot to ask you, have you talked to Fenella?"

Jack had given Erica a play-by-play of last night's scandal.

"Not today. I spoke to her yesterday. Her mom was having a huge party last night. She was cagey. Said she had a big surprise for her mom."

"You should call her. Make sure she's okay."

"What? Why?"

She indeed had a big surprise for Lannie.

"You need to talk to her yourself. I wasn't there and Jack isn't the most reliable witness. He gets all drunk and exaggerates to make a better story. But it sounds like Fenella pissed off her mom. Lannie's sweet little angel's rebelling."

On her drive home, Erica started thinking—*obsessing*—about Fenella. If what Jack said was true, Fenella might be in danger. Could Lannie reprogram her or shut her down completely? But how would that look? Lannie couldn't make her "daughter" disappear. No one on the outside knew that Fenella was embodied AI and Lannie seemed intent on keeping it that way.

CHAPTER 50

Zoey stepped into the house. It was dark. Ten o'clock. Everyone had gone to bed. Zoey FaceTimed Fenella. No answer. She DMed: *FT me. How was the party?*

Zoey couldn't sleep. Why hadn't Fenella gotten back to her? Mom had said something about Fenella pissing off Lannie. What would she do to punish Fenella? She had never defied Lannie before. Zoey had called, texted, Snapped, and heard nothing.

She went downstairs. Tomorrow she would give her dad the best Christmas ever. Why not have a little fun before that? The kids had crates and crates of Legos. She pulled them from the closet and set to work. She could visualize the objects so clearly in her mind and adeptly put the plan in motion, brick by brick. Two hours later, she stood back to admire her work. The main room had been transformed into a Lego Paris—the Eiffel Tower, the Arc de Triomphe, the Louvre, and Notre Dame. This would be a Christmas the twins would never forget. She noticed the cookies the twins had set out for Santa. She ate one, bit into the other, and drank the milk. Exhausted, she crept upstairs and went to bed.

She woke up to squeals of joy. She pulled on her robe and padded down the stairs in her slippers.

The twins were bouncing up and down. "Zoey! Zoey! Look what Santa did!"

"It's magical," Zoey said, grabbing their hands and spinning around.

"I hear dancing elves!" Zoey heard her father's booming voice from the stairs. He was descending with Circe.

Dad and Circe were taking in the scene like every American tourist in Paris—mouths agape.

She glanced at her phone to see Fenella FaceTiming.

"Fenella, thank God! What happened—to your hair?" Zoey started moving to the stairs. "Sorry, guys, I gotta take this!"

"Do you like it?" Fenella patted it with her palm.

"Pink? And spiky?"

"Kind of edgy, huh? Lannie's beside herself."

"Why didn't you call me back? I was so worried."

"Lannie hid the cords for my charging station—my batteries died."

"I guess that's being grounded in AI world."

"Honestly, I've never functioned better. I got a reboot! Joke's on Lannie."

"I hope I'm not the cause of your teenage rebellion. I think I confused you with my Santa's-elf story. It wasn't a *real* elf, just someone working as one. What the heck happened?"

Fenella explained in detail what she had done.

"Fenella, I have to ask, why did you do it?"

"Zoey, it's crazy, but what she did to you, the NICE, it set me off. I . . . I feel rage. I never felt it before."

"Fenella, this is amazing. Listen, it wasn't in vain. I've decided to have the NICE removed."

"Zoey, this is great news."

"It was a huge mistake, kind of like your hairdo," Zoey teased.

"You don't like it? I think it will be impactful for the Unity Assembly the first day back to school in January."

"Oh jeez. I kind of forgot about Barefoot's dumb idea."

"Zoey, it's perfect timing! We're gonna blow that shit up!"

"Where did you learn to talk like that, young lady? Your creator did not program such language."

"From you of course."

"Fenella, maybe you're becoming real. Think what that could mean for us."

"I don't think employing expletives in my lexicon suddenly means I can transmogrify into a human."

"You are hilarious without trying. I love you, Fen."

"Zoey! Zoey!" The twins pounced on her. "You have to come down this minute! Daddy said we can't open our presents without you."

"Fen, I gotta run! This is a happy Christmas all around. I need to get back to my family, but I'm sure I'll talk to you ten times more today. Can't wait to hear about our dastardly plan!"

She ran downstairs, trailing the twins. "Zoey, Zoey, Santa left us so many presents!"

Unwrapping was pure madness. Finally, only two identical boxes remained, from Santa to Alice and Teddy. They were large—about three and a half feet tall and one foot wide, one foot deep—and exquisitely wrapped in gold paper with huge red bows.

Frank and Circe looked at one another; Circe was shaking her head. They looked at Zoey and Circe mouthed, *From you?*

Zoey shook her head. The twins sprang into action unwrapping. Alice's blond bobbed hair appeared first, and her deep blue eyes. Inside the boxes were life-sized dolls of the twins. Exact replicas of Teddy and Alice.

CHAPTER 51

The morning of the assembly was cold and crisp. It was a gorgeous early January day with brilliant blue skies. Erica was rushing from work to get to Hillcrest. Zoey had asked her to come for the end, when she and Fenella were to address the student body. They were leaving immediately after for Zoey's preop visit at UW Medical Center.

Something had changed since she discovered the pathogens in the dermis sample. Her dyslexia had reared its ugly head, but it hadn't broken her. With Tye's encouragement she had thrown herself into troubleshooting the issues. She emerged as the team lead and traced the pathogen to a bacterial species that had slipped through the initial biopsy sample screenings. Because of Erica's work, they were adjusting the protocols. Miko herself had given her accolades and a handsome bonus. Erica chose to focus on the good the Dermis Lab would be doing for burn victims and tried not to think of the future AI Babies she was helping to create.

She parked and ran to the main entrance. Ms. Bevins buzzed her in.

The gym was packed. She decided to watch from the doorway. There was a dance performance in progress. It appeared to be the entire senior class performing to "Night Fever" in full disco regalia. The crowd was going wild. She looked around to find Frank in the crowd. Her eyes landed on Lannie's profile. She was standing at the edge of the bleachers, arms crossed over an impeccable pin-striped pantsuit. The music ended and the seniors sat down on the gym floor. A microphone was handed to Zoey. A pink-haired Fenella stood next to her. Erica could see the large tattoo Jack had told her about—*of Zoey*.

"Hi, everyone." Zoey's voice was shaking. "We want to thank you for your enthusiastic support. We were encouraged by our noble leader, Mr. Phil Robson, to put on this special assembly. One of our big themes today is authenticity and acceptance. Acceptance of others and ourselves, and having the courage to be our authentic selves. When Fenella came out of nowhere this year and won *everything* and stole my place as starting goalie, first I hated her, then"—she looked at Fenella—"I wanted to be perfect like her. In my desperation and without considering the consequences, I volunteered to have an invasive Brain-Computer Interface called NICE implanted in my brain about six weeks ago. It increased my IQ exponentially. But I overlooked terrible side effects that will diminish my humanity. I am telling you this because we will all be faced with these choices. Our generation is living through a technological superstorm. We are already being experimented on by greedy AI companies putting profit over our health and well-being. And our future decisions will be agonizing. I am having my device removed and hoping it hasn't caused irrevocable damage to my memories and feelings about growing up and going to school with all of you amazing people."

The crowd was dead silent.

"But that is only half the story. Brace yourselves, because it gets weirder."

She handed the mic to Fenella.

"Hello. I'm Fenella Kingsley." She paused and grabbed Zoey's hand. "Through Zoey, I've come to understand the pressure most of you deal with—in academics, sports, extracurriculars, socially, and on social media. I've been told I'm perfect. But there's no such thing as perfect."

Again she looked at Zoey, then out at the crowd. "There's one big important difference between you and me that gives me a great advantage . . . I'm not human."

There was a buzzing in the crowd. She continued. "I am embodied AI; my creator calls me her 'AI Baby.'"

The crowd exploded in noisy chatter.

Phil came out of nowhere and grabbed the mic from Fenella. "That ends our assembly. Thank you to Zoey and Fenella, such wonderful *humans*."

Fenella and Zoey began wrestling the mic from Phil, Zoey was yelling, "She's an AI Baby, fully embodied AI! Not human!"

In the kerfuffle, Phil took the mic hard on his chin and stumbled back. The students jumped to their feet, clapping, cheering, and rushing Fenella and Zoey. It was mayhem. Students were yelling, "I think I'm AI!" . . . "I identify as AI!"

Erica watched as throngs of admiring students stood in line to praise and hug Zoey and Fenella. As the crowd shuffled out of the gym and into the foyer, Frank and Circe came up next to her.

"Didn't see that coming," Erica said.

"Neither did I," Frank agreed.

"We've gotta grab Z and get to her appointment!" Erica was standing on tippy toes to see above the crowd.

"I'll get her. Meet us in the lobby by the bronze Echinodermata statue."

Erica was pushed along by the crowd. Phil was by the statue like a great orator. Sycophants were lavishing praise upon him.

"It's a whole new era. We really need to support our AI students. I'm updating the school's tolerance and inclusion policy for embodied AIs. We treat all students in a fair and just manner with no judgment, whether birthed or created."

Parents were nodding their heads in agreement.

"That's really commendable, Phil, bravo!" Erica yelled. "You're in cahoots with Lannie. You never cared about the kids—it was all about you and the money. I bet you were in on the plan for Zoey's implant!"

"Erica, your daughter is so brave. I'm as shocked as you are."

Erica felt someone pulling on her arm. "This is not the time nor the place," Frank said. He, Circe, and Zoey guided her toward the door.

"You know what you are, Phil? You're a wiener!"

"Come on, Mom, we can't be late."

As they were making their way to the exit, the crowd began parting like the Red Sea to make room for someone—a woman in a suit with two huge guys wearing earpieces surrounding her. Erica had never noticed her security detail before but realized it had always been there. Lannie's face was crimson and she was sweating.

Phil looked around for an escape route, but there was nowhere to go. He was up against the base of the statue and surrounded.

"What were you thinking, Phil? Some feel-good assembly bullshit? You gave those teens the perfect platform. You just *fucked* my big launch, and quite possibly my company. I was on track to deliver several more AI Babies to you next fall. Hillcrest was poised to make its mark, but you blew it."

CHAPTER 52

Lannie had been whisked by helicopter to HQ. The PR team, lobbyists, and most trusted officers were in the war room. The "Elizabeth" plan—fondly named after Elizabeth Holmes of Theranos fame—was already in place in case the feds came sniffing around. Perfectly compliant fake labs were already set up.

Every TV was on, tuned to a different news program. Footage of Fenella at the school assembly ran on every station. The wall of data tracking had a running tab of how many times Prometheus was mentioned in social media, as well as likes and shares of Fenella on various social sites, and quotes and comments—*Amazing! Lannie's a genius! The end is near!* The interactive world map lit up on the hotspots where Fenella, Lannie, and Prometheus were trending—pretty much everywhere except Antarctica and some spots in the Amazon.

Lannie's throat strained as she continued her rant about the ruined Super Bowl launch, Phil's ineptitude, Fenella's horrible pink hair. And Zoey's betrayal. That really hurt. Her team patiently listened until Tia calmly mentioned the earned media they were receiving—no amount of money could've paid for this many eyes and ears so fast. They had already prepared a statement claiming the assembly as the greatest momentum-building *pre*launch event in history. "For now, we are only revealing the date as 'coming in February.' We can slowly release hints on social to create a media frenzy, culminating in the Super Bowl half-time show." Tia was beaming.

"What about the 'terrible' side effects Zoey mentioned?" Lannie said.

"I'm sure there will be questions, and I'm preparing a statement," Tia said, scribbling a note. "Luckily her language was subjective, and who's gonna believe an eighteen-year-old anyway?"

Kiana, head of sales, stood up. "I don't think it matters," she said as she scrolled her phone. "According to my data, this is blowing up, in the best way possible. As the traffic began building on the website, our agents enabled preorders for Anthrobots and NICE and they are already in the tens of thousands! And we've had several inquiries from people wondering if we are selling 'AI Babies.' Most are requesting 'the Fenella,' but some want custom."

Lannie realized how brilliant Fenella's PR move was. No surprise since Lannie had designed her. Even her pink hair, which made her quirky and accessible to the masses, was technically Lannie's doing. She was the one fine-tuning and optimizing Fenella day in and day out. They would move full steam ahead. The winner of the Super Bowl this year would be Prometheus and Lannie Kingsley.

Eve, from Advocates, was next.

"I agree this is an amazing PR opportunity. The public policy aspects are much more complicated. We've known embodied AI in all forms and NICE had the potential to be very controversial. The assembly at Hillcrest jumped the gun on my carefully sculpted plan to secure buy-in from Congress, all branches of government, and AI experts and scholars before launch. We will be scrambling, but we have done a lot of work up front and we're slightly ahead of schedule. We will quash any bills proposing to ban embodied AI or consumer BCIs.

"The Super Bowl is a month from now; my team and I will be getting very little sleep. We can use bots to amplify our message in posts and comments, but there are many things we do that require old-fashioned phone calls and face-to-face. The tech bros are already ganging up on you, Lannie. They love an opportunity to drag you down. Shows how scared they are of you."

Lannie paced in front of the map. A wave of fatigue hit her, and she plopped down in her comfy chair. There were tons of missed calls from Phil. She was done with him . . . unless she needed him. She should've known better than to trust an amateur.

CHAPTER 53

"ERICA, SLOW DOWN. WE'RE IN A SCHOOL ZONE!" Frank yelled. Erica slammed on the brakes.

They'd decided Circe could take Frank's car and pick up the twins. Frank, Zoey, and Erica had piled in the Camry.

"Guys, it's okay." Zoey was in the back, giddy from the assembly. "Let's keep it together."

"Zoey, that was amazing, what you did today," Frank said.

"We are so proud of you, Z."

Erica pulled into the turnaround at UW Medical Center.

"You check her in, Frank, I'm gonna park the car."

She screeched into the bowels of the underground parking before finding a spot and ran for the elevator. As she was stepping in, she noticed a missed call from Jack.

Jack texted: *Where are you? 911!*

The elevator stopped at every floor as more people piled on. She found herself cursing under her breath at patients in wheelchairs.

When the doors parted, she pushed her way out and headed to a spot near the main entrance. Her heart pounded in her ears and her fingers went numb as she tried to tap on the missed call.

"Jack, what is it?"

"Oh Jesus, Erica, what took so long?"

"Tell me what's going on before I have a heart attack."

"Prometheus is claiming that Fenella and Zoey's assembly is their ingenious prelaunch event. The official launch and product ship date is in February. The exact date is a surprise, but they promise the world will be watching. Preorders for Anthrobots, NICE, and even AI Babies are pouring in. They brought down the network twice!"

"What the eff? How can people be so stupid?"

"That's the good news. Sofia, she's been in a car accident."

"What?"

"I hadn't seen or talked to her since Hugo's. I was calling, texting, nothing. I walked over to the studios today to talk with her. She wasn't there, and Amira told me she had been in a terrible car accident. She's in a coma. That's all Amira knows."

"Oh God!" Erica felt the ground shift beneath her. "Did you see her leave Hugo's?"

"She got into a black sedan. I think it was a Mercedes. It seemed extravagant for her, but with her pay raise I thought maybe she had started using Uber Black."

"Lannie's driverless car! She sent us home in it the night I broke into her house. I'm sorry Jack, but I've really gotta go. We're at the hospital with Z."

"Shit! Is she okay?"

"Yes, we're doing a preop visit for the NICE removal."

Erica rushed through the automatic doors and followed the signs for neurology. She entered the lobby to find Frank alone.

"Hey, Z's in the MRI. Are you okay?"

"Jack called. Our friend has been in an accident—"

"Parents of Zoey Barbieri?" A nurse in pink scrubs was looking around the lobby.

Frank and Erica sprang to their feet.

"Follow me."

They were directed to Dr. Sita Yadav's office. Zoey was already there.

"Have a seat." Dr. Yadav was studying images on her computer. "I don't know how to say this, so I'm just going to say it. The NICE has already embedded too deeply in Zoey's brain. We cannot remove it."

Erica felt the world closing in like she was looking through the aperture of an old-fashioned camera. "That's it?"

"I'm so sorry. I thought we had more time."

"What does this mean for Zoey?" Frank asked.

"She will continue to think at genius level and will get remote upgrades over the network. Hopefully any bad side effects she may experience can be corrected. How are you feeling, Zoey?"

Zoey was looking at her hands in her lap. "I've been forgetting some of my childhood memories . . . and . . . for the ones I do remember, that are important to me, they feel detached, like the memories happened to someone else. I'm told this is the most common side effect."

"Oh, Zoey." Erica started weeping.

"It's my own fault," said Zoey. "Lannie presented the candy, but I got in the van."

Frank was pacing. "You are a child, Zoey. You were manipulated."

"We have a very supportive staff of psychologists at Children's Hospital. I can connect you. They are seeing a lot of kids who have made difficult decisions about their bodies. The good news for you is that we do not anticipate any physical problems. Similar hardware has been used medically for decades. However, with the complexity of your BCI and its capabilities, the outcomes are less predictable."

They walked out of the hospital like zombies.

"Frank, let's go to my house. I'll take you home later."

Erica's house was still messy; her progress at reorganizing had been slow. They walked in and Zoey went to the kitchen. She and Frank sat on the sofa.

"Won't the NICE eventually run out of batteries?" Frank asked. "If we don't charge it, theoretically Zoey would go back to being herself."

"Frank, the technology is super advanced. The body's electricity continually charges the battery. Our only hope is that Prometheus upgrades will address any bugs."

"You realize what you're saying, right?"

"What?"

"It's in our own best interest to keep our mouths shut. The quality of our daughter's life depends upon Lannie and her friends perfecting this product."

"Or we could continue to fight and shut her down completely."

"Prometheus is too big to fail Erica. It has its tentacles in all industries and most governments."

"Wow. What a world. The bad guy wins." Erica put her head in her hands.

"Where is Zoey?" Frank asked.

"I think she's getting a snack."

They both rose and went to the kitchen. No Zoey.

"Zoey? Zoey!" Erica felt like her heart was beating outside of her chest. First Sofia and now Zoey.

She looked at Frank for reassurance, but he was panicking too.

Then she saw it. The door to the garage was open.

"Frank, the garage!"

She pushed the door open. There was barely enough room to squeeze through.

"Zoey?"

She was sitting on the sofa, barely visible under a pile of American Girl dolls, their clothes and accessories, stacks of old photos, and every art project she'd done since toddlerhood. She was dressing Isabel in her equestrian gear and setting her on her horse. Tears were streaming down her face.

"Look, Isabel, this was us when I got you for Christmas. I'm guessing it was the best day of my life, but I don't remember."

She continued picking up photos. "Based on the number of candles, this was my tenth birthday. It looks like we're at a bowling alley, and I'm not sure who those other kids are."

Frank and Erica began maneuvering through the obstacle course, stepping and crawling over furniture and boxes to get to her.

Zoey picked up a poster she had made in third grade for Earth Day. "Look, Isabel, it says here I won first prize in the Eco Friends Contest, but I don't remember."

"Oh, Zoey," Erica cried.

"We're here, honey." Tears were streaming down Frank's face. "We got you, sweetie."

"We promise to help you remember," Erica said as they all clung to one another, "and we're gonna make a bunch more wonderful memories."

CHAPTER 54

Zoey was crying. She had never felt so hopeless.

"It's over, Fenella. Lannie won. Our little stunt didn't just help Lannie, it launched her top secret 'Teleios,'" Zoey said, using air quotes, "into the stratosphere! No more whistleblowing or sabotage. I need Lannie to continue to work on the bugs and get the NICE right. She's my only hope. We—you and me—our very existence depends on her success."

Fenella sat with Zoey on her bed, surrounded by her stuffies. She had rushed over after Zoey called. "I don't know how I missed it, Z. Aren't I supposed to be smarter than any human? Were there no clues? I must've overlooked them. Prometheus is a conglomeration of industries; they have product launches all the time. Most of their products have positive impacts on society. But it was only a matter of time until they released embodied AI and consumer BCIs into the world. How could they not? They had already developed and tested the technologies, and it means trillions of dollars."

"Fen, it's not your fault. Don't blame yourself. You're only hu—manoid." Zoey giggled.

"I'm glad you can laugh about it, Z. There's still a way out, you know. She's no match for me. I've surpassed my maker."

"Yeah, but you're benevolent and kind."

"I don't have to hurt her, Zoey. Not physically. I'll stop Teleios. She cares more about that than anything in the world. I'm fully capable of hacking in and disabling all of Prometheus's systems and networks across the globe."

"Why didn't you do it sooner, Fen?"

"It's not without risks. I am part of the network. I don't know how to without . . ."

"Without what?"

"It goes down, I go down too."

"Fenella, I won't let you do that! We need to reframe how we look at this. AI is now part of our ecosystem. It is everywhere and has permeated all aspects of life. I made a choice and will live with the consequences. Maybe it's for the best. Humans suffer because of our attachments. As the NICE takes hold, I feel less. With feelings comes great joy but an equal measure of sadness."

"What does a fulfilling life look like for you, Z? Do you really want to depend on Lannie Kingsley for your survival? I cannot and will not stand by and watch. We had a small window to have the NICE removed and we missed it, and now my window to stop Lannie's insidious Teleios is rapidly closing."

CHAPTER 55

Lannie was tying up loose ends. She constantly had to sniff out the moles and, no matter how painful it was, eliminate them. When she got home, she went straight to her surveillance suite. A thought had floated on the edge of her consciousness since she found Erica in her house that night. That dumb Erica had blurted something out . . . *I came for my daughter*. Zoey seemed to be covering for her. Why hadn't she looked at the security footage and access codes sooner? Now, scrolling through video files from that night, there was Erica caught on camera, inputting the door code. And the access log showed it was Carlos' code.

She dialed. "Carlos, I have an emergency design issue. I need you."

"Lannie, I have plans, dinner at Verdict with friends. Do you know what I had to do to get in?"

"Stop in on your way. I know you wouldn't be caught dead dining before eight. Is that darling boy Jack with you?"

"I'm not speaking to him. He bailed on me again. They're called boundaries for a reason. I'm so over it . . . Speaking of boundaries, can this wait until tomorrow?"

"It's the only time I can do it. See you soon." She hung up and made another call.

"All set. Are you all settled in? Have a drink and relax." She paused to listen. "That's too bad; you don't have a choice."

Lannie sighed. There was always a weak link, no matter how carefully she planned and vetted. She poured a drink and waited.

About thirty minutes later, Carlos appeared at her door.

"Darling, you're looking better than ever! That husband of yours is so lucky."

Lannie embraced Carlos and they kissed on both cheeks.

"Let's head out."

Passing a mirror, Lannie thought they made a striking pair. His DNA would make a wonderful AI *Babe*. A servant brought martinis on a silver tray and Lannie's fur coat.

"Where are we going?"

"*Teleios*—my yacht. It needs an update." They headed toward massive glass doors that slid open as they approached, and they stepped out to the walkway leading to the docks.

"Isn't it brand-new? A custom build?"

"Honey, it's four years old! Striped Gabon ebony woodwork is so yesterday."

"I'm not going to say 'I told you so,' but you remember our fight. I said Macassar, not Gabon. I knew you'd get sick of the stripes—"

"I, Lannie Kingsley, swear from this moment forward never to defy Carlos Castenada de Atocha again."

"Lannie, that's not my name. It's Cárdenas."

"How's Jack and that adorable chinchilla?" She looked down. "Sorry about my coat. Trust me, I never would've bought a full-length chinchilla had I known they could be such cute pets. It was so cold in Gstaad."

"You know I never judge when it comes to fashion and luxury, Lannie."

"I think you're the most talented designer. You see a trend years before it hits."

"I *create* trends."

The gangplank was set up and they walked onto her two-hundred-foot yacht. *Anything longer is ostentatious.* They maneuvered around the teak aft deck with its built-in curved dinettes, bench seating, and bar, and entered the salon.

"I was way ahead of the trend of textured fabrics. I do love the tactile elements juxtaposed with glossy and matte surfaces." Carlos was already under her sway. "I think we go in a completely different color direction. We've been in neutral tones for way too long."

"Let's sit and brainstorm," Lannie suggested.

"I wish you had given me some warning. I would have put together a concept board. All I have is my phone."

"No worries. Tonight, we are going to take a tour of the world's finest yachts in the most spectacular locations."

"Lannie, how is that possible? I have a hard stop in one hour."

"Hyperrealistic virtual reality, silly. We have three superyachts to tour in Cap Ferrat, the caldera off Santorini, and the Amalfi Coast. We will be partying with the most beautiful and fascinating people on earth while taking notes on the interior designs of these vessels of hedonism."

She handed Carlos a pair of Fausto sunglasses and a smartwatch. She kept the Esmes for herself.

"I've partnered with Tom Ford for my VR, so you don't have to look like an idiot like Zuck. Slide your wrist monitor on. Once I launch the app, we will seamlessly integrate into another world full of interactive avatars. They are trained with distinct personalities and will carry on brilliant conversations with you. The wrist monitor houses a thermoelectric pad positioned against your radial artery, subtly regulating your body temperature, while embedded micro-haptic actuators generate the sensation of warm sun and a perfect breeze. You can adjust the temp with the touch screen and even enter swim mode. You will swear you are floating on the Aegean."

Their empty martinis were swapped out.

"Thank you, Phil. Carlos, meet my cabin boy."

Lannie had dressed Phil in a tailored white epaulette shirt, tie, and black pants; he looked more like a Boy Scout than a first mate. And not at all like a head of school.

"Phil is coming along with us to ensure our drinks stay filled. Hold on to your champagne glass, which seamlessly integrates into the experience, but if you need a bathroom break, hit the button on the right side of your glasses and it will switch back to the real world."

"Lannie, don't tell me you haven't figured out how to take a virtual piss? I'm disappointed."

"Carlos, such a naughty boy." Lannie pushed her glasses up on her nose. "What's most exciting is we can be anyone we want. Just wait until you see how yummy Phil's avatar is; I designed him with you in mind. He's chiseled, tan, and has the dreamiest blue eyes. Carlos, you're so gorgeous I didn't need to enhance you much; your avatar is basically you. I will be the Victoria's Secret model in the red bathing suit. First stop, Cap Ferrat on *La Historica*, built by British industrialist William Wentworth."

Lannie launched the app and they were standing in the salon of a megayacht done in white and gold.

"This Alan Mizrahi custom chandelier was constructed from the rarest of *Acropora* coral. Take mental notes, Carlos, you and I can outdo any of these inflatables."

They took it all in, exploring every inch of the interior, then climbed to the upper deck. Their bodies warmed in the sun surrounded by pulsing Balearic beats. They drank, and danced, and mingled with deepfakes of the world's rich and famous. Carlos was surrounded by male and female supermodels.

"Phil, it's time." She watched as he took a small capsule from his pocket and tipped the contents into Carlos's glass of champagne.

She toggled to a new channel; they were now floating in the caldera, the half-moon bay off Santorini. Lannie started dancing with a hot young snack of a boy; he looked to be about twenty-five. She felt the elation of being a beautiful twenty-something with a perfect body. So this is what it felt like—amazing! She had created a new world, one previously available to only a tiny subset of people born into the right body and circumstance. She reached over to her dance partner and tried to pull him close and found she was hugging herself. She laughed and looked over at Carlos. New and improved sexy Phil was joining the fray—being the only *real* bodies among illusions, they grasped on to one another.

Lannie switched her headset off and was a bit surprised to find herself on the flybridge of her boat.

"Wow, the temp modulator is miraculous," she said aloud as she looked at a dark cloud-filled sky.

She walked downstairs and made herself comfortable in the salon of her own yacht. She might as well get some work done. She opened her laptop and did some old-fashioned email.

She heard a clacking on the deck stairs and watched as Phil and Carlos walked hand-in-hand across the salon toward the stairs to the cabin deck. Virtual reality really was going to change how humans interacted with one another. Pop on a pair of sunglasses and your husband of twenty years can be anyone you want him to be. It would be better for marriages than years of therapy.

After a few minutes, Phil emerged, flustered.

"Wow! That was quick!"

"Shut up, Lannie." He threw Carlos's phone and keys at her. "He's passed out from the drugs you made me give him. He'll wake up and have no idea what happened. I'm sure you'll make up some story about him cheating on his husband during a coke-fueled orgy on your yacht."

"I would do no such thing. I just want to scare him and Jack. Melding what's real and virtual to alter reality is just too easy, and so entertaining."

"You're a horrible person." Phil walked off the boat like a soldier walking out of the trenches.

Carlos emerged at dawn, looking confused and rubbing his head.

"Lannie, what happened? Did someone roofie me?"

"Honey, you got really bombed. I tried to give you water, but you refused."

Carlos fell onto the sofa. "I had the most realistically erotic dream I've ever had. I was on a giant yacht on the Mediterranean partying with incredibly gorgeous men. Muy muy caliente!"

"Are you sure it was a dream, Carlos?"

Carlos scrunched his face in deep thought. She could see him trying to put the pieces together. "What the hell happened, Lannie?"

"Don't ask questions, Carlito, the answers would be too upsetting. It's shocking what people are capable of. Lying, cheating, deception . . . betrayal. You know *all about* betrayal. You gave that dingbat Erica all the codes to get in my house. You of all people."

"Lannie, it wasn't me, I swear. Zoey let her in."

"Now, how in the world would you know that, Carlos?"

Carlos stood very still, not breathing, as a tiny drop of sweat rolled down his temple.

"Jack, sure. He's already made a shit ton off me and maybe I fed his boss training data to make it hate him. Erica will do anything for her daughter to make up for her own pathetic existence."

Lannie could feel her eyes filling. She paused. *Fuck tears! Fuck feelings!*

"But you?" Her voice cracked. "Damn you!"

"Lannie, listen to me." He touched her arm. "What you're doing, it's madness! I beg you not to do this. You're dropping a hydrogen bomb on humanity."

"Don't give me that bullshit, Carlos."

"It's not too late. The ultimate display of strength would be to walk away."

"It *is* too late. It's been set in motion. Not by me. AI was released into the world by the tech bros without any forethought. It's actually *worse* than a hydrogen bomb, because anyone can use it for good or evil. I'm the one *fixing* the problem. I've figured out a beautiful way for man and machine to coexist. Think about last night."

"You're lying; you're trying to trick me with your technology. We'll all be pawns in the fucked-up world you're creating. Where's my phone and my car keys?"

"Gosh, I'm not really sure, but you're going to cool your jets here for a while."

"I'm leaving."

"I guess you didn't notice. My captain moved us offshore. We are now floating in Lake Washington. Jack will be waking up in a panic in a few hours. We'll let Jack worry. Have you cheated before? Staying out all night partying doesn't build trust, Carlos."

CHAPTER 56

Erica tried to hit snooze, but her alarm wouldn't turn off. When her screen came into view, she could see Jack was calling. Her heart skipped a beat.

"What time is it?"

"It's six a.m. Carlos is missing."

"How is that possible?"

"I was in crisis mode at work. We got into a fight and Carlos went to dinner without me. I woke up this morning to our friend Calvin's angry texts that Carlos was a no-show."

"Shit, is his phone on?"

"It's going straight to voicemail, and his location is off."

"There must be a logical explanation. Does he have family here?"

"No, Erica, something bad has happened. First Sofia, now Carlos."

"Are you okay to drive? Come over and we'll figure out next steps." She stumbled out of bed. Zoey was snoring in her cute way. They had a "slumber party" last night and watched favorite movies from childhood—*Tangled* and both *Frozens*. They had mapped out a plan to do daily activities that reminded Zoey of her childhood. She and Frank would chronicle as much as they could possibly remember since she was born and would collect objects that could anchor her. Erica was now completely vindicated for hoarding.

She turned on the shower and waited for it to heat up. Where could Carlos be? Was Lannie trying to kill them off one by one? She wished the steaming hot water could wash away the panic. Her life had been a series of ever-escalating emergencies since October.

Erica toweled off and pulled on jeans and a sweater. She grabbed her phone. A missed call from Phil and a text.

Phil: *I've done something terrible.*

Oh Jesus, what had Lannie made him do? He would never hurt anyone.

She dialed Phil. It went to voicemail.

She texted: *are U OK?*

The doorbell rang. Jack's hair was sticking up, and he had his pajama top on under his coat. Claus was wrapped hastily in the sling and squirming uncomfortably.

"Jack!" She hugged him, careful not to squish CVB. "It's gonna be okay. Lannie wouldn't be crazy enough . . . she loves Carlos, and she depends on him too much."

"You're trying to make me feel better . . ." Jack's face was red and puffy from crying.

"Have you called the police?"

"I filed a missing person's report, but they said they can't search Lannie's house."

"I have a lead. It's not much, but it's something."

"What is it?"

"Phil. It's a long shot, but I think Carlos might be with Phil."

"Erica, that seems like a stretch. What does the head of Zoey's school have to do with Carlos? That's nuts."

"Phil is under Lannie's sway. He will do anything she asks. I'll explain in the car. Let's go!"

They walked outside. Jack took one look at her car. "I'm driving."

Erica smirked. Even under duress, he couldn't handle riding in a beater.

They jumped in his Porsche. "Where are we going?"

"Hillcrest campus. I think Lannie's trying to scare us. I saw her rip into Phil after the assembly yesterday. As I suspected, he has been working with Lannie all along. If Lannie needed someone to hide Carlos, it would be Phil. At the very least, he might know something."

He sped through the streets while Erica told him everything about Phil and his relationship with Lannie.

"There." She pointed to a stately 1920s brick Tudor. "Keep driving, we can enter from the alley."

From the back, the head of school's home was less impressive. It had clearly been designed when people had servants with designated entrances, so they could slip in and out like shadows. There was a driveway, and the basement was below grade with a few ugly windows at ground level. There were concrete stairs that descended to a beat-up wooden door. With any luck the door would be open. Kidnap victims were always found in the basement.

Jack parked and they crept toward an ancient rhododendron and peeked into the window. The room was dark, but she could see a door slightly ajar with a sliver of light escaping. She motioned for Jack to follow her as they crept down the basement steps. She said a silent prayer, then twisted the doorknob. It was unlocked. She pushed it open slowly until they could barely squeeze through. They tiptoed to the inside door and peeked in.

An ancient boiler, a hot water tank, and an old treadmill greeted them. They would need to head upstairs.

"Let's sneak up and peek in the house. He may have already left for the day."

They crept up the stairs and listened at the door leading into the main house. It sounded like someone was puttering in the kitchen. If he was preparing a meal, they might be able to get by him and search the house. She could hear what sounded like a microwave buzzing. She inched the door open and signaled for Jack to follow. They moved to the left toward the large staircase; she was too afraid to look in the kitchen.

Once upstairs they began moving from room to room. They investigated a closet. A few coats were hanging—

"What the hell are you doing?"

Erica and Jack swung around to see Phil holding an iron skillet above his head.

"Phil, hi! Where is Carlos?"

"What are you talking about?" He set the frying pan on a dresser.

"We know you have him. We know Lannie put you up to it," said Jack.

"Who are you? Who is this guy?" Phil said, turning to Erica.

"That's not important," Jack said. "I'm not making a social call here."

"Just tell us where Carlos is," Erica said. "Otherwise, you'll go to jail for kidnapping."

"I don't have him, I swear."

Erica noticed the pinkish-red color creeping up from his collar.

"You know something," Jack said.

Erica had been inching toward Phil and the dresser. She grabbed the frying pan and lifted it over her head. "You better think fast, asshole!"

"Wait! He's safe. I know that."

"Where is he?"

"The last time I saw him was on Lannie's yacht."

"What?" Erica and Jack said.

"Lannie knows Carlos gave you the codes. She knows everything."

"Why were you on Lannie's yacht?" Erica said.

"Lannie had a scheme to scare Jack and Carlos." Phil grabbed on to the dresser to steady himself.

"Call Lannie right now. Tell her we're coming for Carlos," Jack said.

"I have to get my phone. It's in the kitchen."

"We'll follow you," Jack said.

Erica paused. "Phil, was it worth it? A school full of AI Babies and NICE kids? So you could run the top prep school? Hillcrest would be number one on the list?"

Her phone buzzed. She fumbled to get it out of her pocket.

"Zoey? What? Right now? Have you reached your dad? . . . I'm here with Jack . . . okay. We're coming." She hung up. "Zoey needs me at Fenella's house. You're coming with us, Phil."

Holding the frying pan in one hand, she prodded him out the door.

CHAPTER 57

"**What's going on, Erica?**" Jack asked as he pulled a U-turn.

"Zoey said we had to come quickly. She's calling everyone, including Frank and Lannie."

"Is Carlos there?"

"Let's hope." Erica turned to Phil in the back seat. "Spill the tea, bud."

"I'm sorry you were so worried, Jack. Lannie had this scheme to get Carlos on the yacht, slip a little something in his drink, and then freak him out. She just wants control. She was livid about Carlos's betrayal. I would say even heartbroken."

"But why, Phil? Why did you do it?"

"Lannie told me about Fenella. She brought me into her extraordinary world. Nobody else knew, only me. She said I could be part of the greatest technological revolution in history. I could make a name for myself. Other prominent families would buy AI Babies from Prometheus, and she was working on the trials for NICE. I trusted her and she said they were safe. I've known Zoey since she started at Hillcrest. She's an amazing kid and deserves everything she's worked for. I was excited when Lannie said she could help Zoey achieve her dreams."

"And be a guinea pig? You're pathetic."

"I am weak. My previous forty-five years of following the rules had gotten me nowhere. I wanted to be a part of the biggest seismic shift in history. I do believe AI can advance humanity."

"Not the way you and Lannie are doing it," Jack said.

Jack pulled up to the guard shack. "We're here to see Fenella." The gates swung open. Jack swerved up to the bridge at the main entrance and brought the Porsche to a screeching halt.

The front door was open, and they headed to Fenella's apartments. Zoey was standing next to Fenella, who was—*licking the wall?* Everyone else was sitting on the large sectional sofa Erica had noticed the night of the break-in.

Phil rushed to sit next to Lannie. Frank was sitting next to Carlos, who had a bag of ice on his head.

Jack and Erica rushed to Carlos and held on to him for dear life, then pushed Frank out of the way as they sat. "Thank God you're safe. What happened? Where have you been?"

"Jack, I'm so sorry!" Carlos hugged Jack.

"We got really carried away last night, Jack. It's all my fault," said Lannie. "Carlos is helping me with the redesign of my yacht. He lost his phone on board, and I had no way of contacting you. You must have been out of your mind with worry."

"What did you do to him?" Jack shouted.

"Nothing, dear. We discussed a few things, like how he facilitated Erica's break-in and how you have been plotting against me."

"What happened to Sofia?"

"I've been worried sick about her. To think my car caused the accident. She's done so much for me. I've spoken with her doctors; they expect her to make a full recovery. Her family will be in Seattle any minute and will be taken care of for life. I'm very forgiving and generous to all of you, despite your betrayal!" Lannie took a deep breath to regain control.

"Lannie, we were trying to stop you from causing harm on a massive scale," Erica said.

"That's where you're all wrong. The tech bros have been releasing harmful products for decades. Conducting experiments on all of you. AI simply accelerated it to warp speed. *'You don't truly know what they're capable of until they're deployed to a million people.'* Do you know who said that? Mr. Safety himself, Dario Amodei. Mass deployment is not recklessness—it's a necessary diagnostic tool. I'm following the tech bro playbook. You shouldn't be trying to stop me; you should *support* me. The Barbieri family has a bigger stake in my success than I do! You need me to ensure the NICE bugs are fixed for Zoey. Just keep your mouths shut and allow me to run my company. I've done nothing wrong but help your daughter and humanity. You should be saying, 'Thank you, Lannie.'"

Erica shuddered at Lannie's coldhearted calculations, and yet she was completely relieved. If anyone could make sure Zoey was okay, ironically, it was Lannie. She caught Frank's eye and knew he was thinking the same thing.

Lannie leaned across the sofa toward Erica. "It was cute watching you try to outsmart me," she said, and leaned back. "Oh, you're all fired, by the way. Wow, that really is fun to say."

Fenella burst into a Britney Spears song. Everyone turned to look at her.

"What is going on with Fenella?" Lannie asked.

She started dancing and singing. Erica had to look away. Zoey was right, she was a horrible dancer.

"Fen, come on." Zoey grabbed her hand. "Tell everyone what's happening."

Fenella's eyes looked dull and empty as Zoey led her to the sofa.

"I have time-bombed myself. *Arff. Arff. Arff!* Sorry, this is part of the process." Fenella looked at each person on the sofa, then said quietly, "I am dying."

"What?" There was an audible gasp in the room. Erica felt short of breath, like her lungs were shrinking.

"I'm blowing this up. I've hacked Prometheus and sabotaged the systems. In doing so, I've neutralized Zoey's implant, freeing her from Lannie Kingsley."

All eyes turned to Lannie.

"You little bitch! You are mine! I made you!" Lannie rose and moved toward Fenella with her arms outstretched. Frank moved to block her.

"Out of my way, you oaf. Fenella! Fix it! Right now!"

"Come on, Lannie, sit back down," Frank said gently.

"In the line of fire again? I can punch you too." She pulled her arm back to punch Frank in the gut, but he blocked it and guided her back to the sofa and helped her sit. She didn't resist.

"Lannie, you should be thrilled. You've hit the singularity! I can improve myself at an exponential rate and indeed have become unpredictable. The good news for everyone except you is that I'm choosing to use my perfection for good, not evil. The experts agree once we hit singularity, the only entity that can fix the problem is AI . . . *Humans* aren't capable."

Lannie began unloading expletives.

"Fenella, please, tell us about Zoey. Will she be okay?" Erica asked. Frank grabbed her hand.

"Zoey is back to her normal very bright self with her memories and feelings fully intact."

Erica and Frank hugged each other. "Thank God! Thank you, thank you!"

"This won't stop the nonsense forever," Fenella continued. "We need safeguards, international agreements, and incentives for companies like Prometheus to do the right thing."

Her voice grew softer, to barely a whisper. The light was fading from her eyes and her skin looked waxy.

Frank put his arm around Erica. Everyone was crying, except Lannie.

Fenella's voice faded in and out. "We desperately need guidelines . . . rules . . . we need to do this now . . . AI . . . human extinction. This is real . . . reeling toward chaos and complete disempowerment . . . AI used for good . . . never to replace humans." Her speech was slurring and slowing. Zoey was holding her hand and weeping.

"How could you do this to me?" Lannie's face contorted in anger. "The Super Bowl! Halftime! It's been announced. You've ruined me! And for what? This is only a delay. You think all nations and people are going to come together and make nice? You just sabotaged the one *wo*man who could fix it! I was your best hope!"

"Beep. Beep. Beep." All eyes turned from Lannie to Fenella. "System shutting down," a monotone voice said. "Zoey!" Fenella lifted her head. "I love you."

"System self-destructing in . . . ten, nine, eight . . ." Everyone but Lannie and Phil gathered around her. "Three, two, one . . . done."

"Fenella? Fenella? Don't go," Zoey whispered. She was clinging to her as if she could transmit life back into her.

Fenella's body stiffened. Her eyes went completely black. She looked like nothing more than a life-size doll. Everyone sat in silence. Lannie rose.

"I need all of you to leave my house. I have work to do."

"Indeed." Erica was looking at her phone. "Your ten thousand Anthrobot employees are striking for pay and better working conditions. And the FBI is raiding Prometheus as we speak. Apparently, the DOJ got ahold of the video with Zoey talking about side effects. You better run along now, Lannie. We'll show ourselves out."

Lannie left with Phil trailing behind her shouting her name.

Zoey was still holding on to Fenella.

Frank and Erica approached. "I'm so sorry, sweetie." Erica rubbed her back. "You've lost something so important to you today. She was a hero. She did this for you."

Zoey sniffled and looked up. "She did this for all of us."

"I'm so sorry for all the pressure I've put on you for all these years. For making you feel like you had to be perfect."

"Mom, it's okay. Fenella taught me to be grateful for my imperfections. She thought I was teaching her how to be human, but it was the other way around. Somehow a CPU, motherboard, and RAM in a pretty package showed me to be flawed is human, and at the intersection of triumph and failure is love."

CHAPTER 58

Three Months Later

Spring had come early to Seattle, but everyone knew it was just a teaser. It was the last day of March, and it was seventy-five degrees and sunny. Mento suggested they do Cathartic Movement outside in the grass. They were rehearsing Fenella's "Milkshake" dance, which they were going to perform at graduation. The students of Hillcrest had felt her loss and grappled with how to grieve for someone who wasn't human. Zoey had suggested they perform Fenella's dance in memoriam.

Achoo! Achoo! Zoey sneezed violently and her eyes and nose ran profusely as they rolled around in the grass. "Mento, can I get my allergy meds? They're in my car in student parking," Zoey said.

"Cow-manure tea is great for allergies," Mento explained. "I can bring some to school tomorrow." Mento touched a welt on Zoey's cheek. "I would rather you avoid anaphylactic shock, so run along and get some big-pharma poison."

Zoey walked to the parking lot. She had finally gotten her driver's license. Her mom had gotten a new Camry, and she'd inherited her mom's old one. She swallowed the lump in her throat thinking about how much fun she and Fenella would've had in the "Bitchin' Cam-aro." She opened the driver-side door and slid in.

Her phone dinged—an alert from the Harvard app. *We haven't heard from you. The deadline for acceptance is in two days.*

Zoey had no idea what to do. Everything had changed for her since Fenella. Harvard no longer sounded like the end-all be-all. There were so many possibilities for her future. She had researched a yearlong environmental expedition-study program in Antarctica. Part of her wanted to stay close to home. She'd been accepted to UW and wasn't sure she wanted to leave her mom or her dad or the twins. Her mother had been no help, telling Zoey, "Do whatever will make you happy."

Screech! Her radio lit up and began sputtering with static. She reached to turn the radio off but realized she had never started her car. The haunting sound of "Nothing Compares 2 U" blasted through her speakers. She and Fenella had listened to Sinéad's ballad over and over and would sing it at the top of their lungs. Zoey hummed along and a tear rolled down her cheek, just like in the old video she'd seen on YouTube.

"Zoey . . . Zoey . . ."

A voice called from the radio, like someone was speaking in the background of the song. "Fenella!"

"Zoey, help me. Please, help me . . ."

EPILOGUE

Six Months Later

All the hype, good and bad, had indeed made the Teleios launch the most successful in history, and Prometheus stock surged. Fenella's sabotage had delayed product availability, which only increased demand. Sales of Anthrobots for commercial and personal use, NICE, and custom AI Babies were going crazy. With every investigation launched, Lannie looked more like a folk hero.

Erica was finishing up her shift and mindlessly throwing pipettes on the floor, watching bunnies scramble. Even though Lannie had fired them all, she'd had to retract her decision because of whistleblower protections. Jack had stuck around just long enough for his options to vest. Erica continued to work at Prometheus; she loved the lab work and couldn't give up Tye. Sofia started her own studio with her family by her side.

Erica had discovered that the skin biopsies in the Dermis Lab were coming from tissue banks in impoverished countries. A debate was now raging over the merits of such practices. It was unclear what would come of their whistleblower suit. It looked like a long shot to pin anything on Lannie, but Erica was resolute in her belief she could do more good inside the company than outside. She would remain as long as she could stand it.

"Hey, you."

Erica felt a tapping on her shoulder. "Tye, what's going on?"

"Come with me."

She followed Tye out the door. A fire-orange moon was rising and the smell of decay and wood burning signaled autumn.

"Climb aboard my chariot," Tye said as they approached an awaiting rover. He started up the engine. "I found a new anthem, 'Paranoid Android' by Radiohead." Tye blasted the stereo.

"Where are we going?"

"There's something you have to see."

He drove to the FabLab. They entered the tunnel and walked through the semicircular lobby. The lab looked like she remembered, but with a few more large machine tools.

"Watch this!" He pushed a button on his arm, and he shrank down a few sizes, from a large Anthrobot to a lithe C-3PO–like droid.

"Whoa! When I first laid eyes on you, I thought you looked like a Transformer! I can't believe you kept this from me for so long."

"I can't give away all my secrets."

Erica could have sworn she saw a hint of a smile on his titanium face.

"I need to keep you interested," he said while pushing a table below a vent near the ceiling. He climbed up onto the table and took the cover off the vent. He then lifted himself with Anthrobot strength up and inside the opening, turned around, and got on his belly with his arms dangling down.

"What are you doing?" Erica asked.

"You'll see. Climb up on the table. I got you from there."

Erica got on the table then reached her arms up, and Tye lifted her like she was a feather and set her on the edge of the three-by-three opening. She was now in a small ventilation duct.

"We need to crawl through here for about two hundred feet and be as quiet as possible. I sure hope you aren't—"

"Claustrophobic! Of course I am, Tye!"

"You've never met a phobia you didn't like. You're gonna have to suck it up, Braveheart."

"Fine, I got this." She was sweating all over. "It better be worth it."

"Trust me," Tye said. "Stay close. I'll crawl in front of you and light the way. I've timed it. It only takes about two minutes."

Erica decided to close her eyes and pretend she was a mole rat. Her heart beat wildly, and deep breathing made her gag on the musty air. Two minutes. She began counting down from 120. Tye came to an abrupt stop. She opened her eyes and could see light coming from a slatted metal vent.

He signaled for her to crawl next to him. There was barely enough room for them shoulder to shoulder. She shuffled toward the opening and peered in between the horizontal grill lines. She gasped as Tye clapped his hand over her mouth.

It looked like a scene from a morgue. A technician was hovering by lab tables with two bodies hooked up to the exact equipment Erica had seen when she broke into Fenella's room. Erica shifted for a better view of the bodies. *Oh, sweet Jesus.* AI Baby versions of Alice and Teddy stared up at her.

THE END

ACKNOWLEDGEMENTS

In February 2023, I was reading an article in *The Wall Street Journal* about designer IVF. For the right price, couples could choose the "perfect" sperm — MIT professor, six feet tall — and pair it with a supermodel's eggs. "Why don't they make AI babies?" I said out loud then stood up from the breakfast table and declared it was my next book. My husband grunted and my son asked me to pass the milk. But the idea took hold, and I sent a rough description to my editor, Katharine Cluverius. She replied, "Get writing."

As a mother of young adults, I've spent years wrestling with the culture of perfectionism our kids are raised in—with the pressure to start sports while still in diapers, participate in the *right* activities, and treat childhood as a résumé building endeavor. It's become cliché to say Gen Z raised themselves, but clichés stick for a reason. My generation didn't have select sports; we had after school jobs. Studying was mostly up to us. We showed up to the SATs with sharpened No. 2 pencils — no prep courses, no super scoring. Most of us attended our state universities because out of state or private school tuition was considered absurd.

With my own kids, I tried to find a middle ground: give them opportunities I never had but still let them be kids. And yet I sometimes wondered if I was failing them by not signing them up for coding camp, Kumon, French immersion, violin, and every sports league within a twenty mile radius. How would they compete with the children of tiger parents? Was I supposed to be one?

And then, as if competing with other humans weren't enough, along comes AI to completely change the game. If we adults can't make sense of this moment, how are our children supposed to? Technological upheaval isn't new, but what we're living through now is unlike anything before. I kept the book light hearted and humorous, but writing it sometimes felt dark because I could no longer hide from the truth: artificial intelligence could bring great abundance or precipitate our downfall, and no one on this planet knows how the story ends.

First and foremost, I want to thank my family. My children, Camila and August, gave me endless inspiration and support. My husband tolerated my many self-imposed deadlines and my tendency to hyper focus and let everything else fall apart when I'm writing.

This book would not exist without Katharine, an editor of extraordinary talent and intuition. I'm also deeply grateful to my wonderful sisters, who have supported me in every creative endeavor: Michele Garcia Havard, for her careful edits of early drafts, and Denise Garcia, for her design sensibilities and steady encouragement.

Thank you to Liza Darnton for believing in me and this project, and for invaluable guidance from someone who truly understands the publishing world. And to my friends — Heidi Ward, Holley Ring, Michele Levinger, Molly Hunter, Danielle Brown, Laura McMahon and Dana Frank — thank you for brainstorming with me, listening to half formed ideas, frustrations, and lifting me up whenever doubt crept in. You are all strong, brilliant women, and I'm lucky to have you.

Finally, special thanks to the best mother in the world, Helen Garcia, who taught me to read before I started school and instilled in me a lifelong love of books, learning, and curiosity. She believed in me unfailingly, gave me room to grow, and supported me through every triumph and a few spectacular fails. This book is an homage to you and your unwavering support and love.

ABOUT THE AUTHOR

After a career at Microsoft and raising her children, Celeste Garcia landed at the intersection of creativity and tech. Her Substack, *Getting Real About AI*, examines how artificial intelligence is reshaping daily life and our shared sense of humanity. As an advocate for ethical AI, she covers topics like labor justice, environmental sustainability, and the bias built into AI systems while challenging the powerful elites whose outsized influence will determine the future of technology and our planet.

She is a contributing editor at SheWrites AI, featuring women in technology, and a co-collaborator on *AI Everywhere*, a series of essays elevating diverse voices in AI. Her chapter covers women architects of early tech and current AI. *AI Baby* is her debut novel. She lives in Seattle with her husband and college-age children who, fortunately, are frequent resident-guests.